DEADLY METAMORPHOSIS

Above Angela's cooling body, the chrysalis began to break apart, cracks spidering in all directions along its glossy surface. Within the husk where the woman had found death, there was motion, an unhurried shuffling, then pressure. Like an exquisite butterfly emerging from its cocoon, a new Sil pushed her way free. Headfirst, then arms, reaching up and around to the top of the chrysalis and swinging herself carefully out and down to stand next to Angela's corpse, reborn a fully grown and beautiful woman.

She sniffed the air, and her eyes, steely blue beneath a lovely halo of blond hair, sharpened as she studied her surroundings and the body at her feet. With slow deliberation, Sil bent and began undressing the dead woman.

SPECTRES

And coming soon from Bantam Books

deadrush

SPECIES

A Novel

by
Yvonne Navarro

◆

Based on the screenplay written
by
Dennis Feldman

BANTAM BOOKS
New York Toronto London Sydney Auckland

SPECIES
A Bantam Book/July 1995

ISBN 0-553-57404-3
Published simultaneously in the United States and Canada

Bantam Books are published by Bantam Books, a division of Bantam Doubleday
Dell Publishing Group, Inc. Its trademark, consisting of the words "Bantam Books"
and the portrayal of a rooster, is Registered in U.S. Patent and Trademark Office
and in other countries. Marca Registrada. Bantam Books, 1540 Broadway, New
York, New York 10036.

PRINTED IN THE UNITED STATES OF AMERICA
OPM 0 9 8 7 6 5 4 3 2 1

For my dad,
Marty Cochran.

Who believes in my dreams,
and still helps make them possible.

ACKNOWLEDGMENTS

As with all projects, especially surprises like this one, a lot of people helped in the making. Many thanks to my editors, Anne Groell, Jennifer Hershey, and Jennifer Steinbach, and as always, to my agent and friend, Howard Morhaim. Don VanderSluis and my dad, Marty Cochran, patiently answered another barrage of technical questions. Lots of gratitude goes to Dennis Feldman, who started this whole thing and was always available, and I stand in awe of La Bon Ami, Master Huntress of the "I Can Find Anything Search." Abundant appreciation goes to Jeff Osier, who can remember everything and find out anything, while Linda Schroyer continues her mission of rescuing me in my ongoing war with word-processing software. I was blessed, too, with support and solid declarations of "You can do it!" from more people than I can remember here, but particularly from Don VanderSluis, my longtime friend Wayne Allen Sallee, Janna Silverstein, Amy Wasp-Wimberger, Matt Costello, and Tammy Thompson.

And finally, thanks to Johnny Algiers for the footnotes.

PROLOGUE

♦ **November 15, 1974**
Arecibo, Puerto Rico

From the outside, it looked like another beautiful day in Arecibo. A bustling community settled by the Spanish over four hundred years earlier, the town went about the business of living with a sort of laid-back energy born of a tropical climate and an active industry. Plastics, farm machinery, sporting goods, clothing, and paper were manufactured in the mills and factories, while the largest distillery in the country continued the fine trade of rum-making. At one end of town, the rail yards loaded shipments on trains that would make the trip to San Juan, while at the University of Puerto Rico the students began another round of classes to sharpen their minds for the future.

The residents of the town were used to the huge Arecibo Observatory installation to the north, though many of them never knew or understood exactly what it did. The thousand-foot-wide radar-radio telescope, its antenna structures rising more than half that distance, had been there for nearly a decade and a half but today was like any other in the active lives of the people on the small inlet near the mouth of the Arecibo River.

On this fine and bright Friday, as part of the ceremonies dedicating the newly ungraded telescope, a reel-to-reel tape machine whirred into life in the Observatory's control center in response to the carefully programmed instructions fed to it by the mainframe computer. At the computer's keyboard sat a young man wearing thick glasses, jeans, and a Grateful Dead T-shirt, listening to someone on the other end of a telephone and nodding his head. "Yes, *sir*," he said. His gaze flicked to the industrial clock above the desk, and he watched its second hand sweep around to the sixty mark, then begin another trip. "Sixty seconds and counting." Neither he nor the party on the other end said anything, but the young man did not hang up. Across the room, an older man in a more conservative white dress shirt with the sleeves rolled up checked the position of the tape machine for the third time, then hit the pause button. He looked expectantly at his younger colleague.

Both of them stared at the clock. At minus five and counting, the young man at the computer moved his finger to a strategic position above the keyboard. The older man began counting backward in time with the measured tick of the second hand. His voice was soft and tense.

"Four . . . three . . . two . . .

"One."

The young man at the keyboard pressed the enter key, and both turned to stare at the tape machine as the reels spun into motion and their transmission—destined for the fringes of the galaxy—began. Behind them, data began to flash across the green screen of the computer monitor, far too rapidly for either to read. It didn't matter; they both knew the essence of the message constructed by Frank Drake, Richard Isaacman, Linda May, James C. G. Walker, and Carl Sagan:

A 1,679-bit picture portraying a counting scheme; a description of fundamental terrestrial biochemistry including five biologically significant atoms: hydrogen, carbon, oxy-

gen, nitrogen, and phosphorus; a schematic of the DNA double helix; a representation of a human being, including dimensions; a depiction of the solar system showing that human beings inhabit the third planet; and a schematic representation of the Arecibo Observatory and a description of its dimensions.

The two men were not close. One, a family man with a boy flunking out of high school and a girl doing well in college, thought about how his wife wanted another baby and worried whether the transmission instructions were programmed properly, although he knew the programmer, Bernard Jackson, had done a perfect job. The keyboard operator thought the whole idea was cool, but didn't believe for a moment that anything would ever hear it. He didn't want to be sending messages into the empty reaches of the universe; he wanted to be sending satellites to explore the closer planets. As he sat at the keyboard and kept a close eye on the readouts from the computer tracking the program output, he decided he would reevaluate his major and make sure his education was aimed in the right direction.

While the town of Arecibo went about its daily living, the message of human life began its journey into space.

♦ 1992

Eighteen years had brought a lot of change to Arecibo. Sprawling across the greenery of the Puerto Rican coast, a continually expanding industry had made the town prosper. Operated by Cornell University under an agreement with the National Science Foundation, astronomy students from all over the world now vied for the chance to work in the SETI facility at the Arecibo Observatory.

Miguel Perez had lucked out. The son of a coffee-farm laborer, he had earned a scholarship to the University of Puerto Rico through stubbornness and hard work. His household was poor enough to be considered below the poverty line, and he was acutely aware of the fact that he was the only family member to go beyond the first year of high school. While his peers were studying and compiling the information for their theses in air-conditioned dorms, he did his schoolwork in the hot kitchen of the three-room apartment he shared with his mother, father and two baby brothers, banging out his papers on a manual typewriter his father had found for six dollars in a junk shop.

Miguel was not bitter. Rather, he felt incredibly fortunate—life, he thought, was full of promise and adventure. Someday he would be able to do wonderful things to reward his hardworking parents, and he knew that every day he set an example for his younger siblings. He did not need to have huge amounts of money: the education he was receiving would expand his intellect and care for his future, and his family would nurture his heart. Taking care of his simple needs wasn't even that difficult. Monitoring the computers at the facility for two hours a day gave him enough cash to buy schoolbooks and supplies and help out with the groceries at home. To help Miguel, his mother packed a homemade lunch for him every morning. Today's fine meal was a *carnitas* tortilla and *menudo* soup; the tortilla was long gone and he was savoring the spicy soup while reviewing his spectroscopy notes.

Right now Miguel was alone in the whitewashed room, but Francis Leverton, the American exchange student, would return in about ten minutes. By then Miguel's soup would be gone and he'd be packed up and ready to go; sometimes sitting here by himself for the last sixty minutes of his daily stint—the lunch hour—was tedious enough to make him feel dull and sleepy, and he was looking forward to the return of the two regular staff members and the brisk walk in the sunshine to his next class.

It was time for the final check of his shift, so he swallowed the last spoonful of soup then plucked the clipboard holding the transmission monitor record out of its slot and stood. Filling out the list would start him at the computer to his far left and from there he would work his way across the room. He already knew that his clipboard would look the same as it had every day since he'd started this job two months ago: a line of Xs along the left margin in the "yes" box under the heading *Transmitting Properly*, and three Xs along the right in the "none" boxes under *Signals Received*. Some things just didn't change—

—until a red light began to blink on the receiver four feet away and he saw the needles on the computer recording devices sitting steadily in the center of the red strip that indicated they were active.

Frowning, Miguel thought the equipment was malfunctioning until he checked the electronic readouts and realized this had been going on for at least two minutes and forty seconds. More checks and hastily typed computer commands told him that the signal coming in was not a malfunction, nor could it possibly originate from Earth. Everything indicated that it was a narrow radio wave from space rather than a wide communication band, and *that* suggested that it was from an artificial source, not a natural phenomenon. In short, he wasn't sure *what* it was.

Miguel picked up the telephone and punched in the numbers that would connect him to the office of the head of the Observatory. He had no problem finding the correct number; it was written in indelible red marker across the bottom of every computer monitor in the room. He was particularly proud of his ability to speak clearly and concisely, with no trace of hysteria in his voice as he told the person on the other end that the facility was receiving a transmission from deep space, origin and type unknown. He listened to the man's instructions, said "Yes, sir," and hung up the telephone without a hint of fear in his tone.

While he waited for the Observatory officials to arrive he continued his work, as he had been instructed. But by the time Miguel and his clipboard stopped at the third of the trio of display and analysis systems, his hand was shaking so badly that the X he had put in the "yes" box in the *Signals Received* column looked more like a thick, sprawling arrow.

♦ 1993

"I think I'm onto something," Penny Garnock said. She leaned forward and peered intently at her computer monitor, nose nearly touching the glass. Brown hair the color of grocery bags feathered into her face and she blew it out of the way without changing position.

"You've said that before, wonder girl." What he said aloud be damned, though, because inside Toyo Sagami was cheering her on with everything he had. He'd been at the NSA's Ft. Meade, Maryland facility for two years since transferring from a smaller office in Columbus. This wasn't the first time Toyo wished he'd had the sense to stay put, and he was sure it wasn't the last. But . . . *damn*. Filed with his transfer request to Ft. Meade had been a carload of expectations—transferring so close to Washington, D.C. *had* to mean decoding covert operations plans, terrorist activity logs, you name it. He and Penny had gotten a few minor jobs over the past fourteen months or so, but they always ended up coming back to *this* one. Penny said she felt in her soul that it was based on the English language, but so far neither of them—or the other ten cryptanalysts working on the message—had gotten squat.

Toyo ran a hand through his thick black hair and typed in another experimental ciphertext code, with no result. He sighed; he'd run out of ideas on this project, and spending ninety-five percent of his time working on the same thing really sucked—especially when it was high pressure and higher competition. When the diskful of undecipherable text had first come in from Arecibo, Toyo had wanted more than anything to be the cryptanalyst who solved it. The secrets it might hold were endless—the potential keys to life in the unknown reaches of space, interstellar travel . . . *anything*. The text was undoubtedly an asymmetric cryptosystem and now Toyo wished any*one* would break it—even sexy, shaggy-haired Penny, at whom he stayed perpetually angry because she wouldn't go out with him.

"No, I mean *seriously*." A decade and a half of staring at computer screens had gifted her with bifocals at thirty-nine, and now her eyes—the same beguiling paper-bag tan as her hair—squinted even more behind the lenses. She began banging savagely at her keyboard, and Toyo's heart skipped slightly. She never typed like that unless she was close to success, he'd seen her do it before on the Devon Project—

"I've got it!" Penny said triumphantly. She whacked the enter key with enough force to make her keyboard extender vibrate, then sat back and watched the data on her screen begin to flow. There was a nerve-racking and uncommon one-second lag as the scalar processors in the SX-4 supercomputer worked their way through Penny's final program commands, then Penny threw him a smug grin. At the same time she leaned back and crossed her hands behind her head, her gaze fixed to the monitor. Symbols that had only been a mystery moments before suddenly formed recognizable words: *methane . . . oxygen . . . fuel . . .* and more. When the message ANALYSIS COMPLETE flashed in the bottom left corner, she saved the file, flipped disks, and shoved in the one marked *Message No. 02.92/11/07.* Toyo watched openmouthed as the symbols rearranged themselves and began to spell out the names and specific quantities of minerals, chemicals and enzymes.

"What on earth?" He abandoned his console and scooted his chair next to hers. "I . . . would you look at that!"

"It's a DNA double helix," Penny breathed. Her face was shining. "It's a formula for . . . *life*, Toyo.

"From somewhere out *there*."

1

♦ TODAY . . .
The Mojave Desert, California

"She knows."

Dr. Xavier Fitch jerked at the unexpected sound of Kyle Jacobson's voice, but the lab assistant didn't care. "Don't be absurd," Fitch snapped. "She's sleeping." He bent his head back to his work and Kyle heard him mutter, more personal ranting about all the effort and wasted time, endless hours of research and reams of paper that had gone into this project. Kyle knew he was the only lab assistant Fitch thought might have a passably useful brain, and now he felt foolish, sniveling like a guilty five-year-old caught with his hand on the gearshift knob of the car. He didn't care about that either.

"It doesn't matter," Kyle said softly. "She's not stupid." He ran his fingers through his too-long sandy hair and rubbed them together when they came out oily. His hair needed washing, but he hadn't slept in thirty-six hours or been home since last Thursday—five days. He'd seen his wife a whopping three times since the final phase of the project had begun two weeks ago.

Fitch lifted his pen from the surface of the form he was filling out and from his position at the window ten feet away, Kyle could hear the noise the doctor's teeth made as they ground together. The older man looked as if he were trying to restrain himself, then he gave in to the urge and slammed his pen on the desktop. Kyle jumped and glanced back at him, then turned back to the control booth's window and stared out. After two years the lab still resembled a warehouse more than a scientific center, and no other vantage point in the cavernous room supported that view as strongly as this sealed observation booth. Twelve feet below was the transparent "cage" that had been completed only two weeks ago; clad in a hospital gown—at least it was one of the newer, flower-patterned ones—its occupant sprawled innocently across the width of a white-sheeted cot. Kyle was still stunned at how quickly she'd grown, but the baby-fine blond hair and guileless blue eyes undeniably belonged to a child; he estimated her age at twelve. She could've been an average teenager if it weren't for the dozen or so wires running from the surface of her skin to machines and monitors parked around the interior of the glass enclosure. Other things were scattered around the girl's cot, too: children's picture books and a few soft toys, all examined and discarded almost immediately except for one miniature pink teddy bear. That one was tucked securely within the crook of one elbow as she slept.

"I think I have enough on my mind without listening to this crap."

Fitch's voice was cold and came from just behind Kyle's left shoulder. The younger man couldn't help flinching at the sound; sometimes Fitch moved too quietly, reminding him of an alley cat waiting for a rat to make the move that would turn out to be fatal. The man always seemed to have an unexpected move waiting in the wings. Techs and assistants scurried around the enclosure below them like highway personnel at the site of a car wreck, eyes gleaming with a frightening sort of kill-the-cat curiosity that Kyle found far too morbid. This whole thing bothered him more than it should have—the decoded message and instructions, the girl in the reinforced glass enclosure below, the decision to terminate the project.

Especially that.

"Go down and help them set it up."

Horrified, Kyle gaped at Fitch. "*Me?*" As if she'd heard, the eyes of the girl below suddenly blinked open and looked up, seeking the observation booth and him automatically. Their gazes locked for a fraction of a second, then Kyle yanked his away. "But she trusts me!" he protested. "I can't—"

"You can and you will," interrupted Fitch. "This project is over and those are your instructions."

Kyle opened his mouth, then shut it again. Punishment? Probably; his work here went a lot further back than two years, and if he blew it now by refusing direct instructions, his future would fade to nothing but a gray void. Fitch might think his work was decent—barely— but the wrong response could turn Kyle into just another member of the Fitch Lab Assistant Alumni. He gave a curt nod and headed down to the first level; what he did here today might haunt him for a while, but he wouldn't spend the rest of his life working for Fitch and time would eventually dull the memory.

Sometimes the other workers down here reminded him of androids, robots in sheaths of human flesh doing Fitch's bidding without question or emotion, mobile computers hardly capable of making an independent decision without additional input. In fact, the only thing that seemed alive down here right now was the girl, whom Fitch had code-named Sil for some unknown reason. Fitch insisted that it was nothing more than a randomly assigned computer code, but for all Kyle knew about the older man, the letters could have represented anything from Fitch's mother's initials to an obscure acronym known only to the doctor. In the lab area around Sil's enclosure, the other workers moved with the practiced efficiency of those who had terminated projects before and knew exactly what was expected of them. The main monitors were being shut down by a dark-haired tech whose brilliant white lab coat made his sallow skin look unhealthy under the harsh fluorescent lighting; one by one, the machines inside the glass enclosure went dark as their power sources were disconnected. Kyle could see Sil sitting docilely on her cot, following the shutdown of the monitors with little turns of her head as the power-down made a circle around her confined area. No one that Kyle could see would look Sil in the eye, and from his spot coming out of the elevator he saw her staring fixedly up at the control booth. When he followed her line of sight, he realized she and Fitch were in a staring match, a visual battle for dominance.

"Hey, Jacobson!" Kyle turned and saw one of the labor supervisors directing his men as they connected the feed lines from four slender tanks to closed valves at the bottom right corner of Sil's glass cage. The heavyset man said something into a radio clipped to his left shoulder, then listened and nodded. "Dr. Fitch says he sent you down here to man the valves. We're just about ready."

Kyle nodded grimly but said nothing. It figured; he'd dared to show a little compassion, so Fitch would make him do the ultimate dirty work. By the time he reached the enclosure, Sil was standing again and watching the activities outside her window with narrow-eyed interest. The tanks were in place and the supervisor was doing a final check; clearly visible on the sides of all four tanks were the stenciled words HYDROGEN CYANIDE. Kyle reminded himself that it didn't matter, Sil couldn't read, but when she saw him she tapped urgently on the window and tried to get his attention. He forced himself to meet her gaze calmly, but couldn't hold the connection. Was it fear he saw reflected in those clear blue eyes?

Now the lab area was nearly empty. The supervisor and his workers had made tracks as soon as the last valve was tightened, and the sick-looking medical tech had pulled the last of his power plugs and gotten the hell out. Only a few guards, Kyle, and two or three more technicians stuck it out. And Fitch, of course, lording high above them within his own disconnected world inside the control booth.

Reluctantly, Kyle looked up. Fitch was waiting, his nose practically pressed against the glass, yet the expression on his face wasn't one of eagerness, as Kyle expected. Although his post was a full story above Sil's cage, there was an odd, bittersweet shine in the doctor's eyes that made Kyle wonder for a moment if the older man was crying. Kyle's speculation was shattered by Fitch's curt nod, and the low-pitched murmurs around the room stuttered to nothing as the lab assistant swallowed with difficulty, then quickly—*one two three four*—opened the valves on the canisters. Thick white gas swirled into Sil's enclosure, rolling over her panicked face. Kyle thought he saw the girl swipe at it, but he couldn't be sure; ten more seconds and the glass cage looked absurdly like a huge aquarium filled with clouds.

The deed was done. The technicians and guards around the room began moving again, although no one said anything. Fitch's orders were to leave the cyanide in the enclosure for at least a quarter hour before siphoning it off, and Kyle had already decided that he would be halfway home by then. The lab assistant turned and headed for the stairs, reasoning that his had by far been the worst task; as far as he was concerned, someone else could handle the cleanup. Maybe he'd stop and pick up a six-pack of Bass on the way; that *might* help him get the girl's face out of his mind when he fell into bed.

There was a sound like an explosion behind him, strangely *sharp*, and Kyle spun with crazy images of car crashes in his head, along with thoughts of dialing the emergency code on the intercom. He had time to register the jagged-edged hole in the front panel of tempered glass that made up Sil's enclosure, then the rest of the panel disintegrated with a tremendous *crack!*

The fragments of safety glass held for no more than an intake of breath before they fell, like a hundred thousand diamonds spilling from nowhere. There was a millisecond of beauty as the lovely young girl inside dove through the faux-jeweled waterfall, oblivious to the tiny pieces of glass layering the floor, then the guard closest to the enclosure went for his sidearm. Paralyzed five feet from the stairs, Kyle realized that Sil was holding her breath against the clouds of hydrogen cyanide that were now boiling into the lab. The instincts of the guard headed toward her were not so swift, and he fell forward, dead, long before he could pull his pistol free of its holster.

The alarms went wild. Bells and sirens began blasting from the junctures of the walls and ceilings, garbled voices screaming through the speakers. The girl was still holding her breath, and Kyle tried to follow suit as the cyanide swept through the room. A fool's belated wish, Kyle thought haphazardly as the technicians closest to the glass cage staggered and collapsed; his balance went as dizziness raced across his eyesight and he began to gag. As he went to his knees Kyle knew it was already too late for him and the rest of the room's occupants; Sil ran past as Kyle's vision began a black-and-yellow shimmer, not even sparing him a glance as he retched uselessly on all fours.

It took monumental effort, but Kyle found the strength to lift his head toward the ceiling. His last sight was of Xavier Fitch's grim, white face, staring down from the observation booth.

2

She finally got air when she reached the end of the corridor.

Sil could see the cyanide at the other end leaking from beneath the door she had yanked closed behind her. To her, the fumes weren't white, they were black—*poison*. When the men who had watched her constantly through the flimsy glass walls of her home wouldn't watch her anymore and the malignant-looking clouds began filling the enclosure, only instinct, primitive and previously silent, had saved her. The air saturating her lungs now smelled medicinal, like the alcohol pads the technicians used to clean the adhesive from her skin when they moved an electrode or swabbed her arm when they wanted to take a sample of her blood. It didn't taste good in her mouth or lungs, but it was better than the death-filled air in the lab. She needed to move fast, though, had to stay ahead of the carpet of cyanide gas seeping from underneath the door to the lab and rolling slowly down the corridor at floor level.

Why did they want to harm her? Sil didn't understand the reasoning behind it—especially Dr. Fitch, on whom she had come to depend the most for companionship. True, he didn't say much, but she could *sense* his bond with her, the way he charted her fantastic growth and rapid learning processes, the way he jealously scrutinized the actions of Kyle or any other lab tech or assistant who dealt with her. He had been there when she'd opened her eyes for her first sight of this world—Sil remembered the exact moment—and had held her hand when she'd taken her first tentative step not long after.

And she would never forget that he had been there at the end, too, expecting to watch her die. Betraying her.

There was a door in front of Sil and she hesitated, uncertain. The same kind of stencils were printed on it as had been painted on the poisonous cyanide containers, but the words were different—FIRE DOOR—and no colors leaked from around the door's frame. Since there was nowhere else to go and a backward glance showed the low cloud of black gas passing the halfway mark in the corridor, Sil grasped the silver bar across the door and pulled.

Nothing happened. A knot of panic burgeoned in the center of her chest, identical to the one that had appeared when the sandy-haired technician, her favorite, had turned the knob on the first canister and begun releasing the cyanide into her cage. Sil slammed her hands against the silver bar and had a millisecond to feel foolish as the door opened easily, then she fell forward against the barrel chest of an anxious-faced, heavyset guard headed into the same corridor she was trying to escape. He backstepped twice, then pointed a weapon at her. She glimpsed the words PIETRO BERETTA on one side of the pistol before he leveled it at her face and started bellowing.

"Hold it right there! You just freeze—" He was terrified, babbling like a confused child.

Would he fire? Sil didn't want to find out. She shoved him, faster than he could react, and much,

much harder than she had pushed the door. She didn't know which of them was the more surprised when he was flung a half-dozen feet back. He hit the ground at a bad angle and Sil heard a muffled *snap*, then he went limp. She crouched in front of him, ready, but he didn't move, just sat and stared with his head at an odd angle and his eyes blank and unblinking. Sil prodded him experimentally with one toe; when she got no response, she darted around him.

She'd met the guard at a doorway set about ten feet into the concrete building. Outside, the sight of the sparkling heavens made her falter, its beauty and size so outrageous that it stunned her for a precious five seconds as she gaped up at it. Then she saw a high security fence rimmed with razor wire thirty yards in front of her and headed toward it, an unexpected step onto the paved surface surrounding the building the only thing marring the swiftness of her progress. The fence was all but useless in stopping her, and Sil was up and over it in a matter of seconds, swinging easily over the razor wire. On the other side was nothing but dry, desert scrub stretching as far as she could see, a hundred tones of gray beneath the star-splashed sky.

Then Sil was gone, fleeing into the shadowy arms of the desert night.

Far behind her, lights exploded from the rooftop of the building and new alarms began shrieking in tandem with the muffled clanging of the bells inside. Pools of light spilled onto the concrete from doorways that burst open as guards rushed out, flashlight beams swinging frantically in every direction. More followed, weapons clanking amid harshly shouted orders and static-filled transmissions from walkie-talkies. As she ran Sil heard another, more dangerous sound: the whirring of helicopter blades rising from the helipads on the other side of the complex, their strong Night-Sun spotlights far away but already slicing the air in her general direction. A half-dozen muted hissing noises made her pause and she saw parachute flares dotting the sky close to the building; apparently they had no idea she could run as fast as she had.

Sil didn't know how much distance she put between her and the searchers over the next ten minutes. She knew only that she ran at top speed, pushing her legs and lungs to the limit but not tiring, until the frantic lights and noises surrounding the complex were only silent pinpoints in the black expanse of the desert behind her. She slowed only when she was convinced that she could hide herself among the scrubs and rocks that peppered the landscape, occasionally sending the faraway spots of light a wary glance as she picked her way between the loose boulders and twiggy bushes. Silver gleamed in the ground ahead and Sil stopped and peered at it curiously, finding twin strips of metal that stretched across the desert floor to disappear over an unseen horizon.

Something huge *bellowed* behind her and Sil spun, paralyzed with terror. A vehicle rushed toward her and her brain instantly selected a piece of information from one of the picture books she'd been given—a *train*. She threw herself out of its way before the first boxcar lumbered past, then scrambled back to her feet and sprang for a handhold on the nearest car.

Pulling herself through the first open door she found, Sil searched for a hiding place within its darkest spaces as the train rumbled on into the night.

3

"Get a cleanup crew in there *now*," Xavier Fitch barked into the telephone. The person on the other end said something that served only to deepen the already startling shade of scarlet that suffused Fitch's face. "Oh, for Christ's sake," he yelled, "men are *dead* down there. Of *course* your crew will still need gas masks, you imbecile!" He was shouting when he slammed down the receiver.

Fitch turned back to the window and gripped the sealed edge of the sill, digging at it until his fingernails went white. There were bodies everywhere below. Five guards sprawled at various posts around the large room; three of them had blundered into death at the call of the alarms, while three technicians had crumpled in place, one still clutching his clipboard and pen. And Kyle, of course, lying by the staircase and staring up at him with dead, accusing eyes. Fitch had sent his most competent lab assistant down there out of nothing more than annoyance and now the man was dead. Fitch shook his head; foolish, foolish.

Tension etched its way across his forehead as he snatched up the receiver again. The alarms were mak-

19

ing everything crazy and it took seven rings—he counted every one involuntarily—before he finally got the switchboard operator. By then the fingers of one hand were drumming erratically against the window glass while the other hand was twining around the extra-long cord that ran from the receiver to the telephone's base on the desk. "It took you fucking long enough!" he snarled at the faceless voice. Whoever the woman was, he cut her off when she started to defend herself. "Just get me McConnelly at the NSC—*now!*"

It took so long to make the connection that Fitch was starting to think the operator had intentionally disconnected him, an act he could guarantee would end her government career—menial as it was—forever. Finally, nearly synchronized with the entry of a horde of gas-masked workers into the polluted laboratory below, he heard a series of clicks on the line and a voice spoke on the other end.

"Sir," Fitch said. His voice was shaking for the first time since he'd seen Sil's speedy destruction of the supposedly indestructible glass cage. "This is Dr. Xavier Fitch, Visitor Base One. You asked to be kept in the loop on all pertinent developments." Fitch was fighting valiantly now to keep his words steady.

"I'm afraid we have a serious emergency on our hands."

4

She was floating, weightless, spinning slowly in warm fluid. Water? No, something thicker, more secure, like amniotic fluid in a mother's womb. Drifting without care, sinking slowly toward an untroubled abyss as sight suddenly returned to reveal the barest shimmer of light from far away, the surrounding liquid not black but pale amber. Breathing steadily and heavily, there was a firmness to the sound that suggested stability and size, predator not prey. Shifting, the effort of movement sent graceful tentacles to ripple at the sides of her limited field of vision. A jellyfish passed without pausing at the sight of her, an ancient and beautiful coelenterate, like a multicolored man-of-war gliding undisturbed through its domain. She concentrated then, the passage of instructions along her neural pathways marked by sparkling biolights in her dim golden surroundings. There was a sensation of movement on her left side as something tiny drifted close, a fish lured by the swaying loveliness of her tentacles. Abrupt hunger as the fish nibbled tentatively, the instantaneous release of energy—CRACK!—and the fish jittered and died; the smallest mental command and her appetite was appeased—for now—as her luminous torso covered and consumed it.

21

A *change* in the atmosphere and her breathing accelerated twofold, then doubled again, spurred by the presence of
something dark and sharp in the depths below, bigger, faster,
infinitely more dangerous. She could see it all too clearly, its
lean, arrow-shaped frame rushing through the murkiness,
blind but aiming by sheer instinct, a deadly internal guid-
ance system that would lead it right to her. She tried to spin,
to flee, but she was too slow, grace and beauty exacting a
deadly price in the lush golden environment. Sound then,
growing, and louder than her own panicked breathing, the
enormous reverberation of the creature's charge as it hurtled
toward her, the end of its chiseled head yawning wide, revealing hundreds of glimmering, needlelike teeth—

♦

Sil came awake with a jerk, covered with sweat and
blue eyes bulging with fright, before she remembered
where she was—a boxcar on the train, one of the
empty ones toward its back end. Her skin felt over-
heated from the nightmare, her breathing still heavy
and fast. The steady vibrations through the matted
straw beneath almost lulled her back to sleep, then an
unidentified shape moved in the darkness, coming at
her too quickly and with a moist, sliding sound alarm-
ingly like the one moments ago in her dream. Sil's eyes
widened again in surprise as a man lunged at her, a
hobo wearing a filthy, tattered jacket and grime-
encrusted jeans. She hadn't had much time to think
about her nightmare, but she *had* learned a valuable lesson from it—if she didn't move fast enough, she
wouldn't escape a predator. She jerked out of range as
his nails snatched at her arm and she saw him grin, saw
his nicotine-stained teeth yawn open and glimmer as
gold fillings winked in the wildly flashing red-and-
white lights of a crossroads warning signal. He lumbered forward and clutched at her again, mouth
stretching wider; more glimpses of teeth and winks of
light in a mouth that looked as dangerous as her dream

creature's. She scrambled away and her hand brushed
something in the straw: a liquor bottle, the remnants of
the hobo's evening imbibing sloshing as it wobbled on
its side with the movements of the train. But when Sil's
arm shot forward and she struck him in the chest, the
bottle stayed where it was on the debris-strewn floor of
the boxcar; she didn't *need* a weapon.

The hobo made no noise as his body snapped backward and his face contorted in agony. He fell away from
her almost gently, his weight settling into the small,
uneven mounds of straw with hardly a sound. The
dusty fingers of one hand twitched slightly, mindless
electrical impulses, then he was still.

Heart jackhammering, Sil cowered in the corner of
the car, as far away from her attacker as possible. Was
he dead or would he leap at her again? She waited anxiously, ready to fight, feeling her double-time exhala-
tions slowly return to normal as the minutes slipped by
in the thundering darkness. But nothing about the
hunched shaped moved, and as Sil's fear seeped away
and her nerves calmed, she noticed something odd rising from the slit of a side pocket in the man's jacket,
faint, enticing pink fumes that gave off a maddening
smell. While she was sure the man was dead, she was
still cautious as she crept forward and probed at the
fabric with two fingers, primed to jump out of reach.
Convinced at last, she tore eagerly at the dead man's
coat until she found the source of the appetizing
vapors—a half-eaten hamburger inside a wad of alumi-
nized paper. It wasn't much; three, maybe four bites and
it was gone, barely chewed before she swallowed.

Later Sil found the hobo's ratty travel bag and went
through it. She dug all the way to its grimy bottom, but
there wasn't any more food, and although she opened it
and sniffed the contents inquisitively, the bottle of Mad
Dog lying in the straw held no interest for her. She let
it drop uncapped onto the lap of the dead drifter, where
its contents emptied in steady burbles and diluted the

drying puddle of blood surrounding his torso. Sil did find extra clothes, though, something to substitute for the flowered hospital gown that was all she'd ever been allowed to wear. They were oversized but not hard to figure out; she'd seen the same items on the technicians and guards who had continually come and gone during her short life. The workers around her had seemed to believe she could neither understand them nor think intelligently, so most of what she had learned so far had been on her own, by simple observation and deduction. The picture books had been simple but accurate, and she had a feeling those childish tools would be the ones upon which she relied the most heavily in the very near future. The ease with which she had escaped made her again wonder why Dr. Fitch had tried to destroy her; she believed now that it was because they—Dr. Fitch and the others she had met so far—were weaker than she. There was something else inside her that Dr. Fitch had not intentionally planned to give her, and whatever the mystery part was, it made her better and stronger . . . *dominant*.

When the travel bag was emptied, Sil nearly had a complete outfit. No socks or shoes, but she would deal with that later. The squalid-looking cadaver could keep the ones on his feet right now; they smelled far too repellent to pull free of his body.

Dressed but still *very* hungry, Sil sat back and waited for the train to take her to an unknown destination.

CHAPTER

5

The morning's desert sun was red and bloody looking against the scrub-scattered horizon. Barely risen, its full girth not even clear of the skyline, its rays already coaxed dancing heat ripples from the surface of the earth, warping the shapes of the helicopters and trucks that fanned across the landscape.

Xavier Fitch stood between the set of twin silver train rails, his fists bunched at his sides. The only reason they were able to guess at Sil's direction was the information, sent via a scrambled radio transmission, that a couple of freight trains had made their scheduled runs through here at about the same time as her escape.

"Those trains passed through here over two hours ago," Fitch said thoughtfully. "She could have stayed on . . . or gotten off . . . *anywhere*." Where was the girl now? Perhaps she'd been leaping onto a Utah-bound car even as that foolish search-and-destroy gunner in the Apache chopper had gotten all their hopes up by locking on a target with his chaingun, then pulverizing something in the brush that had turned out to be only a coyote. Fitch recalled the young man's face and how it had turned scarlet when he'd had to report that he'd

25

discharged several hundred .30mm rounds through his chaingun at a twenty-pound canid. He wondered what would have happened had the gunner's target been authentic and found himself shying away from the thought.

The replacement aide assigned to Fitch was Robert Minjha. Dark-skinned and watchful, Robert was younger than Kyle Jacobson and ignorant of the more ... *delicate* aspects of the project. Kyle had known everything about Sil, and it annoyed Xavier to be forced to pick and choose the bits of information he should feed his new assistant. Robert's bright eyes took it all in and hinted that he understood more than what was said, but he didn't question Fitch's orders as much as Kyle had; Fitch thought he was as dull as the sand-colored landscape around them. This time, though, Robert did have a question.

"Is she that fast?"

Fitch hesitated before answering. He could lie, but it would be ludicrously obvious—after all, why else were they looking so far out in the desolate Mojave? All the aides had known about the project from its onset anyway; the current replacements simply hadn't been able to get as close to it before the ... accident.

"Yes," he admitted softly. "She's that fast."

6

Brigham City, Utah reminded Sil, in the most tenuous way, of the complex in which she'd been born, and when the freight train had finally stopped in the rear of the train yard, she had been drawn in spite of herself to the busiest part of the station. Clean, bright, and filled with neatly dressed, freshly scrubbed people, even the travelers seemed to have left their road dirt behind, not daring to bring it into this tidy little metropolis. Sil knew there must have been other hobos in the surrounding boxcars; she had sensed a group of them only one car away, waited to see if their roady curiosity would lead them down the same trail as their now dead comrade. When no one else had come, she had eventually slipped into a fragmented sleep, troubled by broken bits of her previous nightmare.

She didn't know where the hobos had gone this morning—perhaps they had stayed in the boxcars, waiting for the train to carry them to another town or larger city in which they could blend more naturally. Standing on the cleanly swept sidewalk next to the train station, Sil was a flagrant outsider amid the carefully tended pots of marigolds and petunias. Everything about the people

milling past was different from anything she'd ever
encountered—their clothes, the pleasant expressions on
their faces, the way they smiled at each other. Looking
down at the smudged and greasy pants and shirt she'd
found in the hobo's bag and at her bare feet, Sil realized
her hands had started to shake. How long before someone in . . . *authority* began to question her? This was no
dark and private boxcar speeding through the desert at
night; retaliation and escape would not be so effortless in
Brigham City at midmorning.

But it was so *fascinating*. Dozens of people hustled
through the station carrying everything from shoulder
bags and briefcases to overstuffed suitcases they could
barely lift. Others stood in line to talk to a woman on
the other side of a window above which was a sign labeled TICKETS, while yet another line had formed at a
cart painted gaudy red and yellow with western-style
wheels that were far larger than necessary. Her gaze
sharpened as she focused on something inside an oversized glass box on top of the cart—hot dogs, turning
and sizzling on a roaster and sending up familiar feath-
ery fumes, their color a stronger, tantalizing pink that
drifted above the cart like a beacon for the hunger
twisting painfully in her belly.

Sil turned away. Too many people encircled the cart,
and the meat itself wasn't in the open where she could
run by and snatch at it. Dressed in a white coat and a paper hat with points at each end, the man who seemed to
own the cart and the hot dogs was stationed next to it;
the backs of the people in line were blocking Sil's view,
and she had no idea what was required to persuade the
man to give her one. She wandered closer, trying to see,
but the cart and the line were too close to the wall. She
turned away; better to try something more in the open.

After a five-second scan of the interior of the train
station Sil headed toward the snack shop at its other
end, attracted by its brightly decorated window. She
stopped outside the entrance and stared at the posters

crowded on the surface of the glass, photographs of adults eating snacks and drinking sodas, all of which she assumed where available inside. Could she just walk in and take what she wanted? She looked back at the hot-dog cart and frowned; it seemed so, yet didn't make sense, and she was already glaringly conspicuous. But she was so *hungry*. After a moment of hesitation, she decided to go in.

The snack shop was small, shaped like a long rectangle rather than a square. Sil's gaze automatically went to a narrow counter at its far end, where she saw a couple of patrons sitting on stools covered with red vinyl. Behind the counter a teenager with acne-spotted cheeks and hair hanging in his eyes moved back and forth, serving milkshakes and ice-cream dishes with a bored expression on his face. Again Sil saw the pink fumes, this time drifting from the thick glass dishes scattered along the countertop. She turned away; the length of the room, with its only door at the front, made the far end of the shop seem too much like a trap. Staying close to the front seemed her best bet.

The first display she came across was immediately to the right inside the first of the three cramped aisles. The rows of beef jerky and chocolate-chip cookies *looked* edible, but they lacked the lovely pink fumes and smells that she associated with food. Perplexed, Sil gnawed on one fingernail, then touched one of the packets of jerky and made the connection—they were *wrapped*, that was all, covered by a false skin. If she broke through the covering, she would find the food. Satisfied, she tugged half a dozen packets of beef jerky free of their hook, then added as many of the wrapped cookies as she could hold in her other hand.

Now what? Unsure, Sil turned back toward the front of the snack shop and began to move toward the exit. As she stepped into the main area she almost collided with another person and stopped herself just short of instinctively lashing out.

"Sorry," the other started to mumble. It was a boy her own age, trying to walk and tear open the waxy wrapping on a candy bar at the same time. He looked up from his task and his apology stuttered away as Sil gaped at him. She'd never seen anyone her own age before—he looked like a much younger version of Kyle, the sandy-haired lab assistant at the complex who had been her friend until his final treachery. Would this boy talk to her? Could she talk to him?

The boy's lips parted, but he didn't say anything. Instead he lifted the candy bar, something called a Butterfinger, to his mouth. He bit into it, chewing methodically as he scrutinized Sil and her raggedy clothes. His gaze slid to her naked feet, and he looked like he was going to speak when an adult woman touched him on the shoulder. If the woman saw Sil and the condition of her garments, she never acknowledged it.

"Don't eat that until I pay for it," she admonished gently. "Come on, let's go." The boy nodded and folded the excess wrapper over the bitten end of the Butterfinger bar, then followed his mother to the cash register. Sil got another peculiar look from him, then the boy's mother kissed the top of his head as he turned his attention to the man at the checkout counter. Still puzzling over the affectionate ritual, Sil watched with rapt attention as the clerk tapped several keys on the register and a man in front of the woman and boy gave him three folded pieces of paper and some small pieces of round metal. After the clerk handed him a scrap of white paper, the guy left with a plastic bag filled with items—a bag of potato chips, a magazine, a few travel toiletries. Then it was the woman's turn and Sil frowned, trying to watch the boy watch her at the same time as she tried to understand the procedure the woman was following. Rather than the green paper, she offered the clerk a small, colorful plastic card; the cashier accepted it, ran it through a small machine, punched more keys on the cash register, then handed it back—along with the

bagged purchases. Whatever had transpired, it had given
the boy the right to begin eating his candy bar again,
and the Butterfinger was already half-gone before he and
his mother stepped out of the snack shop.

"You going to buy those?"

Sil gasped at the sound of the clerk's voice. She was
standing right in front of him; without realizing it, she
had drifted toward the checkout counter, her contem-
plation making her unwittingly follow the small line of
customers. *Buy* them? It wasn't difficult to figure out
that this was a trading situation—if you wanted something in the store, you gave something in return. The
problem was, Sil still didn't grasp exactly *what*. Green
paper, or plastic cards, yes—but where and how could
she *get* those things?

The clerk started to say something else, then turned
his head toward the entrance to the snack shop as a
group of teenagers came in. Except for being loud, the
four older boys seemed too close in age to most of her
former lab technicians for Sil to pay them any mind, but
the clerk's attention sharpened visibly. While he was
looking elsewhere Sil saw her chance; she dropped the
packets of beef jerky and cookies on the counter and ran
out, her fleet-footed dodge around the older boys making
them whoop in admiration and cheer her on.

◆

She found the boy and his mother again, this time
standing with a trio of suitcases out on the train platform. Far enough away not to be noticed, she watched
as the woman and her son each lifted a suitcase and a
porter picked up the third to help them board a train.
This train was different from the rust-stained boxcar
that had sheltered Sil last night; each car was sleek and
silver and had plenty of windows, and under all of them
the word AMTRAK was painted in sprawling red-and-
blue letters.

After the woman and boy disappeared into the train

car, Sil watched the other boarding passengers thoughtfully. The train, she concluded, was leaving shortly, and with its impression of cleanliness and speed, was an infinitely better way to get somewhere, *anywhere*, as long as it wasn't back to the laboratory. More porters were loading luggage here and there along the length of the train, and as the one nearest her struggled with a particularly heavy wooden chest, Sil snuck past and scooped an undersized blue suitcase from the jumble of bags at his back. She walked away as nonchalantly as she could, dreading the sound of his shout. It never came; relieved, she let her breath out—she hadn't realized she'd been holding it—and boarded the train at a different car, following the mother and son. Half the train car away, she saw the woman and boy open a door and go into a sleeping compartment.

Following their example, Sil strolled down the narrow corridor, glanced around quickly, then slipped into the one next to them. There wasn't much room inside, and what she did find was the antithesis of the environment back at the lab. Everything here was small and dark and varying shades of gray, from the iron-gray vinyl upholstery on the two facing seats to the silvery gray of the metal walls. There was another doorway, half the normal width, on the wall to the right of the window, and when Sil looked through it she found a tiny bathroom with a toilet, sink, and cramped shower stall. Outside the window and a few feet below her compartment, a middle-aged man holding a larger version of the suitcase Sil had stolen spoke animatedly with a conductor, who spread his hands and gestured at the empty platform, then shook his head. As she watched, the train jerked into motion and began to pull out of the station.

A full five minutes passed before Sil felt she could open the suitcase without fear that the train would suddenly stop and someone would start a car-by-car search. She didn't know why, but for some reason she had expected to find clothes inside; instead she discovered a miniature portable television and several stacks of papers held together by rubber bands. The television called to mind the cameras mounted high on the walls of the laboratory at regular intervals, and she turned it on uncertainly, wondering if doing so would enable the men and women at the complex to see where she was. But the image that flickered on was reassuring; the fuzzy but luminously colored cartoon images fleeing across the four-inch screen couldn't possibly have anything to do with the complex in the desert. She pushed a different button on the front and the image lost its color and changed to one of a man and woman kissing; they were dressed oddly, the man's suit and the woman's long, elaborate gown resembling nothing Sil had seen so far. She thought the dress, with its ruffled layers and multitude of bows sewn across the neckline, was pretty but not very practical. A poke at another button and the screen went dark; frowning, she pushed the same button again and the screen lit back up. On, off; it wasn't that hard to figure out.

She set the little television on the other seat, then turned the small suitcase upside down and let the papers fall in a heap on the floor, nearly slipping in the debris when an announcement over the loudspeaker made her jump.

"*Attention, all passengers. The dining car will be closed en route to Las Vegas, but will reopen after the train departs from the Las Vegas station. All new passengers please have your tickets ready for the conductors. Thank you.*"

Dining car? Dining meant food, and Sil picked up the empty suitcase and peered out of the compartment. All of the doors to the occupied compartments were shut and the corridor was dim and quiet, the silence disturbed only by an occasional muffled voice from behind the thin walls. Both ends of the car had aluminum-sheathed openings, but the one toward the front of the train had a sign showing an arrow with a floating knife and fork above it. The other, presumably, led to more sleeping cars.

The dining car was the next one over, and Sil was relieved to find it deserted. It was a lot brighter in here, bigger windows shedding a generous amount of sunlight on the crisp white tablecloths topped with glass salt-and-pepper shakers and white porcelain boxes holding tricolored packets of sweetener. She breathed deeply of the earlier aromas that still hung in the air, a not unpleasant mix of scorched coffee, eggs and overused griddle grease. But when Sil checked, the area behind the counter and cash register was empty. Frustrated, she saw a drawer beneath the cash register and tried to pull it out. When she found it locked, she yanked on it, hard; the front cracked, then splintered open to reveal five compartments, each containing small, neat stacks of the green paper she'd seen people trading for food in the train station—money. She emptied the cash drawer, stuffing its contents into the one front pocket of the hobo's pants that didn't have a hole.

On her way out from behind the counter, Sil spotted another door, one that led to something other than another train car. She tried the doorknob and it turned. What she found inside brought the first big smile to her face since before yesterday's terrible experience at the complex. Food—and lots of it. The storeroom for the dining services was stuffed from floor to ceiling with oversized cans and boxes bearing generic black-and-white labels.

Overwhelmed, instead of tearing into one of the boxes, Sil pulled on the handle of the big refrigerator that was the first object inside the room. What she found was far more suitable than the dry goods on the wall shelves: plastic jugs of cold milk, boxes of raw hamburger patties and uncooked french fries, cartons of fruit juice and plastic cups of flavored pudding. She loaded up her bag with as much as would fit, trying her best to keep quiet and almost blowing everything by dropping a gallon of milk when a conductor unexpectedly passed through the dining car. Her only warning was a whistling sound the man was making with his mouth, a continuous birdlike trilling that Sil found appealing and annoying at the same time.

When the conductor was gone and the suitcase was full, she eased out of the storeroom and headed back to her compartment. The bag was full and cumbersome, though she didn't find it all that heavy. The train, however, seemed to be passing over a particularly rough stretch of track, and she wasn't accustomed to carrying something so badly out of balance. Struggling to get the bag through the doors of the connecting car as the train lurched, Sil froze when a man's hand reached past her and grabbed the handle of the suitcase.

"Let me help you with that." The whistling conductor, not whistling now, smiled affably at her. His friendly brown eyes crinkled around the edges as he gestured at the narrow corridor with his free hand. "You lead, little lady. I'll carry the heavy stuff."

Terrified, Sil forced herself to smile, then stepped in front of him and made her way to the sleeping compartment she had claimed earlier. She didn't care if he was just being helpful; she didn't like him following behind her where she couldn't watch him and wasn't at all comfortable with him carrying the suitcase full of food. How would she explain if the overloaded latches gave out and it opened? On top of that, he was whistling again, and it made her want to turn around, yank the bag out of his hand, and put an end to that irritating shrilling. A more rational part of her brain told her it was fear making her react this way; she stifled the impulse to strike and was rewarded when he swung the heavy bag inside the door to her compartment with a grunt, tipped his hat and went away, pulling the door closed as he left.

Ravenous, Sil started to open the suitcase's latches, then clenched her fists when someone else knocked on the door. "Ticket, please." A woman's voice, muted by the door and the quiet, smoother rumble of the Amtrak train.

Sil quickly pushed the papers strewn on the floor aside with her foot, then opened the door, remembering the announcement that had come over the speaker in the ceiling right before she'd left for the dining car. She needed a ticket to stay on the train but didn't have one to give the young woman standing in the corridor. But she did have money; maybe that would be acceptable. The woman, who was wearing a name tag over her left breast pocket that said A. CARDOZA, gave Sil a bland smile and held out a hand; in response, Sil dug in the pocket of the hobo's dirty pants and came out with a couple of wadded-up bills. She dropped them onto the woman's palm with a hopeful expression on her face.

A. Cardoza looked at the crumpled money on her palm, then back at Sil. "Are you traveling by yourself?" she asked gently. Sil nodded. "How old are you? Eleven? Twelve?" Sil nodded again. The conductor shuffled through the bills, kept two and returned the rest to Sil, who pocketed them. "Tell you what," the woman suggested with a wink as she pulled out a pad of paper, separated a couple of sheets and used a metal device to punch odd-shaped holes in it. "We'll say you're eleven. That way you only have to pay half fare."

She looked at Sil expectantly and Sil hesitated, then nodded a third time. She was beginning to feel like a puppet with a string attached to its neck, but she didn't know what else to do, or what to say. A. Cardoza studied her for a moment, then smiled. "Don't talk much, do you? You must be shy—but that's okay. I was too, when I was your age." Conductor Cardoza backstepped into the corridor and started to pull the door after her, then paused and looked Sil up and down. "Traveling alone like this can be dangerous," she said. "You be sure to keep this door locked, okay?" A second later A. Cardoza shut the compartment door and was gone.

The sound the wooden door of the railroad car made as the Special Operations MP slid it open was like two oversized pieces of splintered wood being rubbed together. That kind of noise belonged in fake haunted houses on Halloween weekends, not on a freight car sitting in the train yard of a clean, sunlit city like Brigham. The door reached its limit with a harsh clang and sunbeams washed most of the inside of the car, giving glaring detail to a man's body—some drifter riding the night train whose luck had run out. It was hard to tell amid the splattered blood, but everything above his sternum seemed to be twisted the wrong way; they could see the rusted—or was it bloodied?—safety pin the hobo had used to keep his pants together, and the matted, graying hair on his stomach, but at the same time they were staring at the back of his shoulder blades and head.

"Our little girl did this?" Standing next to Fitch, Robert stared at the cadaver splayed on the straw-covered floor of the freight car.

"She's not a little girl," Fitch said harshly. "She's not even truly human. Besides, DNA typing of material under the hobo's fingernails proves it was her. He must have grabbed her."

"He probably attacked her." The name tag on the lapel of the second aide said PHILLIP McRAMSEY, but that was all—more, in fact, than Fitch cared to know. Another new aide, replacements for the ones killed at the complex. Workers to do his bidding, and that was all he needed; Kyle had made him feel far too guilty about having to terminate the child, had once even suggested Fitch think of Sil as his daughter. A foolish suggestion, but one that stuck nonetheless and caused him no end of sleepless nights. He still wished he could forget it—especially now that Kyle was dead.

"She could be anywhere," Robert said pensively. He gave the doctor a distressed look. "Chicago, Las Vegas, Los Angeles . . . *anywhere*."

"We should stop all the trains." Phillip scanned the MPs guarding the area, as if looking for someone he could order to do just that. All of them had Army Special Operations insignia on the arms of their uniforms, and all ignored the white-coated lab assistants.

"And have the railroad and local police asking a million questions we can't answer?" Fitch shook his head, shooting McRamsey a disgusted look. "We'll put key personnel at every stop along these lines. I want a team to track her, hunt her down—"

"Jesus," Robert breathed, staring back into the boxcar. "What the hell have we done?"

Fitch started to snap at the interruption, then closed his mouth and gazed off in the other direction, where the train yards ended in sidings that went nowhere and the open plains began. Nothing out there for Sil but pure potential.

What the hell have we done?

Fitch wished he could answer that.

8

"*You came all the way up here to get a cup of my wonderful coffee?*" A pretty woman in her early twenties moved across the tiny television screen toward an extremely handsome man. She was wearing a sweater that seemed loose but tight at the same time—something about the way the fabric stretched across her collarbones and followed the line of her rib cage without really revealing anything. Her skirt was a sensible length, but had that same, oddly sexual appeal to it.

Sitting cross-legged on one of the seats, Sil shoved most of a raw hamburger patty in her mouth without looking away from the screen.

The television woman's companion plastered an innocent smile across his face. "*Does that sound unlikely?*" His smile made him resemble a perfectly chiseled statue.

"*Not . . . entirely.*" The woman tossed her head, swinging a mass of shining auburn hair over her shoulder. Her lips were very red and looked wet.

"*What else would I want?*" He spread his hands in what should have been a demonstration of meekness, but the movement made Sil's eyes narrow. To her, he looked like a predator, someone who couldn't be trusted.

"*I really can't imagine,*" said the woman on the television. She turned her back to the man and began pouring coffee. A foolish movement in Sil's opinion, and she hit the channel button and stuffed the remainder of the meat patty in her mouth. Her fingers had thickened and looked pudgy, too short for her small hands. Two ample rolls of fat had swelled from beneath her chin, and though the dead hobo had been a large man, the waistline of his ratty pants now fit her quite comfortably.

"*When you're tired and need a room for the night, check in!*" A black-and-yellow Best Western sign floated behind a man with a round face and a cheerful voice. Sil found the idea of dealing with him a lot less frightening than the oily-looking man in the coffee commercial. She watched the rest of the ad, which showed a room that included two double beds and extra furniture and was about ten times the size of the one in which she stayed now. At the end of the commercial a series of numbers—$39.95—floated over a picturesque swimming pool surrounded by men, women, and children in very small clothes.

She swallowed the rest of the beef and washed it down with the last of a gallon of milk—her second. The skin of her face felt bloated and tight, ready to explode. Fat had stretched the delicate skin between her eyebrows and upper lids so much that her eyes could open only to slits. Still watching the television, she reached a hand along the seat, blindly searching until her heavy fingers brushed one of the containers of pudding. She snatched it up and ripped off the paper top, using her fingers like a spoon to dip into the chocolate goo. When the contents were gone, she licked as much of it clean as she could, then tossed the container on the floor with the rest of the trash. Floor space on the train was at a premium and there was nowhere to walk now; every inch of the industrial-gray carpeting was covered with stained, crumpled wax squares from the hamburgers, empty juice boxes, and crushed dessert containers. Nestled amid the litter were two of the gallon milk containers, both empty.

Sil looked around the sleeping compartment. She was almost out of food, but she would deal with that only if it became necessary. A different kind of noise from the little television caught her attention and she turned back to it and watched, captivated, as the images of a dozen beautiful women began flashing on the screen. Every one had an abundance of thick, curly hair, each done in a different style and color. *"Curls, girls!"* an excited voice began. *"If your hair and your life need excitement, try this new—"*

The food was gone, but she was sated for now. All that was left was to watch.

And learn.

9

"The things worn around the waist are penis guards."

As always, the front row of the lecture hall was filled with young women. Now they tittered like teenagers at a slumber party, and Professor Stephen Arden smiled indulgently and aimed his laser pointer at the figure in the middle of the screen. An oversized image of himself posed calmly for the camera, undisturbed by the presence of the two nearly naked warriors on either side. Standing here and showing this seminude snapshot of himself with two members of a Brazilian tribe of Yanomamö to his three o'clock class didn't embarrass him at all; it did, however, make him appreciate the wisdom of regular workouts at the health club. He bent over the microphone again. "The women fashion these penis guards for their men to wear to protect their . . ." He raised his eyebrows as one of the more attractive ladies in the front row sat back and boldly met his gaze. He grinned tolerantly and glanced around the auditorium with boyish charm. "Well, I think we all know what they want to protect." He let the pointer doodle around the appropriate area on the screen, knowing full well that it was his own penis protector he was indicating. Another round of giggles, this time more widespread, some "Jesus, enough of this bullshit!" glances from the guys.

They're right, he thought regretfully. Enough goofing off. Time to actually force some knowledge into the echoing brain cavities dotting the audience at his lecture. "In reality, there's quite a bit to fear in the Venezuelan jungle, and particularly in the waters of the Orinoco River. In this particular region, in addition to the other dangers I've already told you about, there's a type of tiny catfish which lives in the river and which is also able to enter a man's body by swimming up the urethra tract and into the bladder. The catfish then stays there as a parasite, feeding and growing, until the man—its host—dies in agony."

"No *way*," one of the students in the front row said. She cocked her head to one side, but Arden wasn't convinced; there was too much intelligence in her dark eyes to pull off this calculated dumb-blond routine. "If they know this can happen, why do they still go in the river?"

"Because, Miss . . . ?"

"Teale."

"Because, Miss Teale," the professor continued, "the Orinoco River basin impacts significantly upon their lives. While they earn quite a bit of their livelihood from agriculture, they also depend upon the river for food, not to mention crop irrigation. This, you see, represents a fundamental difference in cultures, in the way—"

A noise to the left made Arden stop in midsentence and look around. He frowned when he saw Richard Jarelstein, one of his colleagues in the anthropology department, making his way toward the podium. When he reached the spot where Arden waited, Jarelstein nodded at the students. "Excuse us for a moment, please." He turned his back to the class and the microphone and leaned over and whispered in Arden's ear for a moment. Arden's eyes widened and he nodded, handing over the pointer. His class forgotten, he gathered up his papers and briefcase and walked out without further explanation.

Behind him, much to the dismay of the female students in the front row, Jarelstein pressed a button and the slide projector went dark. Jarelstein's voice, coarser than Arden's, rasped through the speakers as he stepped up to the podium.

"That will be all for today's lecture. Professor Arden has been called away unavoidably on business and this class has been canceled until further notice. If this class is part of your anthropology curriculum, please keep an eye on the schedule board. If it does not resume by Monday, consult your course adviser for alternate methods of credit in the interim between now and Professor's Arden's return. Good day."

◆

When the group had started the trip at Lees Ferry, the Colorado River had been clean and cold, the water strained by the Glen Canyon Dam to a sparkling navy blue beneath the high morning sun. Now, muddied miles ago from the juncture of the Little Colorado running in from the Painted Desert, the turbulent, tan-colored rapids at Bright Angel Falls made the river more gorgeous because of its wild glory and return to its natural color. Laura Baker wanted to see everything at once, and she twisted to the right to watch as the thirty-seven-foot silver raft shot past a multicolored outcropping of rock, layers of strata spotted with tenacious clumps of greenery on its steepest face. Her balance on the right tube was precarious and more than a little daring, but she wasn't stupid—besides, their guide would order them all to sit in if necessary. Like the other women on the rafting trip, she was strapped firmly inside a more-than-ample life jacket, and there was nothing at all scrawny about her arms as she gripped the ropes and held herself in place when the raft bucked atop the rapids. The front of the raft dipped, went back up on a particularly large swell, then dropped a good three feet. Laura and the other women screamed with exhilaration, laughing and whooping as the raft plunged through the last of the rapids and slowed, thrown into the calmer waters by the rapids' final push.

Soaked through her T-shirt and cutoffs, Laura grinned as brownish river water ran into her eyes and mouth. She whipped the wet strands of her hair out of her face with a laugh and glanced to the back of the raft, where the hefty, dark-haired guide expertly steered toward the river's center and away from the jagged rocks at the sides of the canyon. Her hands were rope-burned and she was peppered with bruises from being knocked off the side and onto the floor of the raft by a larger set of rapids earlier in the day, and she was having the time of her life.

"That was great, Guida! How far before the next one?" Shouts of agreement from the other women followed her question and made Laura's smile widen.

Guida's hair was plastered to her head like a dark, shining cap. A large Italian woman, her skin was tanned and glowed with an attractive outdoorsy health that Laura—who had red hair and fragile, fair skin that had to be lathered constantly with sunblock—envied. Her return smile showed teeth that were a perfect, bright white against the bronzed skin of her face. "About two miles," she called. "You folks'll have time to relax and you'd better appreciate it. The next set's a big one, with three smaller ones right after." She laughed heartily and swung the raft around until the front followed the Colorado's gentle curve to the west. "After we get your stomachs all shook up, we'll break for lunch along a nice little stretch of beach. Be nice to the sand, 'cause if Glen Canyon Dam keeps running as a peaking unit, there may not be any beaches left pretty soon."

The woman seated behind Laura started to ask a question about Guida's statement, but her shouted words were cut off, swallowed abruptly by a thunderous chopping. The water around them grew turbulent again and Laura saw Guida's face turn toward the sky; she scowled helplessly with the rest of the women at the Huey helicopter descending skillfully toward them, deftly lowering itself between the jutting walls of the canyon. Dismayed, Laura saw a flock of frightened birds take flight from the foliage spreading up the rock face to the west; so much for the undisturbed tranquillity of her vacation. The whole thing was starting to give her a bad feeling in the pit of her stomach.

The sleek black copter now hovered close enough above the raft for the women to see the helmeted face of the pilot and copilot. As they watched, the latter leaned out of the open door and hung over the water, pressing a loudspeaker to his mouth. Laura thought sourly that he looked like a monkey, dangling in the air with a misshapen banana.

"Dr. Laura Baker," the loudspeaker boomed, "please raise your hands." Laura jumped and nearly slid off the side of the tube and into the wind-whipped water as the knot in her gut abruptly burgeoned into outright pain. "I repeat—Dr. Laura Baker, if you are on this raft, please raise your hands. Your expertise is needed immediately in a matter of utmost importance."

"Crap," Laura muttered as the annoyed gazes of the other women turned toward her. "Two years of planning to get back to nature, and I still can't take a decent vacation." No one else heard her, though, and it was just as well. Resigned, she tightened her legs around the float tube of the raft to brace herself, then raised her hands. It was just too damned sad that she'd told the divisional secretary where she was going on vacation.

◆

"Are they still teasing you at work, Dan? The men from the passport identification department?"

Dan Smithson smiled softly. The question was a hard one and while he didn't really want to answer it, he liked the smooth sound of Dr. Roth's voice and wanted to hear it more. Every time he went in for a session, Dr. Roth made him feel calmer, relieved—like letting out his breath when he'd been holding it too long. He opened his mouth to answer, then felt the muscles in his neck and back tense when someone knocked on the door to the office. It couldn't be time for the session to end, could it? He'd only been here a few minutes— they'd just started.

"I won't answer that," Dr. Roth said evenly, noting the look on Dan's face. "Whoever it is can come back at the end of the hour." He paused to reconstruct his thoughts, then continued. "This teasing makes others feel better. If someone else is less, it makes *them* feel more."

The knocking came again, louder, and Dan felt the answer that had been forming in his thoughts sift away, like the powdered sugar falling off the doughnut he'd had for breakfast. He struggled to answer, to ignore the steady rapping on the other side of the fine wooden door to Dr. Roth's office. "They aren't afraid of me. They, uh, they know I won't fight back."

"Dr. Roth, please open the door immediately. It's an emergency." The words were muffled but understandable; with an apologetic glance at Dan, the doctor rose and turned the lock. A man dressed in a dark suit and tie stood patiently on the other side, holding out a wallet bearing an identification card. Dan could see the gold seal shining underneath the plastic sheeting.

"Sorry I have to interrupt," the man said levelly. He didn't bother to introduce himself as he stepped past the befuddled psychiatrist. His face was expressionless but somehow reassuring. "We need your help again, Dan."

Dan sat up and smoothed his shirt self-consciously, unable to mask his grateful smile. Someone needed *him* for a change, not the other way around.

Boy, that felt good.

♦

"Thanks for looking after my cat." Press Lennox dropped his travel bag on the steps and handed his pet to Mrs. Morris, the elderly woman who lived in the town house next door. Mrs. Morris started cooing over Lorca immediately, rubbing the tabby's neck and ears until it purred with satisfaction. Press had to force himself to smile in her direction as he locked his front door. It wasn't that he took her pet-sitting for granted or disliked his older neighbor. Quite the contrary—he appreciated the hell out of it every time she watched Lorca, and thought she was charming company on the rare occasions she stopped to chat. He just knew what was coming, and for some reason it drove him nuts every time she did it.

"We'll take good care of you, won't we, Lorca?" Mrs. Morris rubbed her cheek against the feline's ear and Lorca made an odd noise that was half purr and half mewl. The thing was horribly spoiled to begin with and would be impossible for a week after Press got home.

There was a short, double honk from the gray sedan idling at the curb and Press picked up his bag without turning. "I shouldn't be away long. I'll call you as soon as I get back." He strolled to the car and climbed in the passenger side, reluctantly lifting his hand to wave. Now came the part he hated. It just seemed like such a *stupid* thing to have his big, old tabby do, and it mucked up Press's mood each time he had to watch it happen.

Mrs. Morris smiled cheerily and waved good-bye with Lorca's paw.

Dreaming again, another train station, like but not like the one at Brigham. Not nearly as crowded, and no men at all. Only Sil . . . and several more females, all of whom looked just like her. Were they staring at her? She wasn't sure. She might be looking at reflections, some kind of multifaceted mirror—that could be why they all seemed to return her gaze so fixedly. It was so strange, like being everywhere at once and seeing where you'd just come from at the same time, instantaneously bouncing around another dimension.

The ground rumbled beneath her feet as a train shot from a tunnel at the other end of the station with a cloud of smoke. But the train looked wrong—not like it was a train at all, but a series of skulls, five in a row, chugging and gnashing their murderous way into the station. Horrified, Sil and her look-alikes bolted, but not fast enough to elude the crablike arms that erupted from the sides of each skull and scooped them up like so much easy fodder. She screamed but it was useless; she neither heard her voice nor knew which Sil she was as she was hurled into the air, flying through the smoke belching from the train's smokestack and into a container behind the last of the giant skulls. She landed with a bone-jarring thump and felt herself knocked senseless, *pushed out of real-time sequence. Now she could see the train again but not herself, and she wished desperately for a voice with which to scream as the teeth of each huge skull began chewing in rhythm with the piston's throbbing within the locomotive's engine, each singsong vibration causing a mass of wet, red matter to pulse between the skulls' teeth.*

Hissing and spewing steam, the train began to move into a different tunnel, its gleaming yellowish skull segments undulating one at a time in a caterpillarlike motion, stretching and closing until it pulled itself out of sight after a final, malevolent belch of white-hot vapor.

♦

Another nightmare. Slumped on one of the chairs in her sleeping compartment, Sil opened her eyes unwillingly. She didn't feel well . . . overeating? No, not that . . . nothing about her stomach or body *hurt*. She didn't even feel bloated or full. She was . . . exhausted for some reason. The hunger that had overwhelmed her earlier was gone, replaced by a fatigue so deep that even glancing out the window was an effort.

And she itched *terribly*, her face, her hands, every inch of her skin under the hobo's dirty clothes. Her hands were grimy but they looked okay, and as far as she could tell the flesh was clear and free of bites—that ruled out an insect infestation in the stolen clothes. She studied her fingers. Maybe an allergy, something she'd eaten—

Something below the skin began to move. The itching intensified and her mouth dropped open in shock. The flesh on the backs of her hands was alive with motion, as if unseen creatures searched urgently for a way out. She forgot about feeling drained and leaped to her feet, shaking her hands and arms wildly, bumping from wall to wall in the tiny compartment until she tripped over her own feet and fell, frightened tears spilling down her face. Sil moaned when the skin *there* also

abruptly began to prickle and burn and itch. Was it
moving, too?

She pulled herself to her feet using the door to the
dinky bathroom and staggered inside. Her reflection in
the small square of mirror was the most frightening
thing she'd ever seen, even more terrifying than watching Kyle back at the compound as he'd opened the
valves on the canisters marked HYDROGEN CYANIDE. At
least instinct had kicked in and saved her then; alone
in the middle of the night on this train with only stran-
gers in the surrounding compartments, she had nothing.

The fluorescent light in the minuscule bathroom was
overbright. It hid nothing and Sil nearly shrieked as
she saw her own face. It was teeming with movement,
hundreds of bumps sliding across her forehead and
cheeks, too many dangerously close to her eyes. Panicking, she ripped at one of the bulges, digging a red fur-
row from the bridge of her nose down her cheek. Terror
rocketed through her as a wormlike creature thrust
through the scratch, followed promptly by another,
then another. Pain blossomed throughout her body as
thousands more burst through the fragile skin without
assistance, like being stung by a hive full of wasps.

Wailing with fear, she gagged and tried to pull them
loose, felt herself retch harder as she realized they were
no longer the tiny, maggotlike things she'd first seen.
They had stretched and bonded together; now they
were long worms, still thin but a pallid white, like
nearly translucent ropes twining about her in every direction, growing and slithering from her body on up to
the ceiling. She fought uselessly, struggling to free herself as they grew stronger and wrapped around her torso
and limbs, melding together in an impossibly sturdy
net. Sobbing helplessly, Sil felt her feet lift off the floor
as the worm net began to hoist her upward, tugging
steadily until she bumped against the ceiling and hung
there, twisting in vain as the creatures began to weave

a web of shining, sticky threads. Her voice became hoarse and lost its volume as the strands embraced her chest and hindered her breathing, and was cut off completely when the glistening filaments sheathed her mouth and melted together across the rest of her face.

And Sil was silent at last, wrapped in the glasslike sheen of the chrysalis as it dried.

♦

Nothing moved in the sleeping compartment except for the image on the small television, some rerun of a 1968 episode of *The Prisoner* starring Patrick McGoohan with the volume going full blast. Not loud enough to make the passengers in the compartments on either side complain, it did catch the attention of Angela Cardoza, the conductor, as she passed through the car. She knocked, not too loudly since she didn't want to startle the girl. Kids nowadays could fall asleep with the television or stereo blaring right in their ears, but banging on the door in the middle of the night would scare the heck out of anyone.

"Hello?" she called. "You awake in there, honey? A little late for TV, you know." When no one answered, she automatically tried the door. It swung open without resistance; so much for her earlier instruction to keep it locked. "Hel—oh, for crying out loud. What a mess!"

The only light inside the compartment was the shifting blue white from a little television on one of the seats, the portable kind made for kids and people whom Angela thought were too lazy to read anymore. She picked it up and found its volume wheel, turning it down to a manageable level. If the girl was here, that ought to get her attention. Annoyed, Angela used her feet to shuffle a space through the crumpled food wrappings and empty containers so she could get to the bathroom. Squashed milk cartons and other trash littered every surface of the seats and floor, and if the strange kid had taken off and was hiding in another compartment, guess who'd have to clean everything up?

Already accepting that the girl was gone, Angela nonetheless tilted her head around the wall and through the bathroom door, then pushed all the way in just to see if the girl was lurking in the shower cubicle. The lavatory was half the size of the other room and she almost bumped her head on something hanging over the toilet, plastered in place at the juncture of the wall and ceiling.

Angela pulled back in shock. As she did, her shadow passed across the surface of the object, making it seem as though something inside was doing a restless dance. "What the hell is this?" Angela whispered aloud.

Whatever it was, there was nothing small about it; it stretched from one wall to the other, completely obscuring the upper back ceiling of the john. From where she stood, Angela could see bubbles of reddish fluid flowing under its glassy surface, fanning outward in a pattern like broken capillaries. She gawked at it, too awestruck to be frightened. Something indistinguishable shifted beneath its glistening shell and came close to the surface, breaking Angela from her immobility. She stepped closer, trying to get a better look—was she crazy or had she just seen a recognizable face in there?

A hand exploded from its side and seized her face, long alien fingers moving faster and stronger than Angela could have imagined. Her feet left the floor and before she could scream, her head and neck were yanked into the ragged hole. Her body whipped ineffectually in midair as she fought for freedom, then was wrenched sideways from the neck down. She trembled slightly, then was still. After a moment the unseen hold on her released its grip, and Angela Cardoza dropped to the floor. A three-inch laceration in her forehead bled freely, making wide scarlet streaks in the greenish ooze layering her slack face.

Above her cooling body, the chrysalis began to break

apart, cracks spidering in all directions along its glossy surface. Within the cavity where Conductor A. Cardoza had found death, there was motion, an unhurried shuffling, then pressure. Like an exquisite butterfly emerging from its cocoon, a new Sil pushed her way free. Headfirst, then arms, reaching up and around to the top of the chrysalis and swinging herself carefully out and down to stand next to Angela's corpse, reborn a fully grown and beautiful woman.

She sniffed the air and her eyes, steely blue beneath a lovely halo of blond hair, sharpened as she studied her surroundings and the body at her feet. With slow deliberation, Sil bent and began undressing the dead conductor.

11

Press had been here before but he let the aide they'd sent to greet him on the helicopter lead him to Dr. Fitch's office. The guy was new and Press supposed he was polite enough, but he disliked having a baby-sitter assigned to him when he'd been in and out of the compound more times than—what was the man's name? Robert—had gone to the bathroom since becoming Fitch's number-one assistant. Speaking of aides, Press wondered what had happened to Kyle Jacobson. Now *he'd* been a nice guy, always willing to share a joke to put a lighter side on things. Besides, the main building of the compound was mostly gray glass and metal cylinders connected by causeways, easy enough to get around in once you understood the layout. It was the concrete outer outbuildings that could be a pain in the neck.

Finally, Fitch's office. The room was as stuffy as the doctor himself, Press thought, nothing but paper and business and ten-pound black binders. Not a touch of warmth in the whole setup—even the chairs were uncomfortable. With all the money that got poured into this research center, Fitch could have easily decorated with some wood and an upholstered couch. Stepping into the room, Press stopped short; Robert The Aide hadn't said anything about anyone being at this meeting besides Press and Fitch, but two other men and a woman—a very *pretty* woman—were already seated in chairs around Fitch's desk.

The doctor himself wasn't there, and there were two more empty chairs. Press headed for the spot next to the woman, but paused before dropping onto it. "Are these seats assigned?" he asked with a facetious grin.

The lady smiled back and shook her head. As he sat Press made a quick, furtive examination of the other two men. One was a hefty young black guy with soft, dark eyes, rounded features, and a quick, childish smile. The other, a dark-haired handsome man hardly older than himself, was watching Press and everybody else and cocked an eyebrow when he met Press's steady eyes. They looked over at the woman simultaneously; unimpressed by their stares, this time only one side of her mouth curved in a smile that was just a shade short of derisive. There was no graceful way out, so Press sat, feeling self-conscious.

"Hi." The black man leaned forward, clasping his hands on his knees. His expression was earnest, but bemused. "I'm Dan, Dan Smithson. I . . . don't know why I'm here, but they said they needed me. That it was very important."

The other man tilted his head inquisitively. "What do you do, Dan?" He resembled a doctor making notes in his mental filing cabinet.

"They call me an 'expert at human motivation.' In more understandable terms, I'm an empath." Dan clasped his hands, working his fingers nervously. "Sometimes they show me awful things that people have done. And I try to tell them why." He shuffled his feet, worn sneakers making squeaking noises as they rubbed against each other. "The rest of the time I work in the passport office as an indexing clerk."

Press was curious. "What qualifies you to do that . . . you know, empath thing?"

A slight frown creased the smooth, ebony skin of Dan's forehead. "I . . . *feel* things deeply. They say I have direct access to my emotions."

"Really?" Press eyed him speculatively. "And what am I feeling now?"

He looked like he didn't want to answer, as if he were afraid of violating Press's privacy and alienating him. Finally, out of courtesy, he gave in. "You're . . . like the rest of us. Curious."

"Stephen Arden, Harvard Anthropology Department." The other man offered his hand to the red-headed woman before Dan could continue. "I'm in human research, an expert in cross-cultural behavior."

She shook his hand without hesitation, her deep blue eyes bright with interest. "Laura Baker. I'm a molecular biologist. Why do you think they called us here?"

Press answered that one, the words grinding out of the corner of his mouth around a chewed toothpick as he slumped against the chair back. "If I'm here, the excrement has definitely hit the fan. I'm Preston Lennox."

Stephen Arden leaned forward. "And what exactly is your particular area of specialty, Mr. Lennox?"

"I'm an . . . investigative specialist for the army."

"Really?" Stephen looked intensely interested. "And what does that mean to we the public?"

Press paused for a moment, his glance flicking to Dan. "Let's just say that I have a talent for finding people. That makes me a freelance *solution* for some of our government's problems."

"Really," Stephen said again and folded his arms. "What kind of problems are we talking about, Mr. Lennox?"

For a moment they all thought he wasn't going to

answer, then he shrugged. "Problems," he eventually said, "that nobody likes to talk about."

The look on his face said they'd get no more out of him.

♦

Fitch had the group sent to C-G-1, one of the research labs with a netlink to several eighty-inch NEC projection monitors. When Fitch finally got there, the four members of the team were already seated in the chairs that had been placed in front of the screens. In the rear of the room, a computer technician sat at the unit's console, sequencing the upcoming high-resolution images. From the frustrated looks on most of the faces, Fitch knew the tech had brushed off their questions—as he had been instructed. Smithson, Arden and Baker looked at the doctor expectantly as he joined them, but Preston Lennox—not one of his favorite people, but unfortunately efficient—just acknowledged Fitch's nod with a sort of "Now, what have you done?" sneer. Fitch ignored it and decided to skip the niceties.

"I'm Xavier Fitch," he said. "I'm in command of this operation. Lights out."

A minimovie started on one of the oversized monitors, a spectacular aerial shot of the Arecibo radio telescope and the surrounding forests. Dimming the lighting in the room wasn't really necessary, but it would make the resolution on the screens seem better; Fitch wanted to make damned sure these people missed nothing.

"In November of 1974," Fitch began, "a small group from SETI, the Search for Extraterrestrial Intelligence, used the giant radio dishes at Arecibo to send out a message to whoever might be listening in space. They broadcast about a quarter of a kilobyte of information, including the structure of human DNA, a map of our solar system, the population of the earth—lots of helpful facts like that." Dan Smithson looked at him in surprise and Fitch had to remind himself to keep the sour tone out of his voice. "On March 21, 1992 Arecibo received a signal back from what it believed to be an extraterrestrial source, something from a nonnatural origin. It was also picked up at the Very Large Array in New Mexico and at the Australia Telescope National Facility in Parkes, Australia. The signal—or message, as we decided to label it—came in two sections. Each was repeated twenty-seven thousand times, making it clear that the transmission was intentional."

Dan's attention was no longer on Fitch himself, but on the scientist's conclusion. "They're out there!" he said in wonder. "They really *are*!" He wasn't the only team member with a shocked expression.

"Well," Stephen Arden said, "it makes sense they'd travel by information." His surprised expression had been replaced by something much more contemplative. "It's ridiculous to think they'd come here in some sort of a big metal can. They'd probably be wary—"

"Intelligent life beyond this planet?" Laura's eyes were locked on the computer images.

"Space itself exists far beyond our ability to comprehend it," Stephen remarked unnecessarily. "Why should we be the only life-form capable of intelligent evolution? For us to believe so is the ultimate arrogance." Suddenly his eyes lit up. "Where did it come from? Were you able to find out?"

"No," Fitch admitted. "The means of transmission were indisputably beyond our present ability to trace or decipher. We've had the country's most brilliant astronomers and astrophysicists working solely on tracing its origins since the message's receipt. The best they've been able to speculate is that the sender was somehow able to pull the signal around a series of black holes in a manner of conveyance which we have not yet grasped. The black holes may or may not exist anymore—the *sender* may not exist anymore."

"In other words, you don't know how the hell they got it here. Keep going," Press interjected. He looked bored and Fitch fought the smirk that wanted to slip out. The man—*assassin* was a better term—was still wondering why he'd been called here; he'd learn soon enough.

"As I've said, there were two distinct communications," Fitch told them as the technician waited dutifully. "When the first message was decoded, it turned out to be a superior catalyst for methane. In layman's terms, that means we now have the potential to produce an infinite amount of energy from a clean-burning fuel. This convinced us that we were dealing with a benevolent civilization."

"What was the second?" Professor Arden asked.

Fitch took a deep breath. "The second message turned out to be a new sequence of DNA and the rather . . . friendly suggestion that we combine it with ours."

"Friendly?" Dan asked doubtfully.

Fitch motioned to a double row of heavy binders lined up on the tabletop next to the computer console. "Here's the technical data on the whole operation. You can get feedback on it from Dr. Baker after she has a chance to go through these."

"That'll be fun," Press muttered.

"So you did it." Laura's voice was matter-of-fact. She and Professor Arden exchanged glances. "And then . . . ?"

"The resulting DNA sequence was injected into one hundred human ova." Fitch nodded at the technician; the man pressed a button and the panorama of Arecibo was replaced by laboratory film, less scenic images of microscope slides on a grid marked with three-letter codes. A motorized syringe began moving across the grid, following a preset computer program as it injected the untried DNA into the waiting ova, its maneuvers accompanied by the low hum of motors as the technician at the console punched a few keys and added sound. Each injection generated a tiny flow of iridescent color in the receiving dish. A message typed itself across the bottom of the screen: 93% FAILURE RATE; SEVEN DIVISIONS; TWO ASSIGNED TO LIQUID NITROGEN STORAGE.

"Four of the remaining five divisions deteriorated and were disposed of," Fitch stated, "and we allowed one to grow. Watch very carefully now." On the screen, time-lapse photography showed the minuscule life-form in the dish expanding rapidly. Type ran briefly across the screen: CODE NAME: SIL.

The image flashed and began with a glass container filled with fluid. The mass of tissue was growing incredibly fast, and in only a few breathtaking moments it became recognizable as a human fetus. Even Press leaned forward to watch as Dr. Fitch began a countdown to go with the illustrations, pointing with his finger to make sure they knew which number went with which picture.

"After two hours," he observed. "Now after two days." A newborn floated in the container, and Dan jumped visibly when the infant opened its eyes. Off-screen, somebody lifted the infant gingerly from the fluid and placed it in a waiting bassinet. The person doing it was wearing bulky rubber gloves and a reinforced suit that looked like it belonged on an astronaut.

"My God!" Stephen's mouth dropped open.

Laura sat up straight, her eyes fixed on the screen. "This timetable can't be accurate—the growth is amazing!"

"It's the actual time frame, all right." Fitch sounded grim. "I was there and witnessed it, supervised this footage myself." The image on the screen flicked again, and there was project SIL, now about four years old. "A week," he said flatly.

"It's a girl," Dan said softly. "A miracle."

"Yes," Dr. Fitch agreed. "We decided to make it a girl so it would be more docile and controllable."

This time a glance passed between Laura and Press. She rolled her eyes and Press looked disgusted as he sneered, "More docile and controllable? You guys don't get out much, do you?"

"You kept her caged like that?" Laura demanded. "The whole time? No socialization or interaction with a maternal figure?"

Fitch seemed startled by the question. "Outside of the workers, no. Of course we kept her secluded. We didn't know what we were dealing with here, so we agreed it would be safer to keep her in isolation for two weeks. Our initial assumption was that we were building a creature with which we could communicate, from which we could learn. Because of her half-human lineage, we assumed she would be able to talk to us. Unfortunately, we were not able to convince her to do so." Another image flashed on the screen and the group saw a more mature young girl in a large glass enclosure, Sil at twelve years old. Technicians moved around her, filling out charts and adjusting the dials on the medical monitors scattered around the cage, while guards watched the whole procedure, their expressions mirroring the mistrust on the faces of their white-coated coworkers.

Stephen watched her movements speculatively. "Not much warmth or interaction," he said, "but she can talk, all right."

Laura's forehead creased. "How do you know that? She hasn't said anything. What's to say she understands?"

"Here." The professor leaned toward one of the monitors, paused a second, then tapped the screen. "And . . . here. Watch her eyes. They move from person to person—she's reading their lips."

"Fascinating," Laura breathed. "And in only two weeks."

Suddenly Dan leaned forward, his eyes locked on the film. "She's hiding something."

"You're absolutely correct, Dan." Dr. Fitch motioned to the technician; a few keystrokes and the film shot became another one of Sil, this time asleep under a blanket. The image stopped for a moment, then began to replay in slow motion. "Watch carefully."

For about five seconds nothing happened. Then, concealed beneath the white blanket, something sharp jutted from the girl's back, its silhouette lean and long, like a pointed spike. In an instant it was gone and the line of her back was smooth again, the normal spinal curve of an adolescent.

"What the hell was that?" Press demanded. His full attention was on the screen now, his light blue eyes sharp in his handsome face.

"Rewind the tape," Stephen ordered. "Run it again." The technician obeyed and the five of them watched it carefully. Even with image enhancement and stop motion, whatever came out of her back was so fast that all they got was a brown-black blur on the screen. "Watch her face while it's happening," the professor pointed out excitedly. "Look at her eyes. She's undergoing REM— rapid eye movement. She's dreaming."

"A nightmare?" Laura asked. "Maybe what happened was an anxiety reaction to her dream."

"Makes me pretty anxious," Press muttered. His gaze sought Fitch's and the older man nodded.

"It had the same impact on the research team, and the result was the decision to terminate the physical experiment until we could conduct further theoretical research. We needed to determine more about what we were dealing with—"

"No kidding," Stephen interjected, his eyes bright.

Dr. Fitch's expression darkened. "This is what happened when we attempted to terminate the project."

The footage shifted into a replay of Sil's escape and the volume escalated as the computer presented the viewers with full details. "That's Kyle," Press said somberly as the security camera showed Fitch's former assistant sinking to his knees, retching miserably, then toppling forward. "I wondered what happened to him."

"This is very bad," Dan said. "Those people—"

"Are all dead," Fitch said.

"So it—she—got away," Laura said quietly.

"*It*, and yes." Fitch's mouth turned down farther and Dan winced openly as the next footage gave the team a gruesome view of a twisted, blood-streaked corpse. "And yesterday morning the body of a transient was found in a boxcar on a siding near Salt Lake City. Preliminary DNA tests indicate the man was killed by our creature."

"Nice kid," Press remarked, pointing to the bottom part of the shot. "Look at the food wrapper next to the man's body in the lower right of the screen. It's on *top* of the puddle of blood—she slaughtered the guy, then stayed next to him and ate his food."

"Not exactly a promising start to her tour of the country. Have you found any more bodies?" Stephen asked.

"Not yet."

"You will," Dan said unexpectedly. All eyes turned toward him, but he didn't seem to notice. "Her eyes are in front. That makes her a predator. Predators have their eyes in front so they can judge the distance to their prey."

Press touched his own eyes thoughtfully, then frowned. "What about the dinosaurs, the ones who were meat eaters? They had eyes on the sides of their heads."

"They don't qualify for modern equations because they've been extinct for so long," Laura answered when Dan looked stumped. "Besides, the dinosaurs were reptiles. In the modern world, Dan is mostly right."

"And where did you pick up this information, Dan?" Professor Arden asked.

"I saw it on a documentary on the Discovery Channel," Dan responded with a touch of pride. "I thought it was really interesting."

"Why did you say he was 'mostly' right?" Press asked Laura.

"I think what Dan picked up from the program he watched was information on stereoscopic vision in the order of *carnivora*, a category of carnivorous mammals—a good portion of which has stereoscopic vision. There are, of course, predators in other orders— reptiles, rodents, and fish, for instance. Just as not all mammals with stereoscopic vision are predators, not all predators have front-facing eyes. Only those preda- tors whose primary hunting sense is *vision* have front- facing eyes and stereoscopic vision; on the other hand, having both doesn't automatically mean the animal is a predator. Primates, for example, are largely vegetarian, yet they are mostly associated with stereoscopic vision because they evolved in trees. Thus they needed stereo- scopic vision for exceptional depth perception."

"Stereoscopic vision?" Dan asked.

"The ability to see things in three dimensions," Laura clarified. "Stereoscopic perception is possible be- cause of binocular vision, or the ability to use the im- age seen by both eyes to result in a single view that appears to have three dimensions . . . which is where it ties into the program you watched, Dan. If one animal is incapable of accurately judging the distance to an- other, it cannot be a predator . . . because it could never catch its prey."

The scenes playing on the computer monitor ended and they all blinked as the lights came on. Fitch turned to Press. "Mr. Lennox, as a nonscientist, are you at all clear on what's happening?"

Press glowered at him from his slumped position on his chair, his face cold. "Oh, I think so, *Doctor* Fitch. In layman's terms, you made a monster with a formula from outer space, it's escaped and is going around kill- ing people." He fixed each of the others with a glance. "Now you want *us* to hunt it down and kill it."

"You have quite a talent for simplicity, Mr. Lennox," Fitch said peevishly.

"Thank you."

Laura ran her hands through her hair in a gesture that seemed more disheartened than anxious. "There's no way we can capture her and keep her alive to study further? I mean, she *is* half-human."

There was a hushed moment as they all considered this. Dr. Fitch looked as though he wanted to agree but oddly, didn't dare. After they'd all thought about the idea for a minute, Press stood, ready to leave. "Laura," he said quietly, "I think this is strictly a search-and-destroy mission." His gaze brushed Fitch then wandered to the floor, and he didn't look back up.

"They've never asked me to find anyone they didn't want killed."

12

Looking at Union Station for the first time through a slit in the curtain, Sil could see that this was a world apart from Brigham City, Utah. In fact, she thought the population of that entire town could have been outnumbered just by the people milling about on the platforms here as they waited for trains to arrive and depart.

Before leaving the sleeping compartment and its decaying contents behind, Sil smoothed the front of her new conductor's uniform and checked to make sure the fanny pack was adjusted properly—her hips were slightly narrower than A. Cardoza's had been. Stepping off the train, she followed the rest of the disembarking passengers down a ramp to a tunnel that apparently led to the main station.

The main building was immense, nearly overwhelming. The elaborately adorned ceiling was so far overhead it was dizzying, and Sil tried to focus on the smaller things going on around her in an attempt to give her mind time to get used to the frantic pace: off to the side of her a little girl smiled and held tightly to her mother's hand; just ahead a man in a plain, navy-

blue suit and dark glasses headed purposefully toward
her—

Sil tensed, waiting for a confrontation. It never
came; instead, the man passed without comment and
went up to the woman and daughter. They exchanged
a few words and he flashed a small identification card,
then steered them in the direction of a door marked
ADMINISTRATION. For the first time Sil noticed more
men, similarly dressed, herding a group of girls between
the ages of eight and fourteen. Then it hit her and she
felt a moment of triumph—these men *were* looking for
her, but they thought she was still a child! She could
walk right past them and they'd never be the wiser.

But she couldn't relax. She sensed someone watching her and turned nonchalantly; a good twenty feet to
her left was the boy from the snack bar in Brigham
City. He recognized her—or thought he did—and was
tracking her with wide, bewildered eyes. Tall and stunning in her new clothes, Sil gave him a confident return smile. As the boy's mother grasped him by the
hand and led him away, she did a smart spin on her
heels and blended into the crowd hurrying down the
hall to the main exit.

And, with a thousand other people, headed into the
streets of Los Angeles.

♦

"May I help you, dear?"

Sil glanced up as she flipped through a rack of
dresses. The woman who'd approached her was older
but heavily made up, and Sil blinked at her spiked,
burgundy-red hair and slick, flowing tunic with clash-
ing swirls of purple and chartreuse. Off guard, she
grabbed at the next hanger and offered it to the
woman. "This one."

The clerk read a tag on the neck of the dress, then
looked at Sil. "I take it you're buying this for someone

else?" She gave Sil's tall figure a quick appraisal. "It's nowhere close to your size."

Sil turned back to the rack and chose another. She held it up and raised an eyebrow.

The clerk shook her head, slipped Sil's original pick back into place, and did the same with her second choice. "That won't do either, I'm afraid. Come over here." She motioned to a different section, then gave the younger woman another once-over. "You're more likely to find something under size eight than in sixteen, dearie. Look." She plucked a hanger from the rack and held it up. "This one's just like the one you had."

The pink satin was identical, and Sil had a moment of mystification until the concept of size slipped into place in her mind. She reached for the bridesmaid's dress and the clerk put it into her hands, then guided her toward a curtained cubicle. "Go in there and try it on," the woman advised. "This is a consignment shop, so all sales are final. You'll need to be sure it fits before you leave with it." When Sil hesitated, the clerk gave her a motherly prod. "Go on now, dearie. Don't be shy—I'll make sure no one walks in on you."

In less then three minutes Sil was back at the counter, arrayed in good-quality pink satin. The dress was an off-the-shoulder style with a bodice that gathered snugly below her breasts and fit her exceptionally well. She'd buckled the conductor's fanny pack around her waist again, this time with the pouch in front; now she dug into it and pulled out the wad of money stuffed inside. The clerk opened her mouth to speak, but Sil pushed all the bills across the counter and started to leave.

"Wait!"

Sil stopped and turned back. She stood, shoulders rigid, while the woman counted the money.

"You want to be more careful about your money, honey," the clerk said kindly. "Most ladies don't . . .

ah, *wear* a bridesmaid's dress out of the store." This close, Sil could see that the woman's eyelashes were unnaturally thick; she'd painted the lids and lashes with two different colors. The woman endured Sil's inspection patiently. "Are you foreign?" she finally asked.

Sil cocked her head and considered this for a moment. "Yes," she answered. The clerk handed her back several bills in change and Sil folded them and tucked them into the fanny pack.

"Do you speak much English?" the clerk asked.

"Yes," Sil said. "I can talk."

The older woman studied her silently for what seemed to Sil to be a very long time. At last the clerk sighed. "You want to be careful here, okay, dear?"

Sil nodded, her expression absolutely serious. "Yes," she agreed, "I know. Be careful."

◆

Sil had been walking for most of the day, and now the rays of the late-afternoon sun topped the mountains and slanted over the peaks and valleys created by the buildings along the boulevard. Her senses were nearly burned out, overloaded with information and images, sounds and half-completed impressions. People were everywhere—too many to count, too many to understand. In the doorway she was passing was a man who made her think of the transient whose body she'd left in the railway car. Though the memory was fuzzy and fading more with each hour, she was certain that this person wore more clothes, layer upon layer—far too much for the warm climate. Instead of the semiprivacy and somewhat questionable safety of a moving boxcar, the man, whose face was deeply lined and grizzled, slept in the open next to a battered grocery cart piled with tattered-looking plastic bags.

As Sil passed him she jerked in surprise as another man, this one in a motorized wheelchair, sped by on the sidewalk. She gawked after him, then almost got pushed off the sidewalk as a door burst open in her path. A man and a woman spilled out, clutching each other and laughing amid the driving beat of heavy-metal music and the scent of liquor. His hands were all over his companion, but she didn't seem to mind; with Sil only a few feet away, the woman spun the guy to face her and kissed him deeply on the mouth, her tongue darting past his lips. Sil watched, fascinated, as they embraced and leaned against the building, then she stepped around them and kept going.

♦

The hours rolled by. Now it was full dark and Sil was on a different street, a magical place called Hollywood Boulevard. At dusk she had been in a different, quieter area, where the streets were not as brightly lit and there were fewer people. Lush green trees had lined the sidewalks and dotted the yards of well-kept houses, a few dogs had barked angrily at her from fenced-in yards. It had been lovely to look at, the houses covered with bougainvillea with full, ruby blossoms, and pepper trees dotting the lawns, their spicy scent drifting past and mixing with the sweeter smell of the flowers. All in all a pretty but boring neighborhood, with none of the exciting neon lights and hard sexuality that surrounded her now. Erotica was everywhere here—oozing from prostitutes prancing along the streets and calling invitations to passing drivers, painted larger than life on luminous billboards packed into every available advertising space, staring seductively from magazine racks.

In the midst of it all were youths still bordering on childhood. Ranging in age from eleven to their early twenties, the older ones had personalities and expressions far different from the boy she'd nearly spoken to back in Brigham City and the occasional child she'd noticed in the residential section earlier in the day. And there was the youngest yet; at the bus stop in front of her Sil saw a beautiful young woman with long, shapely legs wearing tight, cutoff jeans and deep red high heels. A guy stood next to her in a sleeveless T-shirt and jeans nearly as tight as hers. His muscular arms were covered in colorful tattoos and Sil watched, entranced, as the serpentine figures twisted each time he moved. When the bus came, the woman turned enough for Sil to see that she held a sleeping baby wrapped in a soft pink-and-yellow plaid blanket. She bent her head and nuzzled it on the cheek; when the infant waved a chubby hand in response, the guy grinned.

They climbed onto the bus and were gone just as a pregnant woman swept by in the crowd, her three other children following obediently, hands entwined in a connection that led ultimately to their mother. A few paces away another couple went in the opposite direction, the stroller the man pushed in front of him holding identical twin boys with wheat-colored hair and innocent brown eyes.

Sil watched it all, drinking it in, trying to learn. Everyone around her seemed to have a place to go and a companion to go there with. It was obvious that those who were alone were shopping—they put on their best clothes and donned makeup and jewelry, then prowled the streets, looking for the right someone to buy or take. It didn't seem that hard, if you had the right tools.

Two giggling girls spun to a stop in front of Sil, whispering to each other and pointing as they looked in the window of the shop behind her. She followed their lead, wondering what they were laughing about—her? She touched the front of her pink dress, comparing it with the more outlandish outfits of the girls at the window, but they paid her no attention. She watched them from the corner of her eye until they moved away, then moved to where they'd stopped in front of the display window. Her eyes narrowed as she scanned the vibrantly colored clothing behind the glass. These things seemed much more suited to the environment, and made the satiny yards of material she wore look childishly flamboyant. Before she went inside, she backed away from the window and looked up at the fancy lettering that composed the name of the store, trying to understand it.

FREDERICK'S OF HOLLYWOOD.

13

"Looks like she had a party," Stephen said as the team filed into the sleeping compartment. There was barely enough room between the two seats for all of them to stand and their feet were engulfed in the litter piled on the floor. A miniature television on one of the seats was tilted on its side and murmuring some lame afternoon soap opera; Dr. Fitch reached over and thumbed the on-off button. The strange and nearly intolerable smell that had permeated the compartment and seeped into the rest of the train car was a cross between rotting eggs and scorched sugar—to say nothing of the slowly bloating contents of the lavatory.

Press edged around the rest of them and poked his head into the bathroom. "Some party." The others peered around the door, then recoiled at the sight of the woman crumpled on the floor, clad only in a bra and panties.

"Something . . . *bad* happened in here," Dan whispered. His skin had taken on an unnatural grayish color.

"No shit," Press muttered as Fitch bent and inspected the corpse.

"Crushed her larynx." The doctor stood, then saw what the others were staring at.

"What *is* that?" Dan asked. He'd backed out of the bathroom to get away from the body, but he could still see the area at the top of the bathroom.

Arden inspected the mass of shredded fibers fastened to the wall and ceiling. "I think it's a chrysalis—a cocoon."

"So what are we looking for now?" Press asked sardonically. "A giant moth?"

Laura fingered one of the dried strands speculatively. "Well, whatever it is, she'll be fully grown now."

"What makes you so sure?" Fitch asked. "We're not exactly dealing with known factors here."

"No," Laura agreed, "but the purpose of a cocoon— *usually*—is to provide an environment which protects a young larva while it metamorphosizes into an adult. Then the adult's main purpose is to procreate."

"We're not talking about a vermiform creature, Dr. Baker," Fitch said dryly.

"Vermiform?" Dan looked at them questioningly.

"Wormlike," Laura explained. "And while that's often the case, there are a few creatures that don't resemble worms that undergo a pupa phase. For instance—"

Press broke in. "I hate to interrupt your scientific discussion, doctors, but maybe being fully grown is how she got by our people. We were looking for a child, remember?"

Laura started to say something else, then put a hand over her mouth and nose. "Ugh, this smell is awful. I can't stand it in here anymore."

"I'm with you, Dr. Baker." Fitch and Arden stepped away from the door as Press offered his arm to Laura and she leaned on it gratefully. "Let's all get out of this death box and get some fresh air."

◆

"Okay," Xavier Fitch said when they were outside and had rejoined the waiting aides and the MPs who had cordoned off the area. The warm morning air, filled with the smell of diesel fuel and exhaust, wasn't as fresh as Press had suggested, but it was a damn sight better than the stench of the soiled sleeper compartment on the train. "Any more ideas about the cocoon?"

Laura took a deep breath, her expression easing. "I think she's used the chrysalis stage to jump-start through puberty. Not only has she probably developed into a fully formed adult, we have no idea what she looks like anymore."

Stephen held up a bag loaded with items he'd gathered from the train compartment. A drink container with a straw through the top, an empty package of french fries, and a pudding container were only some of the trash visible through the clear plastic. "This is amazing," he said. "It takes us years to do it, but she's learned to read in only a few hours."

"Physical acceleration, maybe," Laura said. "But what makes you think she can read? There's no proof that her learning capabilities developed at the same rate."

"Yes, there is," the professor insisted. "Look at what the contents of the bag say—insert straw, pull tab, tear back. Nothing in here is ripped or chewed. She read and followed the instructions."

"But how would she have *learned?*" Press demanded. "Nobody's been teaching her the alphabet."

"Not here," Dan cut in. "But I'll bet they gave it a good try back at the compound."

They all glanced at Fitch and he nodded. "Of course we did. One of the primary objectives of this project was to communicate with the creature we created, but she never tried to speak or gave any indication that she understood what we said."

"She didn't have any reason to," Dan said. "Now she's on her own. What she didn't pick up at the compound she probably got from television. Infomercials, for instance—a lot of those are closed captioned. All she had to do was watch."

Press turned to Phillip McRamsey. "Amtrak has verified that the woman was a conductor?" The aide nodded. "Get her credit cards and identification into your computer right away. There's no sign of a purse or a conductor's pack on the train, so we have to assume Sil took them, although she probably won't use them for a while."

"Why not?" Stephen asked. "My guess is she'll want to dump the conductor's clothes and get something that will help her blend in with the rest of the city."

"True enough," Press agreed. "But Amtrak's human resources department also mentioned that everybody got paid first thing this morning and a Thillens Check Cashing Service truck was waiting for the train employees at the forty-five-minute stopover the train made in Ely, Nevada. Because of their mobility, most of these men and women cash their checks for up-front money, then deposit the bulk of it when they get back to wherever it is they call home. There was probably a nice wad of cash in the conductor's pack."

Phillip scribbled notes on his clipboard. "I'll see to the plastic and identification."

"This woman is vicious," Dan said. "She's killing people but doesn't have any sense of remorse."

"Great. She'll fit right into L.A." Press's tone was caustic.

"So this is it." Fitch folded his arms stiffly. "Los Angeles—where the battle will be fought and won."

"Battle?" Stephen looked slightly frightened. "I don't think you understand, Dr. Fitch. This city is *perfect* for Sil. It's the metropolis of the future, with a huge and totally mobile population. Anything goes and everyone's a stranger. Whatever she does, no one will notice—everything is acceptable, nothing is taboo." His cheeks were pale. "What's to stop her?"

Press's face was rigid. "We are."

♦

The Biltmore Hotel was spacious and opulent, more than a little surprising to most of the members of the team. Built in 1923, the hotel's lobby had twenty-foot ceilings that boasted elaborately carved moldings and patterns, as well as sections with huge, backlit skylights inset with milk-colored textured glass. Constructed in an age in love with the Italian Renaissance, the brass-and-glass entryway was flanked by huge, pale pillars and carefully tended shrubs in oversized pots.

It was an astonishing place. The span of ten minutes that it took to get everyone's luggage unloaded from the two government-gray sedans that had carted them here wasn't nearly enough to gawk at the main floor. All too soon Robert Minjha joined the group waiting by the bellboy's cart onto which their baggage had been stacked. As he passed out room keys, Dr. Fitch addressed the team.

"Our laboratory, Visitor Base One, is being temporarily established at an empty virus research lab at the University of California. Most of the equipment has already been moved, and the rest is being transferred as we speak. The entire setup should be operational by eight o'clock this morning. That gives you just enough time to get your luggage to your rooms. Everyone is to be out front in fifteen minutes."

"Really." Stephen Arden looked draggy and still half-asleep, as if he needed another three cups of coffee. "And what exactly are we going to do once we get to this laboratory?"

"Process the evidence, of course," Fitch said impassively. "Everything we collected from the train."

"Of course," Press said dryly. "The evidence— chocolate-pudding containers and frozen french-fry wrappers. Why didn't I think of that?"

"I have a suggestion," Laura Baker said. "Why don't we try growing the creature with a full strand of its own

DNA, rather than halving it with human DNA. If we make up a version without mutating it with our characteristics, we would be better equipped to investigate its vulnerabilities."

"I—I don't know if we should." Fitch looked taken aback. "If we consider ourselves mutations, or at least regard the human DNA which we combined with the alien DNA to have mutated *it* . . . we've got a lot to consider. Mutations are generally weak, defective. Most don't survive—"

"Yet this one did," Press commented. "I'm out of my field, but that seems to indicate it would be an extremely strong creature *without* our help."

"Even so," Stephen cut in, "we could deal with it—"

"I disagree entirely," Press interrupted hotly. "I've never heard a more dangerous proposal."

"But Laura's idea does make sense," argued Stephen. "We'll never get anywhere if we don't see what this creature looks like without a human life-form behind which it can hide. To see it without its camouflage would be our best weapon." He glanced meaningfully at each of the others.

"All right," Fitch agreed reluctantly. "Maybe Dr. Baker has a point. At least then we'll know what we're dealing with."

Press opened his mouth to object, but the arrival of the elevator, crowded with civilian passengers from the lower floor of the hotel, stifled the rest of his remarks.

14

"When we pierce the cells, the alien DNA will be introduced into the host specimen. The specimen has been contained in a nutrient solution which will provide the appropriate sustenance to promote growth and cell division."

Press could tell from Laura's tone of voice that she was used to explaining her procedures to an audience; more than likely, she often had assistants and grad students watching her methods and asking questions while she worked. Right now the group was in the observation room in an unused portion of the Virus Research Lab at the Los Angeles campus of the University of California. Laura was operating two levers—they looked like joysticks—and controlling the precise movements of a mechanism within a glass box inside an isolation chamber from which they were separated by a five-foot-square quartz window. A lab worker with a name tag that said MICHELLE PURDUE stood to the side, ready to assist. Gathered around, the team watched the process on two video monitors mounted on the console directly in front of the controls. One recorded the overall layout of the isolation chamber, while the other showed the viewpoint of a smaller, high-resolution camera integrated within the microscope and mounted inside the glass box to show the actual process of injecting the DNA.

"If we're not using human cells," asked Stephen, "what *are* we using?"

"Bat."

"Why bat?" asked Press. "Don't experiments like this generally use amphibians? Or rats?"

"I don't like bats," Dan said. He was looking at the monitors as if they were showing scenes from a particularly scary movie. "They can fly."

Laura smiled a little. "True," she agreed, "but they're small and not very strong. Our host cells were limited to what had been prepared and was still available at this lab. We can't exactly go to a pet shop and buy prepared embryonic cells."

"I can't believe the biology department didn't have any frogs," Press argued. "I'm with Dan—bats would be last on my list of choices. Besides, I thought we were going to try and see what the alien would look like by itself. Won't it end up looking like a bat this way?"

"It might," Laura said. "But without host cells from the original species itself, we'll never be absolutely sure we're seeing its true form anyway—who's to say that the DNA sequence we received accurately represents them? Even if it does, we have no idea what to expect—what if it's twenty feet tall? Our own safety mandates we mix the alien DNA with *something* known. We all know what a bat looks like, so we'll be able to pick up any differences immediately. My thinking is that the alien DNA will be the more advanced anyway, thus any resemblance to a bat will be recessive. And without human intelligence, the resulting creature won't know it can or should change its form—it will simply look like what it *is*. There are canine cells, but the resident DNA was removed before the viral studies shut down, so we can't use those—we'd have to insert a complete strand of DNA instead of half and run the risk of creating a creature we can't control. We also considered using human cells, as Dr. Fitch did originally. Increasing the number of alien chromosomes and decreasing the number of human might make the creature less intelligent, but remember the footage of Sil's reaction to her nightmare at the compound? The resulting creature could, again, be too large to control, and the aliens are obviously *quite* intelligent. In any case, the equipment needed to process a human cell and remove its DNA was moved elsewhere when the research here ended—and, of course, we have no idea if our alien-to-human chromosome ratio will produce a viable mix. We'll have to make do with what's available, and I'm afraid human isn't one of the options. Plus there are other things to keep in mind."

"Such as?" Press's eyes were keen.

"Thinking this through more carefully raised the possibility that the alien in its natural state might not be able to breathe this atmosphere," Laura pointed out. "That alone is sufficient to explain the message suggesting we *combine* DNA from the two species. In its true body, the life-form may not be able to exist on our food, and there's always susceptibility to viruses and bacteria to which the existing life-forms on Earth are immune. Did you know that hydrophobia—rabies—never existed in Hawaii before outside explorers 'discovered' the islands?"

"Which brings us to these cells," Fitch added. "Apparently this lab was working on studies involving hydrophobia—rabies—before it closed down. There were several host choices, and bat seemed the least offensive, taking into consideration size and strength."

"What were the others?" Stephen asked.

"Dog, raccoon, and skunk," Fitch said. "Are we ready?"

"Raccoons are nice," Dan suggested.

"They're too smart," Laura said absently. "They learn

very quickly to open things. Dogs are too large, and I don't think we want to deal with a skunk hybrid." She flicked a switch, then nodded. "Here we go."

All eyes went to the smaller monitor as the mechanism moved into place to inject the DNA into the host cell. "Right . . . ther—*damn it*." Laura released the controls and sat back, disgusted.

"What happened to the picture?" Dan glanced through the widow into the empty isolation chamber, then gave Laura a perplexed look.

"Modern technology at its finest." Stephen sniffed. "Looks like you're out a microscope camera."

"Do we have a replacement?" Laura asked Dr. Fitch.

Fitch looked stumped and Purdue answered for him. "Sure, we have a stand-in. But it will take some time to get a technician here to replace it."

"Why do we need a tech?" Laura complained. "We have this problem at my lab all the time—everyone does. Camera replacement is a simple chore, standard operating procedure."

"Meaning you can do it?" Fitch asked dryly.

"Of course, if someone's willing to pitch in a pair of hands to hold the top of the box open."

Press took the toothpick he'd been chewing out of his mouth and flicked it at a nearby trash can. "Let's not have a big conversation about this. I'm your man. Let's do it and get on with the show."

"Camera's right here," the lab worker said. She plucked a sealed cardboard box off an overhead shelf, slit the top open with a pair of scissors and pulled out a new camera. "You guys sure you want to go into the isolation chamber?"

Laura took the camera from her and checked it quickly. "We'll be in and out in no time," she said. "Normally we wouldn't do something like this in an isolation chamber, but we're dealing with DNA, not airborne viruses. Let's go." Press followed her obediently to the heavy fire door separating the isolation chamber from the observation room. Fitch pressed a button on the control console and the door slid open; they stepped through and it closed behind them and locked with a clang.

"*Can you hear me?*" Fitch's voice sounded metallic and strangely high-pitched as it reached them through an unseen speaker. "*We can see you both through the window, but I need to know if the speaker is working properly.*"

"It's working," Press said loudly, glancing around in a futile effort to pinpoint the source of Fitch's voice.

"You don't have to shout," Laura admonished. "He won't have any trouble hearing you if the speaker's in working condition at his end. We'll be able to hear everybody out there as well."

"Oh." He and Laura stepped to the table bearing the glass minicrate and Laura handed Press the camera to hold. About three feet square, the box was made of heavy, sterilized glass and the top was hinged and locked down with two substantial wing nuts opposite the hinges. Press watched as she struggled to unscrew them, then tucked the camera under one arm and pitched in. Together they lifted the lid, then he held the disabled camera in place while she disconnected it. When it was free of the box, he lifted it out and slid the new one in position. She quickly pushed the video cables into their connections and stepped back. Suddenly, she jerked.

"Hey—"

"*Christ!*" Fitch screamed over the speaker. "*We've got a picture. The process has already started—get the top back on!*"

Press was grabbing for his side of the crate's top when the organism in the petri dish became visible to the naked eye. Already a smushy, brownish-pink crust was rising, pushing up and out like a defective loaf of bread. "This is incredible," Laura breathed. Despite her astonishment, she moved swiftly to help slam the cover

over the rapidly expanding mass. The wing nuts were still in Press's hand and he slid one in place and tightened it, then bounded to Laura's side of the glass box. "No known form of life can multiply this fast!"

"Wonderful." Press pushed the other locking mechanism home and ground his teeth as the wing nut fumbled around in his grasp. He let out a yell when it slipped out of his fingers and dropped to the floor. "Shit!"

She didn't need an invitation to join him on the floor in a frantic search. On the table above them, Press heard a click and knew instinctively that with no wing nut to hold it in place, the second locking lever had slipped to the side; it wouldn't take much—a little leverage against the bottom of the case, for instance—to force the unlocked end open. Something else wormed into his hearing, beyond the unexpected thundering of his heart and the rasp of Laura's panicked breathing somewhere off to his right. Dan's voice, sounding clear and inescapably correct:

"I think Laura and Press should come back in here now."

"Where *is* that damn thing?" Press cried. "I—"

"There!"

Laura jabbed a finger to the left of his field of vision and he snapped his head in that direction. Two feet away, three—it didn't matter; his fist closed around it and he leaped to the table, jammed the lock in place and spun the wing nut on the end of the screw. He sucked in his breath as he realized what he was staring at: a miniature chrysalis, like the ravaged one they'd found in the bathroom on the train. The microscope's camera—the reason they were in the isolation chamber in the first place—had immediately been rendered virtually useless by the cocoon's size.

"Amazing," Laura said from beside him. "It's like watching a fetus grow without the protection of a womb."

"Or a spider entombing its dinner," Press retorted.

"*Dr. Baker, I'm not sure this was such a good idea.*" Fitch's metallic-screened voice sounded stiff.

"*What do you think it is?*" asked Dan in a worried tone.

The next voice was Stephen Arden's. "*That's the million-dollar question, Dan. Laura?*"

"I can't answer that," she said without taking her eyes from the vibrating structure shifting within the glass box. "I've never seen anything like this." She stepped back involuntarily as an area on the side of the chrysalis split and something whipped out of it and cracked against the glass top, making the box vibrate. Another snap and the cocoon broke apart entirely.

"Jesus," Press muttered as a queer, batlike face momentarily flattened itself against the underside of the glass top. Nothing remained of the creature's chrysalis but fragments littering the floor of the cage. "Let's get out of here."

"*I don't like this,*" Dan said abruptly over the speaker.

"Let's go." Press took Laura's arm, then both he and Laura recoiled as the face squashed itself against the glass again and then shrieked, a circular mouth ringed with pointed teeth clicking savagely against its enclosure. Before they could react, there was a blur of motion from the box's interior and something—a spike-studded tail vaguely reminiscent of the shape that had bulged from under the sleeping Sil's sheet—snapped forward and hit the glass with a hefty-sounding *click!* Press and Laura stood, frozen, as it happened again—*click!*

Jolted into motion, the two flung themselves backward as a spiked tail struck at the glass a third time. This time the box shattered under the force, and Laura screamed as the life-form, a grotesque shape similar to a bat with tentacles and a barbed tail, catapulted from the enclosure and straight at Press. He threw himself to the side and into Laura as the creature sailed over his shoulder. "Come on!" he shouted as the bat-thing fell.

It struck the concrete floor tiles with a sound like an oversized rattlesnake's tail and quickly righted itself; hissing, it sped under a wooden table at the rear of the isolation chamber.

Bubble lights at ceiling height in each corner of the chamber began to pulse red in time to an onslaught of earsplitting sirens. Fitch's words came clearly over the speaker despite the noise, sounding professional and far too cold.

"*I've hit the automatic clock,*" his disembodied voice said. "*You have two minutes to destroy it. If you can't accomplish that task within that time frame, I'll have to burn the room.*"

Laura gasped and Press spun and glared at Fitch through the window. Affixed to the wall just below the video camera was a digital clock already descending from 2:00. "*What!*"

"*I'll have to burn the room,*" Fitch repeated. Through the clear quartz glass, his expression was utterly bland, while Stephen and Dan were gaping at him with slack-mouthed dismay. "*You've got less than two minutes to kill the creature.*"

"Bull*shit!*" Press stalked to the door, Laura on his heels, her gaze flicking around the chamber. "Open this door, damn you!"

"*I can't do that. It might escape. I have to follow protocol.*"

"What fucking protocol?" Press roared. He hauled vainly on the door handle. "Open the door, Fitch!"

"*The protocols by which these experiments are run.*"

Fitch sounded absurdly patient and Press wanted to scream; more than that, he wanted to wrap his hands around the older man's neck and see if he could twine his fingers together like he was praying.

"Why the hell didn't you tell us that before you suggested we go in here and replace the camera?" Laura demanded through the window. "What were you thinking, anyway?"

"*I think you should let them out.*" Although they could see him clearly, Dan's voice sounded tinny and faraway, as if he'd been pushed off to the side. "*Please, Dr. Fitch—*"

Fitch's words cut him off. "*There's nothing I can do now. You're wasting valuable time.*" At the end of the word *time*, Press heard a scurrying sound from under the table. Laura pulled him farther away from it.

"I'm scared," Dan said shakily.

"*There are two incineration lines running to the isolation box.*" The lab worker's frantic voice came over the speaker, overriding all other sound from the control room. "*Green is oxygen, red is gas. Disconnect the red one and try to use it as a flamethrower. You'll get gas through it as long as you keep a finger pushing on the safety valve at the end of the piping. Hurry—you've only got a minute and forty seconds!*"

"Fitch, you son of a bitch," Press growled at the camera. He sprang to the box and ripped the red connection free as Laura opened the valve. Gas hissed and Press dug in his pocket and came up with a Bic lighter; he thumbed the strike wheel and a small jet of flame shot from the line. He and Laura whirled, but the life-form was nowhere to be seen. "Where the hell'd it go? Here—" He tossed Laura the lighter. "Hang on to this." He dropped to his hands and knees and crawled forward, trying to keep the flame directed away from him. A faint hiss came from his right, then another, much louder than the sound the gas made spilling from the open line. Press scuttled backward as he saw the creature fastened to the inside of one of the table legs; at the sight of Press, it scooted along the underside, going as far back as it could.

"Don't let it eat anything," Laura said urgently. "It might not be all the way through its growing phase—we mustn't let it get any bigger before we can get out!"

Revolted, Press peered under the table. The life-form

was there, in the shadows at the far rear. Wood splintered and Press saw with horror that it had appendages resembling arms and was ripping away at the bottom of the tabletop. Then it got worse, as the thing's back split, revealing another circular tooth-filled mouth. Like obscenely blooming flowers, two smaller openings unfolded on either side and the creature began voraciously stuffing the pieces of broken wood into the three openings.

Press didn't hesitate. He aimed the flaming end of the gas line at the creature and thrust it forward, stretching as far under the tabletop as he could without actually crawling beneath it and trapping himself. The small jet of flame barely licked at the thing, and it screeched and scampered away. As Press scrambled out from under the table his gaze skipped to the LED display of the clock: 1:15 . . . and passing far too quickly.

Press yanked the table recklessly aside, but their creation was gone. "Fitch, you bastard, open the fucking *door!*"

There was a pause, then Fitch's voice came over the speaker a final time.

"I'm sorry, Press, Laura. I simply can't do that."

◆

"*Please*, Dr. Fitch," Dan pleaded. "Look at them in there—you can't just burn them up!"

"It's out of my hands, unfortunately. Sometimes we have to do things we don't like."

"Like annihilate a couple of people innocently following your instructions?" Stephen asked furiously. "You sick bastard, you'd do it and stand here and *watch*? Where's the damned button for the door? *I'll* open it. You can say I forced you—"

A scream from the intercom made them all suck in their breath. The window showed a view of most of the room and they could see the life-form, now nearly two feet long, clinging to the front of Laura's dress at thigh level, the rims of its mouths pulsing as it clawed its vaguely tadpole-shaped body upward with newly developed pincers. Press vaulted over the upended table and wrapped a hand around its tail without faltering, slipping his fingers neatly between the razor-edged tips and its main body. He wrenched it off Laura and rolled with it, hollering as the thing's claws and mouths snapped viciously at his face and the spiny tail whipped in every direction.

Every time Press managed to push it off, it came back, each time a little stronger; he'd dropped the gas line when the creature had gone for Laura, and now she picked up the line and used the Bic to relight it. Forcing the safety valve down, she tried to track the erratic path Press and the life-form made around the room in a vain attempt to burn it without charring Press in the process. Hissing fiercely, the thing went for him again; bellowing, Press finally got another decent hold on the tail and flung it as hard as he could across the room. On the screen, the three men in the observation room saw a fish-eye view of Press and Laura's predicament as the creature skidded across the concrete floor and hit the wall, stunned. When the couple sought the clock on the wall, they seemed to be staring beseechingly straight into the main camera. Then the alien squirmed across the floor again, and both Press and Laura leaped out of its path as it inflated something around its neck—a flesh sac of some kind. The sudden pouch made it appear four times its original size.

Nine seconds to go.

"Get out of my way, Fitch," growled Stephen. He stepped toward the console, then stopped short when Fitch pulled a pistol from his pocket and aimed it at him. Stephen found himself looking down the barrel of a small, stainless-steel AMT .45 Backup. Only about six inches long, it was formidable enough to make him freeze. On the other side of the window Press used the end of the extinguished gas line to stab suddenly at the life-form. With only a few feet between it and them, the rigid metal tube sank deep into the inflated pouch, popping it with a sound like a dud firecracker. The creature howled in pain and backed up half the width of the room, then began to advance again, spitting and clicking its teeth.

"Stay there, Arden." Fitch's face clearly finished the sentence: *Or I'll shoot*. A single bead of sweat made a crooked path down the doctor's left temple.

Six. Five—

Dan looked around wildly. So many buttons on the console! Which one opened the door? Professor Arden knew, but Dr. Fitch wouldn't let him do anything. Paralyzed with indecision, he saw the LED display drop to four, then three. He was horrified when the older man moved his free hand to a position over a bright red button. That button could only be one thing—death for Press and Dr. Baker—but Dr. Fitch was carefully watching both the screen and Professor Arden. Michelle Purdue stood to the side with the dazed grimace of a woman in shock.

Two . . .

"No—you shouldn't!" Dan slammed into the older man just as his hand was descending. His larger size gave him an advantage and the two men bounced off the console and crashed to the floor; the doctor's .45 went spinning harmlessly across the floor, well out of reach. Still, the smaller man must have had some kind of martial-arts training in his past; he freed himself from Dan's clumsy grip easily and tried to scramble across the floor, headed back to the console and the incineration button.

He made it to the edge of the table and got a hand at table height before Dan charged him again, this time using all his weight in a simple wrestler's body drop that successfully pinned the man to the floor. With Dan's second rush, Stephen sprang to the console and found the switch that released the door to the isolation chamber. He flipped it and the door slid open.

"Come on!" Stephen screamed into the microphone on the console. *"Get out of there!"*

Press and Laura tumbled through the doorway and Stephen hit the switch again. The door closed, and above the harsh sound of Press and Laura breathing, they all heard a muffled thump as the life-form collided with the other side of the fireproof steel door.

"Enough of this shit," Press snarled. He stepped over Dan and Fitch and swatted the incineration button; for a second nothing happened, then the views through the window and on the monitor went an eye-blistering orange red as the interior of the isolation chamber was engulfed in flames.

"God, that was so *close*," Laura managed. She hung on to the side of the control table, gulping air.

"You okay?" Press asked her as he extended a hand to help Dan to his feet. His breathing was still fast and audible, but the cool demeanor had already returned. "Everything in working order?"

Laura sucked in a healthy lungful of air and held it, as if she were intentionally heading off hyperventilation. At the beat of four, she released it and smiled widely at Press. Her hair was a vivid, shining strawberry blond in the light of the inferno coming through the quartz window, and Dan gawked at her, a little dazzled by the transformation. "Yeah. Just peachy."

Press was still holding on to Dan's hand, and now he squeezed it harder and clamped him on the back. "In your whole life, Dan," he said seriously, "if anyone— *anyone*—ever treats you badly, I want you to call me. You understand? You're one helluva guy, Mr. Smithson." Dan beamed at the praise, then flushed as Laura nodded enthusiastically.

Fitch slowly climbed to his feet under the glares of all four team members. Press's face twisted and he balled his fists and took a menacing step toward the scientist. "Get a grip on yourself, Lennox," Fitch said quickly. "I hope you all understand that I had no choice. Because of Sil's escape, protocol dictates that I was to burn the room in two minutes if something—anything—went wrong that might endanger the rest of the complex again." He walked across the room, picked up his pistol, and slipped it back into his pocket without comment.

Press started to say something pointed, but Dan's soft question silenced him. "Protocol?" Dan looked questioningly at the doctor, his boyish face bewildered.

"I didn't know protocol meant killing the people on your own side."

15

When Sil got back to the Sunset Palms, the motel she had chosen earlier in the day, she had to dodge around a couple of police officers on the sidewalk in front of the small, slightly seedy building. Seeing them made her hesitate at first, but they were engrossed in questioning a hooker, and if they noticed Sil and her overloaded shopping bags they gave no indication. She heard little of their conversation, but the word *murder* caught her notice and stuck; between what she'd learned from the small television on the train and these two uniformed men, it reinforced the idea that what she'd done to the hobo—an act she barely recalled— and the female conductor were unacceptable things. These policemen were agitated and demanding, and the woman they were interrogating appeared frightened. It was no stretch of the mind to realize that she'd have to be careful of her behavior in the future—and watch for signs of retribution from whatever authorities might be involved in capturing her and returning her to the complex . . . or worse.

Inside, Sil pulled the remaining money from the fanny pack and stepped to the registration desk. The guy behind it flipped through an issue of *Rolling Stone* with a bored expression and didn't acknowledge her. He was in his twenties and not very clean, with lank blond hair and a space between his teeth that he probed idly with his tongue. Not sure what to do when he ignored her, Sil pushed the folded bills toward him without speaking and waited, her mind on the city of Los Angeles and the imposing mountains that over-looked the municipality from nearly every angle.

Finally, he looked up. His eyes widened and he dropped the magazine and hopped to his feet, slicking back his greasy hair with both hands in a pointless at-tempt at vanity. He wasn't tall, and the sight of her Amazonian figure made him gape stupidly for a few sec-onds; then his mouth snapped shut and he scooped up the cash and began counting it. He kept almost all of it and, that done, gave Sil an odd grin that she didn't find particularly pleasant.

Still, she gave him a shy smile in return.

◆

Sil had picked up as much research material and cloth-ing to go with it as she could and still leave what she guessed was enough money to pay for the room. The concept of counting still eluded her, but while every-body else seemed to do it naturally, maybe it wasn't im-portant in the scheme of things as they were working out for her. The cashier at one boutique had patiently gone through the bills and returned the excess to her, pushing back the white piece of paper with numbers printed on it that said PAY STUB. "You probably ought to keep this with your records," she'd said around a smack of bubble gum. Sil had nodded agreeably and pocketed it. Records? What did that mean? When the clerk at the next store had handed it back again, Sil dropped it in the trash on her way out. How important could it be if no one would take it in trade?

But the conductor's money had bought a lot of

things while it lasted, almost more than the dingy-sheeted double bed in the motel room could hold. There was a lot to learn, but the magazine stands along the Strip had proved a limitless resource; spread at one end of the bed, flipped open to the most important pages, issues of *Ms.*, *Cosmopolitan*, *Playboy* and *Chic* showed Sil everything she needed to know about how to dress. She'd bought the magazines and settled on a bus-stop bench to study them page by page. By the time the sixth or seventh bus driver had shouted angrily at her, she was ready to go shopping.

Now, hours later, her treasures were waiting. There was a mirror on the back of the closet door, and although it was pitted and dark with age, Sil could finally see how she looked. Standing in front of it, naked except for black patent-leather high heels, she examined herself. The reflection in the mirror showed a tall, slender woman with straight blond hair and striking, almond-shaped azure eyes, wide set but large. Her skin was clear and smooth, and she had fine, high cheekbones and smartly arched eyebrows. Full, firm breasts, a tiny waist and lean, shapely hips completed her appearance. Her gaze slid to the bed and the piles of satin underthings and tight outerwear that waited. She plucked a pair of shiny black panties from the heap on the bed and held them up.

Once wrapped, she'd make a lovely package.

◆

Dressed at last, Sil was on her way out of the room when she saw something on the edge of the dresser. Partially hidden by the lamp, it had escaped her attention and now she picked it up curiously. There wasn't much to the device; several rows of labeled buttons took up most of its surface, with a line of larger ones on the left side. The button at the top left was red, so Sil pressed it to see what would happen.

Behind her, voices exploded out of nowhere. Startled, she hissed and spun, then saw that the television had come on. She'd seen the set earlier but had been too engrossed in learning how to dress to register exactly what it was. Now she grinned and experimentally pressed another button, then another; like magic, the picture flashed into something different every time Sil tried a button. She loved it—what a wonderful teaching tool! She drank in glimpses of every channel she could find—so many more than the smaller television on the train. Men, women and children doing so many things, singing, screaming, building. She even found a program about something called earthquake preparedness—what was an earthquake?—that she puzzled over for quite some time before moving on. On the screen, men and women always seemed to be doing a dance around each other, sometimes blatant, sometimes so subtle it could barely be discerned, a sort of silent mating call that left Sil breathless and filled with yearning as she watched. On one channel the words FIVE MINUTES XXX FREE PREVIEW! ($7.95 AUTOMATICALLY CHARGED TO YOUR ROOM AFTER FIVE MINUTES) flashed across the screen and eventually went away as, entranced, Sil spent a quarter hour observing a man and woman strip completely, then copulate in full view of the camera. The sight filled Sil with strange, hot desperation; she needed to be a part of that world no matter what, to possess a man in the same way, to *mate*.

From union, she knew intuitively, would come reproduction.

◆

The greasy-haired guy at registration called to Sil before she could get out the front entrance of the motel.

"Uh, 'scuse me . . . miss?"

Now what did he want? He looked . . . *nasty*, and smelled worse. She was tempted to keep on going and leave the idiot stuttering behind his desk, then decided doing so would only draw unwanted attention. Reluctantly, she veered to where he waited. His gaze skittered up and down her figure as though she wouldn't notice, resting furtively on the cleavage showing above her low-cut black blouse before moving on to the high, cleanly muscled thigh that disappeared beneath the hem of her miniskirt.

"You got a charge on your room here." For emphasis, he poked at the screen of a computer monitor that was covered in smeary dust and dull nicotine stains. "I'll need your credit card number for the in-ci-den-tals." Sil cocked her head; he seemed to have trouble pronouncing the multisyllabled word. His cheeks were pitted with old acne scars and deepened with color at her frank gaze. "Movies, long-distance calls," he rushed on. "Damage to the room and sh—stuff. You know."

Sil regarded him uncomprehendingly, then zipped open the fanny pack and offered him the few remaining bills, the same ones he'd returned to her when she'd checked in.

He shook his head. "No can do, lady. Gotta have the credit card. Zip-zap."

"Zip-zap?" Now she was even more baffled.

The registration clerk cracked a smile, obviously amused at his own label for whatever it was he was trying to convey. His teeth were as yellow as the discolored casing of the computer and she could smell something warm and rotting on his breath—the food from his last meal, lodged in his unbrushed teeth. "Yeah, honey. Zip-zap, Amex, Visa, MasterCard. Plastic."

Plastic—now Sil understood. Unzipping the conductor's pack, she fished out a plastic card with a logo that matched a small, pyramid-shaped sign on the desk, a MasterCard. She extended her hand and he took the card and nodded; when he sat and began punching keys on his keyboard, she zipped the fanny pack closed and walked out. She was only a few yards down the street when the guy from the motel dashed out the door and bounded after her.

"Hey!" he called. "Wait up!"

Sil paused for him to catch up, frowning slightly. Did

he want more plastic? There was another card in the pack, a Visa. She could give him that one too, if necessary.

But the clerk only waved the MasterCard she'd given him in front of her face. She accepted it reflexively, waiting to see if he wanted something else, but he gave her only another oily smile. "Hey, Miss Cardoza— Angela—can I call you that? You wouldn't wanna have your credit card falling into the wrong hands, if you know what I mean." His smirk stretched wider, as if they shared some secret, and Sil felt her lips turn down in distaste. She didn't know what *in the wrong hands* meant, although his words implied that his were the *right* ones. Right for what?

"No," she said, "I wouldn't." She stared at him for a moment, then made a decision. "Where is a good place to meet a man?"

The clerk's leer dropped away and his mouth fell open. "A guy?" he asked stupidly.

"Yes, a man," Sil repeated.

The clerk used his hands to slick back his hair again, then tried to look thoughtful. "Well, there's a lot of guys at the ID around the corner on Formosa." Sil gazed at him blankly. "It's a club," he said uncertainly. "You know—drinks and music and shit?" She finally nodded. "Yeah," he continued, "you won't have any problem finding somebody there, plus it's ladies' night—they'll let you in for free. If you can't find what you're looking for," his glance turned lecherous, "you just let me know, okay?" He blinked at her, his gaze darting lasciviously down her figure. "You can't miss the place. You'll see the line."

"Good." Without saying anything else, she turned back the way she'd been going before he'd stopped her, tucking the MasterCard back into the fanny pack as she walked. Sil thought she heard him mutter something that sounded like "Ungrateful bitch," but when she glanced over her shoulder, he was already gone.

It took Press a long time to answer the telephone. Fitch could imagine the guy in his room, sprawled across the bed in front of the television. He'd probably have the Sports Channel on, some used-up former athlete with a toupee blathering on about this year's rising basketball star. But Press was a thorough if not always obedient worker; no doubt the photographs of the destruction at the compound and the two killings were spread across the bed with him—along with a few empty beer bottles.

"Yeah?" Press's voice sounded groggy.

Finally, Fitch thought with irritation. "The conductor's credit card has turned up at the Sunset Palms Motel in Hollywood," he said curtly. "The van's out front and ready to roll. We're leaving in thirty seconds, so—"

There was a sharp crash on the other end and the line went dead. Fitch winced at the noise and pressed his lips together, then headed toward the van, grinning at the thought of Lennox cussing in his room and trying to shake the sleep out of his head enough to function, tripping over smelly bottles as he searched for his shoes.

Well . . . maybe not. The man *was* a professional, after all. While the others climbing into the van looked pressured by the sudden orders and still muddled from sleep—Dan was carrying his socks and shoes—Press was probably already fully dressed, completely alert and in the elevator on his way down. Still, Fitch would bet Lennox really hated him right now, or at least a little more than usual. And that was okay.

The feeling was mutual . . . for *all* of them.

♦

"Well, here's a classy place," commented Press. He jerked his chin sardonically at a dirty window and ledge on the left side of the building. "What do you say—let's go for the drive-up room." Dr. Fitch ignored him and steered the van under the arch above the driveway of the Sunset Palms Motel.

"Why would she stay here?" Dan asked, craning his neck in an effort to see out the side window. "The Biltmore's much nicer."

"She wouldn't know any better, or care," Stephen answered as Fitch brought the vehicle to a lurching stop. The team scrambled out and headed toward the motel's front door, where the clerk stood waiting, his hands jammed into the back pockets of his jeans.

"The woman claiming to be Angela Cardoza—what room is she in?" Fitch grabbed the younger man's arm. "We don't have time to waste. You were notified—"

"Hey, man, let go." The clerk shook him off. "You're gonna wrinkle the shirt. I know who you are."

He made an exaggerated show of straightening his sleeve and Press stepped forward, a black scowl twisting his features. He was easily a head taller and thirty pounds more powerful than the motel employee. "We're not screwing around here, buddy."

The greasy-haired clerk blinked and held up his hands. "Take it easy, man. She's gone, anyway—took off right before the card number came up as stolen."

"Where's her room?" demanded Stephen. "Did she leave anything in it?"

"Nothing," the clerk said slyly. "I checked."

"Yeah, I'm sure you did," growled Press.

The smaller man shrugged. "Hey, go and see for yourself."

"I intend to," Press declared. He brought a hand down on one of the guy's bony shoulders in a pseudo-friendly gesture, but hard enough to make the joint give an audible pop. The weaselly man gasped as Press squeezed and beamed at him companionably. "In fact, I'll do that personally a little later. You'll be a swell guy and make sure everything's there, won't you? You know, all that stuff the . . . *maid* probably moved?"

The clerk's Adam's apple bobbed jerkily as he swallowed. "Sure, yeah, sure. I—I can do that." They all heard his sigh of relief as Press lifted his hand and folded his arms.

"That security camera up there," Stephen said, pointing toward the ceiling. "We'll need to see the film."

The clerk shook his head. "Forget it. I'd have to—"

"Oh, I think you'll do whatever it takes," Fitch snapped. He pushed his face close to the other man's. "Or haven't you got a clue yet? Maybe you'd rather explain to the owner that your failure to cooperate is why I had the place shut down for the next two weeks. And maybe you'd like to do *that* from the comfort of a federal jail cell."

"Okay, okay!" The clerk threw up his hands. "You got it—gimme five minutes." He stalked through a door off to the side that had a handwritten sign marked EMPLOYEES ONLY taped on it and they heard him rummaging around and cursing under his breath. A couple of minutes later, just before Fitch was about to start screaming at him, the guy came back with an ancient black-and-white portable television balanced atop a battered, bottom-line-model VCR.

"Hurry it up, would you?" Fitch glared at the man, and Stephen grinned to himself as the clerk seemed to downshift visibly, moving even more slowly than before.

Finally he got everything plugged in and turned the set on, then hit the play button on the VCR. He fiddled with the fast-forward and rewind buttons awhile, then paused the machine. "There," he said, "that's her."

"Is this the best picture you can manage?" Laura asked, peering at the small screen.

The clerk folded his arms peevishly. "This ain't a video store, honey. What you see is what you get."

"And there's certainly not much around here to *see*," Laura said with a pointed look. She turned back to the screen.

"Do you have any idea where she went?" Fitch asked. His eyes were glued to the picture. "Even a guess?"

"Yeah—well, maybe. She said she wanted a good place to meet a man, so I told her about the club around the corner, the ID." For a moment the group fell silent and the clerk looked at them, perplexed. "What's so strange about that, right? The way she was dressed, I figured her for a hooker, though she looked like she'd be a little pricey for this place."

"Give me the tape," Fitch said. The guy opened his mouth to argue then thought better of it, and ejected it from the machine. He handed it over. "We'll send this to the lab and have it enhanced, see if we can get a better look at her." He glanced at the other members of the team. "In the meantime, next stop—

"The ID."

17

The ID was L.A.'s biggest club, and the sight of it dazzled Sil. Converted from an old movie palace, the outside looked like something she'd seen during her television scans, only on a smaller scale. Around a massive, arched entrance, graystone walls rose three stories above sidewalks inset with glittering mica. As the clerk had told Sil, a line of people stretched three blocks back from the club's entrance, and she simply walked beside the line until she found the front doors. Compared with some of the women standing sullenly in line, her outfit was nearly conservative. Her legs, though, were better than most: sheathed in a nearly transparent fabric of shimmery black gold, they were long and sleek and impossible to ignore. As it turned out, they were her ticket to get in.

"Hey, you. Legs." A big-muscled bouncer with a thick, flat-topped crew cut guarded the club's entrance. He gestured at Sil and flicked his head in the direction of the dark doorway behind him. "You're in."

Sil smiled at him and walked purposefully forward, oblivious to the jealous mutterings from those still forced to wait at the front of the line. Passing through the heavy, beamed doors was like nothing she'd ever experienced; inside was a huge room, crashing with movement and people and flashing lights that periodically tried to blind the patrons. Presiding over everything was the music, immense and relentless, pounding from dozens of unseen speakers in the high, blacked-out ceiling, sending waves of energy coursing through the atmosphere. Sil hesitated just down the wall from the entrance and looked around, formulating her next move. In the center of the enormous area was a giant, circular bar made of diamond-plate sheet metal and chromed railings. Suspended above it, a line of television monitors followed the generous curve of the bar, all screens showing sexy but dated images from black-and-white movies. Above those, midway to ceiling level, were two all-but-naked dancers bathed in multicolored lights while their hair blew in all directions, swept by the brisk currents of concealed fans.

For a little while Sil gawked, excited by the motion and hundreds upon hundreds of people, women dressed in every imaginable kind of clothing, men cruising along, their eyes flashing with sexual energy. Eventually she pushed her way to the bar. When somebody got up, she seized the opportunity to sit among the other women preening around the bar, watching as some bounced with the music or twined their fingers in shining curls, while others dipped their fingers in glasses filled with strawberry-sweet drinks and chewed their bottom lips engagingly.

Sitting straight on her barstool, Sil realized that her low-cut black silk blouse covered her far more than any of the clothing worn by the females around her. She crossed one long leg over the other, exposing more smooth thigh, but it wasn't enough to attract attention. A woman with blond hair, like hers but considerably longer, drifted past with a lazy sway in her walk. Sil saw several of the handsome men milling around the bar turn to watch, saw their gazes drop to the woman's midriff, skin bare and tanned below a tight, cherry-colored tank top. Sil's own blouse was tight but masked far too much; in one smooth move she pulled it free of her skirt and slid it over her head. Underneath she wore a black lace bustier trimmed with a thin, gold ribbon that perfectly complemented the tight miniskirt and shimmery stockings, and no one appeared to notice the blouse she let drop to the floor behind the barstool.

As Sil scanned the crowd a nice-looking guy with brown hair locked eyes with her. She looked boldly back, then blinked when, after about five or six seconds, he dropped his gaze and turned his back, shooting a final, mystified look in her direction. She couldn't understand it—what had gone wrong? Brow furrowed, she watched him openly for some time, noting that every time he looked over at her, he seemed increasingly uncomfortable. Finally, Sil saw him catch the gaze of another woman, just as he had with her. But this woman didn't hold his stare as obviously as Sil had; instead, she met his eyes, then fluttered her lids and looked down at her drink, repeating the ritual several times. At last the guy walked over and started a conversation as he slid into the space next to her at the bar.

Sil's eyes narrowed as understanding dawned. The males needed to feel *dominant*, and her refusal to look away had made her seem too brazen, too *strong*. She would not make the same mistake again.

"What'll it be?"

Sil swiveled on the barstool, then realized a bartender had stopped nearby but was talking to someone else, a young man with sun-streaked hair and a face that was attractive enough to be on one of the television screens with which she was becoming so enamored. The guy felt her gaze and smiled at her. "Hi," he said. The bartender shrugged and moved away to wait on someone else.

"Hi," Sil said in return. She gave him her best smile then carefully averted her gaze for a second or two.

He turned in her direction and casually leaned an elbow on the bar. His skin was deeply tanned and his teeth were very white. Despite his closeness, the color of his eyes was impossible to see because of the wildly flashing lights. "Where're you from?"

"I'm . . . foreign," Sil answered. She fingered a strand of her hair as she tried to plan her next words.

"Really?"

Sil wasn't sure whether this was the right thing to say, but she never got the chance to find out. As she opened her mouth, still not sure what her next words would be, another girl weaved through the crowd and stumbled into the man standing next to Sil. Quite pretty and apparently drunk, she had auburn hair that fell past her shoulders in thick waves and cascaded onto a full bustline that was nearly coming out of her black leather vest. When the man who'd been talking to Sil caught the girl's arm and helped steady her, the other woman gave him a moist grin. "Hi," she said. Her voice sounded vaguely slurred. "I've got a party to go to and no one to take me."

"I'll take you," the guy said immediately.

The girl's smile widened as Sil watched, stunned. "Will you? Cool!" She found her own balance and tossed her hair. "I have to go to the little girls' room first, okay? You wait here. I'll be right back." She veered into the crowd.

Sil looked at the guy, but his back was to her as he motioned to one of the bartenders. Outcompeted by the other woman, Sil was already forgotten. As she heard him order something called a "Jell-O shot," Sil slid to her feet, ran her hands down her hips to straighten her skirt, and headed for the rest room.

◆

The rest rooms were on the lower level, down a flight of bottom-lit stairs that were never meant to be negotiated with a stomach full of alcohol—at least it seemed that way to Sil as she watched the drunken girl from the bar wobble down them as a few other woman staggered up. Sil followed the auburn-haired beauty into the women's room and squinted at the unexpected bright white tiles, relieved only by an occasional framed movie poster bolted to the wall. The stalls were off to the side, floor-to-ceiling enclosures—little rooms—that reminded Sil of the tiny bathroom on the train but without the luxury of a sink or mini–shower stall. For the moment they had the rest room to themselves, and Sil's competitor stopped at the mirror and dug her hand inside her tight leather vest, giving her breasts a few practiced tugs that resulted in a cleavage far more generous than before.

As she turned to go into a stall, the young woman saw Sil waiting for her and scowling. Her response was a self-satisfied smirk. "Whatever works, right?" She didn't seem nearly as intoxicated as she had upstairs, and Sil's expression went icy and full of hate. The girl shrugged, unimpressed. "Hey, honey, all's fair in love and war." Ignoring Sil's glare, she ducked into the closest stall and shut the door.

Sil slipped into the one next to her and carefully pulled the latch closed, wondering where she'd heard that saying before. Perhaps it had been on the television, during one of those innuendo-filled daytime shows about men and women that she'd watched on the train. It didn't matter now, and what bothered her more was not understanding exactly why she had disliked being called *honey* by the woman who was now singing to herself as she used the toilet in the next stall. Sil could hear the words—

"Touch me now, stranger, it's time to explore. . . . My body is your ship into which—"

Barely aware of what she was doing, Sil calmly punched through the wall separating the stalls. Despite Sil's earnest efforts, the screaming, bleeding girl just wouldn't fit through the hole Sil had made in the wall-board.

◆

The noise and blazing streaks of colored light in the nightclub's main room was an assault after the clean, eye-popping whiteness of the rest room. Sil almost didn't see the handsome man standing casually by the top of the stairs. When she did notice him, she ducked her head and glided back into the shadows for a moment, where she could study him without being seen. As handsome in a dark-haired way as the guy she'd be talking with before the drunken girl had intervened, this guy struck Sil as more intelligent and watchful . . . *cunning.* Dressed in a tuxedo as though he'd just come from somewhere special, he surveyed the crowd with the air of a predator familiar with the hunting ground; Sil found the aura of shrewdness that surrounded him immensely electrifying.

Stepping out of the darkness, she intentionally swayed into him as she passed. "Whoa!" He laughed as he held out a hand to steady her. "Better find your balance before you try those stairs again, babe."

"Hi," Sil said. Her voice didn't sound as slurred as her previous rival's had, and she hoped it wouldn't matter. "I've got a party to go to and no one to take me."

"Really?" The man's dark eyes sharpened with interest and he slipped an arm around her waist. His breath was warm in her ear. "Well, my name's Robbie and I've got a car that says I'm your transport. Where's the party?"

"I . . . don't know. I can't find the address," she added quickly. Sil hadn't thought about anything beyond the borrowed phrase, but that didn't seem to matter to Robbie. He simply laughed.

"What the hell, baby. Let's go—we'll make our own."

♦

"Here it is. What do you think?" Robbie opened the door to his convertible and looked at Sil expectantly. She didn't understand the question, so she nodded agreeably and climbed into the passenger seat. He closed the door for her, then came around and settled behind the steering wheel. "It's a Puma. I special-ordered it."

"Puma?" She'd thought a puma was a type of cat, but apparently that was incorrect. Sil slid her gaze over the inside of the automobile, watching as he inserted a key into the ignition and turned it, learning the process as the engine started and he shifted into first gear and pulled out of the parking spot, then left the lot behind. It didn't seem to take substantial intelligence to operate the car—hand-eye coordination, attentiveness to your surroundings, memorizing what the various knobs and pedals did. She thought she could do it if she had to.

"Yeah," Robbie continued as he steered smoothly into the flow of night traffic on La Brea, then turned left onto Hollywood. "From Brazil. Not too many of them around."

"It's very . . . orange," she finally said.

Robbie chuckled. "Yeah, it is. Like I said, you don't see a lot of 'em. So what's your name?"

"Sil." A familiar sound above them made Sil's head snap up. A helicopter sped by far overhead, then joined another hovering somewhere behind them, spotlights probing the street from which they'd just come. Were they from the complex? Had they been able to trace her here?

"Wow," Robbie said, acknowledging the copters with a nod, "check it out. There's always some action going on in this part of town." His disinterested expression didn't match his enthusiastic words. Then he brightened. "Wait'll you see my place . . . uh, Sil." He gave her a sideways glance. "It's on Chalette Drive, built on the side of a hill. When I turn out the lights, you can see all the way to the ocean."

Sil nodded again, still keeping one ear tuned to the fading sounds of the helicopters. What was the *ocean*? For a while the street signs had continued to read SUNSET BLVD. and follow a line of apparently endless parking meters, then Robbie had passed a corner called Fairfax. On it was a cylindrical building made of glass, and she looked back and saw a sign in front of the building that read DIRECTORS GUILD OF AMERICA. Then he turned and began weaving the car along a dozen smaller, curved streets. It didn't take long for the noise of the helicopters to disappear entirely, but she was still disappointed to leave the gigantic billboards and the bright clubs and stores behind.

"Don't talk much, do you?"

Sil shrugged, hoping that gesture would suffice. She wasn't sure what to say, what he wanted her to say, what she *shouldn't* say. She knew that there was a sort of ritual that was usually applied here, but she was at a loss as to the finer points of it. The television—her best teacher—had shown her the basic biological steps, but not much else. She had a lot to learn.

The Puma had been climbing steadily for several minutes, and suddenly Robbie used a turn signal and veered into a carefully landscaped driveway. Farther up, at the peak of the hill and lit by strategically placed yard lights, a blue-stained cedar A-frame with huge windows waited. Robbie stopped the Puma in front of the lower-level garage and pressed a button on a device clipped to the driver's-side sun visor; the double-wide garage door rolled smoothly up. He pulled in and hit the switch again to close the garage, then killed the engine and came around to open Sil's door.

"Home sweet home," he said cheerfully. "This way." Sil followed him to a set of steep, wooden stairs, looking curiously at the unfinished garage, with its open wood framework and scores of hardware items hanging and stacked on shelves everywhere. Robbie waved a dismissive hand at it. "Don't look at this mess. I hate screwing around with garage stuff. Come on—wait'll you see upstairs." He pushed through a door at the top of the staircase and motioned for her to follow. As she stepped through he snapped his fingers. Soft track lights winked into life on each side of the living room, following the high peaks of the ceiling until they met. Robbie snapped his fingers again and a stereo system against the far wall lit up, spilling soft music into the room from surround-sound speakers. On the other wall, in the center of two sets of patio doors, was an unused fireplace faced by two expensively upholstered Papasan chairs. Surrounded by deep brown leather couches, a thick, twelve-by-twelve area rug the color of café au lait dominated the room. In the rug's center rested the highlight of the room, a circular coffee table made of heavy, polished copper, a lovely disk with hand-beaten designs that rested on a dark wooden base. The muted track lighting made it sparkle.

Robbie grinned at her, showing capped, expensive teeth. "You like it?"

Sil nodded amiably. "Yes. It's very nice."

"Great." Robbie watched her for a second, then made a mock fanning motion in front of his face. "Whew," he said nonchalantly. "I'm all hot and sweaty from the crowd in that place—what a madhouse. I feel like a shower." His eyes, a clear gray color she'd never seen before, glittered in the subdued light. "How about it, beautiful—you want one?"

Sil smiled hesitantly. A shower?

"Tell you what," Robbie said easily. "I'm going to take one. Join me if you like, or take one later. If you'd rather get something to drink, the fridge is off the living room. Help yourself. No problem."

"No problem," Sil echoed, watching as he headed toward the bathroom, stripping off his clothes and leaving them in a trail across the living room. She followed him through the living room and into the master bedroom's bathroom, liking the sight of his muscular back and lean hips. He grinned at her, completely at ease in his nakedness, and ducked quickly into a overly large shower stall separated from the rest of the bathroom by a seven-foot wall of glass blocks. The blast of the water startled her for a moment, then a cloud of steam rose above the stall, billowing out and up toward an exhaust fan embedded in the slanted ceiling twelve feet above her. She could see Robbie's silhouette, distorted by the glass blocks; moving back and forth under the hot water, he was humming huskily as he lathered up with some kind of scented soap. The smell reminded her a little of the scattered spots of greenery back in the desert surrounding the complex—earthy and exciting.

Sil's breathing sped up, kindled by the sound of Robbie's throaty singing, the clean, steamy scent of his soap and the erotic glimpses of skin shifting in and out of view through the glass wall. Her face began to flush as the temperature built in the bathroom, and after a few moments she went to the bedroom to wait for him. The bed was ridiculously huge, covered by a thick comforter in a sizzling dark Persian print with a dozen matching throw pillows. She ran a fingernail slowly across the bottom of the comforter, listening to the sound it made and being careful not to tear the fabric. She felt as wet and sultry as the moist, heated air in the other room.

She couldn't wait for him to finish his shower.

18

Press was the first one out of the van when it screeched to a stop in front of the ID. The club was certainly striking, and the bouncer who stood at the front of the waiting triple-deep line of club goers—a standard Mr. Muscles weight-lifter type with a California tan—managed to look bored and vaguely menacing at the same time. When the guy ignored the government card Press flashed in his face and tried to stop him at the door, Press thought he finally knew how stereotypes were born, especially when he saw the name BRUNO embroidered across the breast pocket of the bouncer's Ralph Lauren polo shirt.

"Tonight's guest list only," the bouncer rasped. "Get in line."

"Can't you read, pal?" Press snapped. He flicked his identification card again, this time close enough to Bruno's nose to make him blink in surprise and jerk his head back. "Government. Now get out of the way." He pushed around Mr. Muscles without waiting for a go-ahead.

"Wait a minute, jerkoff—" Bruno wrapped a grizzly-sized hand around Press's arm and tried to pull him back. Press's hands were already positioning to give the idiot a hapkido joint lock that was guaranteed to make him let go in a hurry when the inside of the ID erupted in screams. Bruno's mouth opened and shut several times in rapid succession, and he forgot all about Press and his government card as people started barreling out of the club. "Hey! Hey!" Bruno bellowed. "Hold it— what the fuck's going on? What—!" His braying ended in a *whump!* as someone's pointy elbow accidentally caught him just below the sternum. The pain made him do a fast spin and he found himself face-to-face with Dr. Fitch and a stream of aides and armed military personnel. "*Shit!*" he squawked.

"Round up everybody!" Fitch shouted to his charges. "And I mean, *everybody*. Nobody leaves the club until I say so!"

"Coming through, coming through," Press yelled, trying to be heard above the chaotic, bizarre mix of laughter, deafening music and screams. "Come on," he hollered. "Get out of the way! Let us *through*, damn it!"

"I'm *telling* you, Vicki says she talked to the girl who'd seen the body in the bathroom," a female voice whispered on Press's left, practically in his ear. "Blood *everywhere*." Before Press could turn his head, the speaker had vanished into the confused crowd. Abruptly the hammering music stopped, leaving a noticeable pulse in his head; voices immediately rose to fill the void, escalating precariously toward shriek level.

"EVERYONE, PLEASE STAY CALM. YOU ARE NOT IN ANY DANGER." The master sergeant in charge of the MPs had come up with a bullhorn and, much to the outrage of the bartenders, was now standing on top of the circular bar in the center of the immense room. "THERE'S NO REASON TO BE ALARMED; YOU'LL ONLY BE DETAINED A FEW MINUTES. TO EXIT, PLEASE FORM A SINGLE FILE LINE AT THE DOOR AND BE PREPARED TO SHOW TWO PIECES OF IDENTIFICATION, ONE OF WHICH MUST BE A PHOTOGRAPH." Press

saw him hop nimbly off the bar and stare down the few
people who dared to question him; at the entrance, the
exit line was already forming.

"Why the mass exodus?" Laura asked from behind
him. Dan and Stephen were on her heels, with Fitch
not far behind.

"I haven't verified it," Press said with a dark look,
"but I think a woman's dead in the rest room. Want to
bet it's our girl's handiwork?"

"The bouncer says the rest rooms are downstairs,"
Fitch informed them. "Stairs are all the way to the
right rear."

The team saw the sign for the rest rooms and made
their way to the stairs with no trouble. Press was surprised to find the stairs oddly deserted, free of the usual
gapers, as though someone had announced it was the
source of the bubonic plague rather than a murder.
He sprinted down to the landing and ducked into the
women's room, scanning but finding nothing in the
front area by the sinks and mirrors. To his right was another room, this one filled with the kind of high-
privacy toilet stalls that ran from floor to ceiling, like
little rooms with actual doors and knobs. Both rooms
were tiled in a white so bright it made his eyes ache, a
decorating move probably meant to put a little wakeful-
ness in an intoxicated patron. The snowy tiles made it
real easy to spot the large, black-red puddle of blood
leaking from beneath the closed door of one of the
stalls.

Press tried the door—locked—then banged on it,
though he knew it was useless. When he got no response, he lifted a booted foot and gave the door a
sharp kick just as the rest of the group filed into the
rest room with the club manager at their heels.
"Uh-oh," he heard Dan say unhappily. The flimsy lock
cracked away and the door flew in, then hit something
soft with an unpleasant thud and rebounded to a partly
open position. When Press eased his head around its

edge, the dead eyes of a once pretty young woman with wavy auburn hair stared back at him. Wedged between the toilet and the wall on Press's left, there was a hole in her back that made it obvious something . . . *big* had pierced her from behind; ripped from her body, her spinal column was draped across her feet in a bloody line. Blood had splattered the inside of the stall and ringed a jagged-edged crater in the wall.

Press ducked out and stepped to his left, but the adjoining stall was empty. Not so much as a droplet of blood marred the pearly tiles of the back wall or floor, or around the break in the wallboard. He didn't know how she'd done it or why, but Sil had murdered the woman in the next stall without even getting her hands dirty.

◆

"Everyone checked out," the MP sergeant told Fitch. "She must have left before we made the place." Fitch nodded morosely as Press joined him at the entrance. "We already searched the building from top to bottom, but we could do it again."

"Forget it," Press said. "If she wasn't in the club when we took it, she sure as hell isn't going to come back. Come on, Doc. Let's go talk to our pal Bruno. Maybe he remembers her."

"I don't see how that's possible," Fitch said cynically. "How many women come in here each night?"

Press plucked a toothpick from the bar as they passed it and stuck it in his mouth. "You never know until you ask."

Bruno the bouncer was still positioned out front, except now he'd rearranged the waist-high metal stands and velvet cords to make it obvious that the ID was closed for the night. People milled by the front, gawking and whispering about the ambulance and military vehicles double-parked on the street and the stone-faced MPs guarding the entrance. Adding to the fray were a half-dozen L.A. police cars, red-and-blue bubble lights strobing everything around them. When Bruno saw Press and Fitch coming his way, a grimace twisted his face. "So you didn't find who you were looking for," he said flatly.

"No." Press worked the toothpick from the left to the right side of his mouth, then back again. "We're looking for a tall, blue-eyed blond woman, five-ten or so, wearing a black blouse and black miniskirt. Any idea who she left with?"

Bruno rolled his eyes and shot Press a contemptuous glance. "You're bullshitting me, right? Must be a thousand blondies going and coming every night, and seven out of ten of 'em leave with some dude to screw. Not exactly news around here."

"I told you," Fitch said. "We're wasting our time."

Press ignored him and chewed his toothpick thoughtfully for a second. "Okay, let's go at it another way. How about the regulars, the guys on the know who get in every night? No losers." He tapped his wristwatch. "It's still early. Any top attractions leave before their normal time?"

"Assume he's socially adept," said Stephen over Press's shoulder. "He'd have to help her out because she's inexperienced."

Bruno looked nonplussed. "You mean like a virgin or something?"

Press shot Stephen an annoyed glare. "Yeah, something like that. In other words, we're looking for a guy who'd be friendly to her, not a totally conceited asshole. And like I said, he'd be leaving earlier than usual."

Bruno scratched his head for a moment. "I'm thinking, I'm thinking." His broad face brightened. "Hey— Robbie Llywelyn, he left with a blonde. Kind of early for him to blow the joint, too."

Press snatched the toothpick from his lips. "This Mr. Robbie Nice Guy, is he on your mailing list?"

Bruno grunted. "Hell, yeah. He's been a regular for years. All I know is that he lives in Hollywood Hills, but the boss'll have Robbie's address in the office." The bouncer shook his head. "But I'll tell you this, Robbie's a pro player. If you've got some idea that you're gonna stop him from doing her, it's probably already too late."

19

It wasn't long at all before Sil heard the water stop running. She could hear the man moving around, still singing softly to himself, but she wasn't sure what to do next. Should she go into the bathroom, or wait until he came to her? The choice was taken out of her hands when Robbie stepped out of the bathroom, clad only in a pair of loose gray sweatpants. Sil had never been this close to an undressed man before, and she couldn't help but stare at his body. Well-defined muscles stood out on his arms as well as his chest and belly, which were covered with an appealing layer of silky dark curls. His lips turned up when he saw her standing by the bed, exposing engaging dimples in cheeks that were starting to shadow with a day-old growth of beard. In his hands was a thick towel, and he took a final swipe at his wet hair, then tossed it aside and folded his arms.

"Take off your clothes," he said evenly. "I want to see you."

Sil nodded and reached to unhook the bustier that she'd worn as a blouse for most of the night. Her fingers were clumsy, trembling with a combination of relief and excitement, but at last she managed to unfasten it

120

Scientists observe the creature as she sleeps in her glass enclosure.

Twelve-year-old Sil and her creator, Dr. Xavier Fitch (Ben Kingsley).

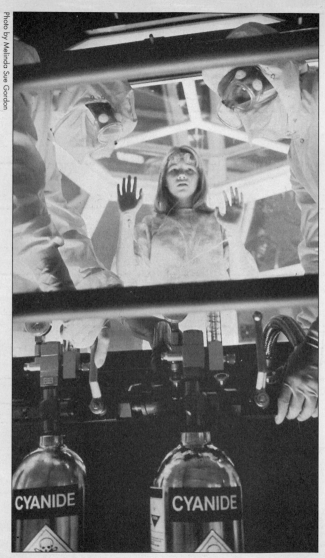

Sil watches the lab technicians prepare to terminate the project.

Sil dives through the tempered glass of her enclosure.

The search team. *Left to right:* Alfred Molina, Marg Helgenberger, Ben Kingsley, Michael Madsen, Forest Whitaker.

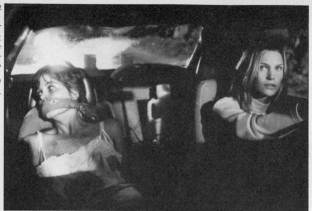

Sil (Natasha Henstridge), now fully grown, takes a hostage.

The search team finds another victim.

Sil changes
her identity.

Sil as Nicole.

Sil and Laura meet in the hotel bathroom.

Ben Kingsley as Dr. Xavier Fitch.

Laura searches for Sil beneath the streets of Los Angeles.

Arden meets a beautiful woman.

Photo by Melinda Sue Gordon

Laura and Press find they have something in common.

and drop it to the floor. She'd been afraid that he
would need to be convinced or, worse, he would reject
her as a mate. Obviously, that wasn't going to be a
problem.

"Very nice," he cooed. "Now the rest of it."

She could hear his breathing escalate from here, and
without breaking eye contact her hand moved to the
zipper on the skirt, then froze. A frown slid over her
lovely face as the pupils of her eyes contracted visibly,
like an animal pinned in the roadway by the sudden
light of an oncoming truck. A pale mist was oozing
from Robbie's body, thick and light green, like the
steam from a boiling vat of algae-clotted water.

She bent to pick up the bustier. "Drive me back,"
she said coldly.

Robbie's jaw dropped. *"What?"*

"I said, drive me back."

His lips drew into a hard, thin line. "What are you
talking about? You knew what we came here for—hell,
you came on to me."

"And now I don't want to."

He stepped toward her and she backed up, step for
step. "All right," he said coolly, "you've said the oblig-
atory no. It's duly noted. Now come here."

"I want to *go*," Sil insisted. "I don't want to be here
anymore."

"It's too late for that, baby." Robbie's voice was different from the suave guy she'd met at the ID, chilly
and implacable. "You're not going anywhere."

Sil stared at him as another new lesson sank in, an
unknown point of no return. Tension was building inside her, knotting her shoulders and making her head
pound. That terrible green haze was still radiating from
every pore of his body; he was unhealthy, diseased. She
didn't want to touch him, let alone mate. She tried to
take a step toward the door that led to the living room
and ultimately out, but he moved in front of her, making himself a human obstacle. "Maybe you didn't hear

me the first time," he said icily. "I said, you're *not* leaving. If there's one thing a man can't stand, baby, it's a cockteaser."

Neither of them moved. Five seconds went by, then ten. "All right," Sil finally said. Her fingers had curled into claws and wouldn't slacken; she hid them behind her back so he wouldn't see. "Whatever you say."

Robbie's rigid expression relaxed and he closed the distance between them and put an arm around her. "That's better," he said. He was taller by a good four inches and had to tilt her face up to his for a kiss. "Come on, baby. Loosen up and have a little fun. I know what I'm doing—I'll make you feel real good, I promise."

His mouth closed over hers and his tongue pushed past her lips. Sil had to fight the urge to gag as that horrid, sickly fog enveloped her. After a moment she pushed the memory of the green mist aside and surrendered to the impulse of self-preservation rising inside her; closing her eyes, she let her tongue reach for his mouth as she enfolded him in her arms. A feeling, huge and dark and indefinable, rocketed through her body, making her spasm and clutch Robbie closer.

Robbie's eyes bulged. He tried to scream and couldn't as Sil's tongue unfurled, filling his mouth and throat as he struggled desperately to get free. He couldn't break her crushing embrace, so he punched her twice in the back of the head, the only part of her that he could reach. Useless—she didn't even feel it, and before he could manage a third strike, Sil's tongue burst from the back of his skull, spraying the rich, Persian-motif comforter with blood, gray matter and bits of dark-haired scalp. Robbie convulsed in her arms and went limp, and Sil found that when she let him go, only her bloody tongue, long and barbed on the end, held him upright.

An automatic push of will and it retracted, whipping back into her head and taking a good chunk of

Robbie's brains with it. His body toppled sideways and Sil leaned over him and spat out the filth in her mouth, retching violently as she tried to cleanse herself. Out of breath and splattered with his tainted blood, she stepped over the body and went into the bathroom, stripping gratefully before stepping into the sumptuous, glass-surrounded shower. A little experimenting with the knobs and she managed to enjoy a nice, hot shower to wash away Robbie's repulsive touch.

20

"Well," Laura said dryly, "if she hasn't guessed we're after her, I'm sure she knows now. Every house on that hill has a clear view of both Loma Vista and Carla. With this kind of equipment, anyone could see us coming for miles." She swiveled on the front seat for a view out the rear window of the van. Seven army vehicles of various sizes chugged up the hill behind them; even with their lights on dim, the troop would be impossible to miss.

"There's no other way," Fitch said. He sounded like he was trying to talk with his jaw wired shut.

"It doesn't matter," Stephen stated impassively. He was staring absently out the window. "She won't be thinking about us right now anyway. Her behavior is clearly indicative of a desire to reproduce, to breed."

"So tell us something we don't already know." Press looked moodily out the window.

"Don't you think she'll be here?" Interior lighting was minimal and Dan's ebony face was nearly invisible from his seat in the midsection of the van. "Why wouldn't she?"

"If she's mated successfully," Stephen murmured, "she could be long gone."

"Mating doesn't mean she'll have a baby right away, does it?" Dan struggled to unsnap his seat belt, then scooted forward until he could lean between the two front bucket seats. The dashboard lights gave off a low, multicolored glow and Laura could see rivulets of perspiration sliding slowly down Dan's forehead and temples. His fear-filled voice made it clear that it wasn't the warm night or the unaccustomed humidity in the air making him sweat. "She's half-human, so she'll have to wait nine months like us, like a normal human woman, right?"

Laura didn't answer right away. She could feel the others on the team waiting. "I don't know," she finally admitted. From the far backseat, Press made a fake, sardonic sound that was supposed to pass for a cough but sounded more like the throat-clearing noise people used to politely inform you they know you are lying. It was unfortunate that he wasn't directly behind her where she could smack him for being so damned insolent. "From what we've seen of her growth and the growth of the creature at the virus lab, probably . . . not."

Dan sat back, speechless. Fitch's voice cut through the sudden silence as he braked sharply and spun the wheel to the left through an entrance gate in a long, wrought-iron fence. "Everybody get ready. This is the driveway to the house."

◆

The house, Press soon discovered, looked like a standard A-frame from the front, but had its ass end propped on stilts buried deep in the side of the hill. Below was a sparkling, panoramic view of Hollywood Hills; to the northwest, the freeway was a vibrating ribbon of light in front of an exotically shimmering glow that could only be Universal City. Quite a view, Press thought sourly, and one good mud slide would make Mr. Robbie Nice

Guy kiss this happy little homestead good-bye. In the meantime the stilts did serve a purpose by giving Press and the two Special Forces men following him a perfect place to shimmy up to the cantilevered deck. Once they were on top, all three crouched for a moment to get their bearings.

"Your move, Lennox," the one closest to him whispered. "What's your plan?"

"You go to the left, and you go to the right." Press peered toward a sliding-glass door about four yards away. He pointed at it. "I'm in through there. You've been briefed on what the woman looks like. If you see her, shoot to kill. Let's—"

"Dr. Fitch said to try to take her alive." The second man was little beyond a black-on-black phantom a few feet away. The low light spilling onto the deck from the patio doors barely showed him carefully positioned on the rim of the deck. Nothing moved inside.

Yet.

"Fitch is a fool and not here doing the cleanup on his own dirty work," Press hissed. "Try it and she'll kill you before you can change your mind. Now *go!*" They melted into the night without further argument and Press crept to the door that looked out over the deck. Just for the hell of it, he gave it a try. More stupidity; it slid open easily, as if Press and his men were the only ones in the world who could shimmy up a rough wooden pole. He opened it only enough to slip through and close it behind him, pulling his SIG-Sauer P229 free of its holster before he was all the way into the living room.

Nice decorating, Press thought as he covered the length of the room in a running crouch. Wish I had that coffee table. He halted soundlessly at the juncture of a small hallway and another door. Because of the angle of the hall, he could see nothing past the doorjamb except another open door. It was well lit and he could hear the sound of the shower running all the way out here. Gun cocked and eyes fixed on the door that obviously led to the bathroom, Press glided around through the opening and almost stepped on the body of a man with half his head gone.

He barely stifled his yell of surprise and did a fast, quiet dance around the dead man's limbs as he tried not to step on the arm and leg outflung toward the hall. Was Sil in there? Discarded in front of the bathroom door was a crumpled black brassiere, the kind with underwires and heavy fabric that faddish women were wearing as blouses these days. There was something oddly . . . *smeary* about it, and Press had to get practically on top of it to see the blood, soaked into the black fabric so heavily it was leaking out the other side.

Robbie apparently didn't believe in air-conditioning, or maybe he'd intended to open the patio doors during the planned romp on the still-made bed. Between the sneaking around and the steam roiling out of the bathroom, Press could feel his shirt starting to cling to the center of his back. Despite the tension and warmth, his grip on the .357 SIG was still dry and his sight was steady, but his mind was giving him a snippy and utterly useless reminder that he'd never gotten around to switching his SIG-Sauer semiauto for the fully automatic Heckler & Koch MP5SD4 he'd set aside back at the complex. If he got out of here alive tonight, he'd have one of Fitch's nagging little aides go back and retrieve it for him . . . *if* this job wasn't over by dawn.

With the water running like that, the air would never uncloud enough for him to get a clear view. "Fuck it," Press muttered, and darted into the vapor-clogged bathroom. The sound of the shower was thunderous in his ears, hammering right along with his heart. Taking a deep, moisture-laden breath, Press leaped through the door, hit a vanity with a black-and-gold marble top, and brought his pistol up and ready to fire as he ricocheted into the glass-enclosed shower.

The *empty* glass-enclosed shower.

"Shit," he said in a low voice. He yanked the .357 SIG away from the spray of water—long past being anything but lukewarm—and found the knob to cut off the pressure from the shower head; the ensuing silence gave him a ringing sound in his ears, like standing next to a dam when they cut the water flow. His shirt was soaked, his hair was plastered to his forehead . . . hell, even his shoes were squishing. To top it off, he could hear enough voices coming from the rest of the house to tell him that Sil was definitely not around.

It looked like he was going to have to ask for the fully automatic after all.

♦

"This woman is a cold-blooded killer." Press was talking *at* Xavier Fitch rather than to him. "She—"

"Is not a woman," Laura reminded the group. "And you should stop thinking of her as such."

"But you just said *her*," Dan said in confusion.

"She *is* a female," Laura explained, "but she's not human because she was created with alien DNA. She uses our human form as a costume only, a camouflage to walk among us. She does not necessarily *think* like a human, at least not all the time."

"Which makes her all the more dangerous," Press cut in. He looked like he wanted to throttle Fitch. "One of those soldiers told me your orders were to take her alive. Are you out of your fucking mind? How many more people have to die because of your moronic experiment?"

Fitch didn't look a bit intimidated, just preoccupied. "I don't understand how any of this has to do with reproduction, or her desire to reproduce," he said eventually, reaching to massage his temples. "First she kills a girl at the nightclub—a total stranger from what we've been able to ascertain. Then she finds a man and gets him to take her someplace private, and ends up murdering him, too."

"I'd say she fits the classic definition of a psychopath," Stephen said. "There's nothing to inhibit her—no moral sense, no social structure—"

"She wasn't exactly smothered with motherly love by Xavier," Laura said caustically. "Nor did he teach her any manners." She met his annoyed glance evenly.

"She'll kill if she feels threatened or wants something," Stephen continued. "Anyone who gets in her way is going down."

Dr. Fitch frowned. "Gets in the way of what?"

"Of reproduction," Laura said impatiently. "We talked about this earlier, when Stephen first mentioned it in the van. And he was correct—she's in the mating part of her life cycle."

Fitch pondered this for a moment. "I suppose you could be right," he conceded. "But why kill that girl at the ID? What purpose did that serve?"

Stephen opened his mouth, but Laura beat him to it. "Sexual rivalry," she said. "The girl must have gotten in her way, stolen the attention of someone Sil was interested in. She invoked a sense of jealousy in Sil, plus she was an obstacle. Therefore, she was eliminated."

"Exactly," Stephen agreed. "Again, she fits the classic definition of a psychopath—no inhibitions, moral sense or social structure. She'll kill for any number of reasons. In response to feeling threatened, as a means to obtain something she desires, or just for convenience—if someone is in her way or is keeping her from accomplishing what she wants, she'll cut them out of the picture. Simply touching her the wrong way could be enough to set her off."

"She's certainly hard on the competition," Press said with a raised eyebrow.

"You're saying that now she's managed to mate?" Fitch asked. He looked repulsed and enthralled at the same time. And something else, too, that Laura found hard to define . . . proud, perhaps?

Laura saw Press glance at the corpse on the bedroom

floor, then shake his head. "No. Doesn't look like a successful mating to me."

"How would you know that?" In spite of herself, Laura was fascinated by Press's no-nonsense perceptions.

"He's still got his pants on," Press said wryly.

"The killing could have been afterward," Laura suggested.

"I doubt it," Press replied. "Bed's still made and the only piece of clothing our creature left behind was a blood-soaked bra." He wandered over to the bathroom door and looked in, checking for anything that might have been missed in the previous excitement and now dissipated steam.

"She must be very frustrated," Dan said.

"Aren't we all," Stephen said sourly.

"Frustration can be the worst state of mind for anyone," Dan continued, "especially someone socially unstable. Emotionally, it's the root of all evil."

"That's right on the money, Dan." Stephen tried to grin, but the dead body on the floor made the smile sag before it reached the professor's eyes. "We're all frustrated in one way or another."

"Yeah, well, bully for us," Fitch said uncharacteristically. "In the meantime let's get back to Sil. If she didn't mate with this guy, what was her problem? He was here, she was here, the moment was right. So what happened?"

Stephen was at a loss. "I have no idea. Everything I know says she should have gone for it. It looks like they were even starting."

Laura chewed at her lower lip and studied Robbie's body. "Maybe *she* rejected him. We can test him for hereditary diseases—bad heart, defective liver, something that would make him an unacceptable mate. She's probably got sensory faculties far more advanced than ours—or far more basic, depending on how you look at it. Rats, for instance, can sense disease or genetic damage in potential mates."

"I think I found the problem," Press said. He held up a syringe and an empty vial bearing a white label with blue-and-black lettering on it.

Laura extended her hand and he dropped the vial onto her palm. "*Novolin 70/30*," she read. "This is insulin. *70/30* is a combination of two human-derived types. Our man here was a diabetic; that would make him an unacceptable mate." She handed the vial back to Press and he ducked into the bathroom; the resulting *clink* told her he'd tossed the glass vial and used syringe back into the wastebasket.

"So why didn't she just walk out?" Fitch asked, exasperated. "Why did she have to kill him?" Laura held out her hands in the standard "I have no idea" gesture.

"Well," Press mused, "it looks like he could have been between her and the door. Do you think he tried to stop her?"

"Some men don't like to be rejected," Dan put in. "They tend to get insistent. Maybe he was one of those."

"Well, we're not going to find her here," Fitch said. He spoke rapidly to an aide waiting for instructions a few feet away, the second guy who'd joined them back at the freight train. "Dig into this guy's history and find out what he drives, then put an APB on it, stat."

"It's already been done," McRamsey said. "He drives a Brazilian kit car called a Puma. The DMV records indicate it's bright orange."

"I guess she's not so docile and controllable, is she, Doc? What now?" Press had found another toothpick and shoved it between his lips. His hair had finally dried into an uneven bunch of dark, curly tufts, and he sounded absurdly like a cross between a thin-lipped Clint Eastwood and Bugs Bunny. "We could head back to the motel. I'll bet you my next paycheck the clerk's come up with the stuff Sil 'didn't' leave behind." He gave them all a dark, lazy grin.

"That's as good a place as any," Fitch said. He looked questioningly at Laura.

"I'm guessing as much as anyone else, Dr. Fitch," she said. "We should examine the things she left behind anyway." She shot a penetrating glance at Press. "*If* she did."

Press gave her a smile that was just short of insolent. "You wait and see, Dr. Baker." He flicked the toothpick from one side of his mouth to the other without touching it. "I think you'll all be quite surprised at what we find."

21

Sunset Boulevard at night was a riot of color and sound and never-slowing movement. The Puma was a nice sports car, a little two-seater with a black interior and top that contrasted nicely with the bright orange paint job. The top had been down when Robbie had last driven it, and Sil liked it down, liked the way the warm California wind picked up her hair and made it drift on the air currents rolling over the car. She sure hadn't gotten that kind of freedom looking out from the glass box back at the complex.

Traffic was heavy and the car was forced to slow until Sil had to work the clutch constantly—stop and go, stop and go. Prostitutes and cops were everywhere, everyone trying to look like they were someone, some-*thing* else; johns toured the area, trying to invent new ways to elude the no-cruising ordinance that went into effect at ten P.M. Men looking for women, women looking for women—with all those people milling around, it was a wonder that Sil spotted the first plainclothes security man on the corner a block away from the motel. Dressed in slacks and a sport coat and sitting on a street bench eating popcorn while he browsed through a magazine, she couldn't believe he didn't realize he was ridiculously conspicuous amid the scantily clad women and leering men in muscleman T-shirts and shorts. More security guys dotted the sidewalk, but none of them noticed the Puma and Sil squeezed the car into the left lane of traffic and accelerated. When she saw a break in the oncoming cars, she jumped the red light with a left turn.

She wound her way southwest through a number of smaller streets until she came to La Brea and followed it south, just because she liked the name. She recognized the expressway emblems from the television and decided she would keep going until she found the Santa Monica Freeway that the signs advertised, but when she reached the entrance ramp she was forced to detour around it. Wide-eyed when she saw the huge, twisted metal supports and cracked concrete, Sil cruised through the underpass of the massive structure and painstakingly mouthed the words on the signs: DETOUR—EARTHQUAKE DAMAGE—USE ADAMS BOULEVARD TO EXPOSITION—FOLLOW THE SIGNS. She still didn't know what an earthquake was, but she'd just gotten a lesson in what it *did*.

At last Sil was on the freeway, the night wind blowing in her hair as the automobile sped easily along. More signs flashed by, and one in particular intrigued her: PACIFIC OCEAN/SANTA MONICA PIER, 6 MILES, followed by an arrow in the direction in which she was driving. Robbie had mentioned this, and Sil still wondered about it. This ocean, did it have anything to do with an earthquake?

She would drive there tonight, she decided. There was so much to see and learn, so much to do.

Top on the list and much harder than she'd anticipated, was to find a mate.

22

The greasy clerk at the motel was gone, replaced by the night staffer, who was a no-nonsense middle-aged man who looked like he was an ex-marine and introduced himself as Raymond. He gave Press's hand two hard pumps and ignored Fitch altogether as he produced a room key from the cash drawer and tossed it to Press. "Seven-B," he said flatly. His face was bland but his eyes were small, dark pebbles, intelligent and sunk deep in his skull. "Henry—that's the guy who was on shift when you folks were here—and me had a little talk about the stuff that was in there and how it oughta be back in the room when you folks returned."

Press nodded his thanks and didn't insult the man by asking if that meant Sil's belongings were there now. The motel was crawling with Special Operations men trying to look like nonchalant businessmen. Press thought they fit in about as well as a Scandinavian blonde at a seminar on African-American genealogy.

Sil's motel room was right on line with the rest of the place—small and slightly seedy, clean on a surface that masked years of poor-quality care and cheap cleaning materials. The curtains were drawn and the room's

only lamp wasn't much help in the lighting department; it made the frayed, dark-colored bedspread look
mostly black and didn't even have enough output to
fully illuminate the tiny closet. All of the things that
Sil had apparently purchased with the cash from
Angela Cardoza's paycheck had been dumped in a pile
on the double bed. Press and Stephen went through it,
with Stephen marveling over the speed at which Sil
seemed to be learning the technique of sexual attraction.

Press lifted a piece of lingerie with one finger and
raised his eyebrows. "Bet you can't guess where this
came from," he challenged.

"Frederick's, I'd bet," Stephen answered.

"Oh, *please*," Laura said in a disgusted voice from the
bathroom doorway. "This isn't a game, you idiots. That
alien—or she-thing or whatever you want to call her—
could be killing someone right now. Or even worse, reproducing."

"What do you think, Dan?" Fitch surveyed the drab
room. "Any guesses on where she'll go?"

"What do *I* think?" Dan looked carefully at each of
his team members. "I think she's probably tired and
wants to find someplace safe to rest. Didn't your tapes
from the complex show her sleeping a lot?"

Fitch rubbed his jaw. "Yes, but she's older now, already through her growth stage. She won't need to
sleep as much."

Laura's voice drifted out from the bathroom. "But
Dan's right; the human part of her will still require a
certain amount."

Dan went to the window and parted the drapes so he
could peer outside. "I think she won't come back here
while all our cars and people are lined up out front."

"You're assuming she can find her way back."

"Why wouldn't she?" Stephen asked. "She can understand and speak English, shop and use a credit card.
She rented this room on her own and also took her last

victim's car, remember? If she can learn to drive that quickly, there's no telling what else she's capable of. Besides, most intelligent life-forms find their way to and from their lairs unconsciously. It's only humans that place so much value on actual locations and addresses." He sounded disdainful.

Dan wandered over to the open bathroom door. "What are you doing in here, Dr. Baker? Did you find something?"

"Yes." Laura had pulled on rubber gloves and was using a cotton swab to dab at a small spot of red on the toilet seat.

"What is it?"

Laura dropped the soiled swab into a plastic bag and carefully closed it. She held it up to the dim fluorescent bulb that buzzed over the sink. "It could be blood," she said thoughtfully. "This would seem to indicate that Sil's body follows an animal's reproductive cycle."

"Who said anything about an animal?" Dan looked confused. "I thought she was part human and part alien."

"She is." Laura peeled off the gloves and dropped them in the wastebasket next to the toilet. "But we know nothing about the alien part, remember? Perhaps the alien part of her reproductive makeup resembles the estrous cycle of some of the animals on this planet. If that's true, we've got to find her before she completes it, before she breeds."

"And what if we don't?" asked Press from the doorway. Fitch and Arden came over to listen. "Let's not bullshit around. For all we know, she could be banging somebody right now. What if she *does* manage to mate?"

Laura lowered the bag. Her navy-blue eyes were troubled and faraway. When she spoke, her voice was barely audible.

"Then I guess we have no idea what we're up against."

23

A new dream, bringing new sensations. Heat suffused her as something stroked her flesh, making her dizzy and breathless, teasing her until she strained in response. Something huge and indefinable, multilimbed and shimmering with translucence, encircled her, made her feel safe and desirable, and so very, very hot, as though every cell in her body was suffused with electricity. The other creature was like her but unlike her, a male counterpart tailored to fit her body in every respect, sliding inside her with a burst of exquisite sensation, spinning and spinning until she felt she would explode into the silky warmth of the endless amber atmosphere surrounding her—

◆

"Uh!" Sil sat up with a twitch and tried to free her mind from the last of the dream's arousing images, feeling too warm in the jacket she'd filched from Robbie's closet on the way out of his house yesterday. She'd pulled the Puma into a space in this parking lot last night after staying on the freeway until it ended abruptly at Fourth Street. At Fourth, she'd continued to follow the "Ocean" signs, turning left on Colorado and staying on it until the signs and the street changed, evolving into something called the Municipal Pier and Santa Monica Beach. She'd wanted to explore last night and had actually gotten out of the car before feeling the full impact of fatigue. So much had happened yesterday—she'd needed rest, not confrontation with the subtle, roaring sound surrounding her in the darkness. With the stars and sliver of moon obscured by gauzy clouds, she'd climbed back into the Puma and surrendered to the need for slumber.

Now it was sunrise, and a painfully blue morning sky dotted with pink-splashed clouds stretched as far as Sil could see over the biggest body of water she had ever imagined. She could see the waves start, so far out, watch them sparkle in the sunlight as they swelled to a frothy white head then foamed away on the sand. The air was tinged with salt and still cool, but starting to bend toward the warmth that would come in a couple of hours. Surprisingly, this was the first time she'd ever smelled the ocean; up to now, the aromas in the air had ranged from diesel fuel to eucalyptus, and she had the idea that once the day and the traffic got going, the faint, clean smell of the Pacific would be overwhelmed even at its shoreline.

From her place in the parking lot, Sil saw a woman wearing a bulky T-shirt walking along the otherwise deserted beach at the edge of the water; a hundred yards from the pier, the woman stopped and began to pull things from an oversized tote bag. When she had set up a mini—lawn chair and draped it with a towel, the woman stretched her arms toward the sky and pulled off her shirt, revealing a sleek red-and-gold athletic swimsuit. After tucking her hair into a tight bathing cap, the woman waded into the water to thigh height, then dove under, reappearing ten feet away and working through the waves with strong, sure strokes. Entranced by the swimmer's skill, Sil watched for a good ten minutes, feeling the warming air build beneath the

rayon jacket and wishing she hadn't left her blouse at
the ID so she could be free of it. She watched the
swimmer for a while longer, a wistful look on her face,
then got back into the driver's seat of the Puma. She'd
wasted enough time; now she had to go and find the
rest of her life.

♦

The Puma quit running less than a half mile down the
Pacific Coast Highway. Sil coasted to the side of the road
and inspected the dashboard and its gauges, turned the
ignition key a couple of times, tested all three foot pedals.
Nothing happened; the only thing that continued to
work properly seemed to be the optional items—the fan,
windshield wipers, and the radio, which was like the tel-
evisions but without a picture. When the engine died,
the needles on the gauges had dropped all the way to the
left, except for the needle in the dial to the right of the
steering wheel. That one stayed where it was, resting on
a red *E*. Baffled, she climbed out and left the little orange
convertible behind.

The car had made Sil feel secure and quick, and
leaving it behind was unfortunate. She started walking
in the direction she'd been driving and a sign informed
her that in another mile she'd reach San Vincente
Blvd. Suddenly it was all too strange, too *much*, and Sil
did an about-face and strode back toward the pier and
Santa Monica Boulevard, passing the disabled Puma on
her way to territory that was at least somewhat familiar.
It was a slight risk, but as long as she didn't return to
that motel or the Hollywood area, she figured she was
safe. After all, there must be hundreds of thousands—a
million—people within the limited areas she had
crossed.

To find her, a lone woman amid the multitudes,
would be a feat, indeed.

24

"Okay," Stephen said, "let's see what we've got." Gathered around him at the computer workstation one of Dr. Fitch's aides had assembled in Stephen's room, the rest of the group watched the monitor as he called up the security tape footage from the motel. McRamsey had turned it over to somebody else for enhancement, but the results were disappointing. "There she is," Stephen said. "At least, as much as they could get of her." He punched a few keys and the image on the screen froze; a few twists of his wrist and a double click on the computer mouse and he was able to zoom in on the facial area and blow it up to ten times its former size.

"That's helpful," Press sneered. "Christ—she looks like a specter from a 1920s silent movie."

Laura squinted at the screen. "You can't even make out her face. Magnification just makes it worse."

"No kidding," Stephen said.

"The video enhancement didn't come out that well," Fitch agreed. "The boys at the photo lab did the best they could—"

"Geez," Dan interrupted, "I saw a movie on television once where they got a full photograph of Kevin Costner from just the backing of a Polaroid picture."

"—in the time they had," Fitch continued, shooting a stern look at Dan. Stephen saw the younger man duck his head, but he could have sworn Dan had a mischievous glint in his eyes. He was glad to see the empath finally feeling more at ease with the rest of the team.

"Well, the features aren't very clear," Laura said, "but everything else we've got suggests she's in her early twenties. Does that sound right?"

"Yes," Stephen replied. He folded his hands and rested his chin on his fingers. "Which means her reproductive system should be fully activated."

Laura reached over his shoulder and maneuvered the mouse for a few seconds, trying unsuccessfully to sharpen the image of Sil's face. She gave up. "At the rate she's grown, her biological clock must be on hyperdrive."

Stephen looked troubled. "I think Laura's correct. Despite her half-alien heritage, we've been on the right track—mostly—as far as projecting her motivation. Her sole objective seems to be to mate and reproduce. That's what she was trying to do at the ID, and that's what she'll continue trying to accomplish until she succeeds. The girl she killed at the club was . . ." Stephen hesitated, trying to find the proper word. "A *deviation* on how we anticipated she would behave, but looking back, it was almost predictable."

"But still unavoidable," Press added.

"Exactly."

Stephen turned back to the keyboard but stopped when Dan touched his shoulder. "Let me ask you this," Dan said. "What if we aren't ever *able* to catch her? I mean," his gaze skipped to Fitch, then back to Stephen, "Dr. Fitch and his people made her, then let her get loose. Maybe if we stop chasing her, she'll stop killing. Can't we just learn to live with her?"

Stephen shook his head immediately. "I don't think that's the point, Dan. Everything we know about her indicates that *she* doesn't want to live with *us*." Stephen hit a few keys and Sil's image disappeared, then he began typing rapidly on the keyboard. Data screens began to flash across the monitor as Stephen worked his way through programs. "I'm going to access Harvard's system through Internet and show you a program I developed using existing ecological data, hypothetical situations, and a software package a lot like the Sim Earth program developed by Maxis."

"Sim Earth? What's that?" Dan's gaze was riveted on the screen.

"It's a software game that let's you invent a world of your own," Laura said. "You control the atmosphere, the ecology, the life-forms, everything."

"You play God, in other words." Press's eyes were shadowed as he glanced at Fitch. "Sort of like the grand doctor here."

"I resent that," Fitch said hotly. "You don't—"

"The program I'm calling up is a more serious version of that concept," Stephen interjected, cutting off the quarrel. "We designed it three years ago to see what would happen if a new species was introduced into a closed ecological system."

"Such as ours," Laura said.

"Exactly." Stephen didn't look up. "It uses factual data which presently exists and mathematical statistics to accurately predict future situations. It can also recreate past occurrences. The factual data can be manipulated to project hypothetical futures."

"What kind of futures?" Dan asked.

"The kind that we could be up against if this creature—Sil—were to reproduce," Stephen explained somberly. He flicked his wrist and the pointer on the screen responded by expanding another window from the upper right until it filled the viewing area. "What I'm calling up is an existing model that was designed three years ago. It has some ... *enlightening* descriptive examples." In front of the team, the monitor dissolved into a detailed geography map.

"That's a map of New Zealand," Dan said.

"Yes, but on the screen is a model of how it existed a thousand years ago," Stephen told them as the image on the monitor began to change. "Our base for the program is the Maori, a Polynesian people who migrated to New Zealand half a millennium ago, possibly earlier. What you're seeing is a computer-generated time line of their migration starting at about the beginning of the eleventh century." Stephen began to move the mouse again, flicking on boxes and instructions too fast for any of them to follow. "We could spend a lot of time exploring the negative and utterly shameful effects the British had on the Maori culture and social structure when they began arriving in the seventeen hundreds, but I don't think that's a good archetype. The Maori are still in the struggle, although they're losing. Rather, let's look at the impact the Maori people had on the moa." He typed a final instruction, but didn't hit the enter key. Instead, he swiveled on his chair so he could look at them and punctuate his narrative with gestures, the teacher in him coming to the forefront.

"Moas were large, flightless birds native to New Zealand. Some scientists believe there may have been as many as twenty-five different species of moa, all of which are now extinct."

"All of them?" Dan looked surprised.

"Yes. The smallest moa was about the size of a turkey; the largest was bigger than an ostrich, perhaps ten feet high and two hundred pounds plus. Their size was deceptive, though; they were docile herbivores, more like giant chickens than anything else, surviving successfully on the islands for millions of years."

"And here come the Maoris," Press said gloomily.

"Exactly." Stephen rotated his chair until he faced the computer again. He pressed a series of keys. "The indigenous species—moas—are green. The predators are red."

"The Maoris," Dan said.

Stephen nodded. "Watch what happens." He flicked the mouse and the cursor jumped to a button at the upper right that said START PROGRAM. When he double-clicked the mouse, a counter appeared in place of the button. Starting at 1,000, it began to roll forward by tens.

The screen map flashed and the earth tones of the geographical format shifted to green, except for the highest mountain ridges. At the eastern edge of the islands, a few red dots appeared at the lips of protected bays. The dots began to expand to small patches as on the map the Maori established colonies and instituted landholding. As the counter rolled into 1,100 the red began to expand rapidly, forcing the green into retreat. For a brief moment the green dots expanded on the mountain ridges, then the red tide overwhelmed it again.

"If I were to add a third color to represent the arrival and beginning colonization of New Zealand by the British in the mid–seventeen hundreds," Stephen said a little dreamily, "say . . . blue, you would see a triple impact. The green would retreat before the red, and the red would begin to disintegrate, more akin to a thinning of the herd than outright exhaustion of the species." The counter turned over to 1,300; wide-eyed, they all watched as scattered outposts of green remained in the isolated valleys, then fell before the spreading mass of red.

"Wow," Dan breathed. He leaned on the edge of the computer table and Stephen saw that Dan's hands were shaking. "This really happened to these birds?"

"Yes. Keep watching." As the computer counter hit 1,500 the red color swept into the mountain passes and flooded the last of the valleys, swallowing every spot of green in its wake. A few dots of green materialized now and then in the remotest areas, and then, when the computer counter stopped at 1,740, the final green speck had vanished. Red blanketed the islands from nearly coast to coast. "And finally," Stephen said softly, "the extinction of the moa."

"That's a lot of chicken dinners," said Press. "Brutal. Mankind certainly wasn't the saint in this saga."

"There are no saints in biology," Laura remarked. "Only survivors."

"It's the history of life," Stephen responded. "A species will expand unless something stops it from doing so. In the case of the Maori, they ran out of moas."

"The moas are all gone?" Dan asked. "Forever?"

"The larger ones were extinct by the end of the seventeenth century. A few of the smaller species may have survived into the nineteenth, but not beyond." Stephen cleared the screen and punched in a new set of instructions. "You've seen what people can do to animals; now watch what people can do to people."

Fitch leaned forward, his eyes sharpening. "What are we looking at, Arden?"

"The Ainu," Stephen answered as the computer image shifted to a different map, one showing the four major Japanese islands. "Physically unlike the Japanese, they spoke a different language with a number of dialects. Their customs were unique and their religious beliefs centered around the forces of nature. They were masterful hunters, fishermen, and trappers until the Japanese migrated to Hokkaidō and attempted to settle them with agriculture." This time the computer counter ran to 1,995 before it stopped, leaving a weak scattering of green dots amid the overlay of red on the islands. "Unlike the moas in New Zealand, about fifteen thousand Ainu still exist in Japan, but hardly any of the survivors are of pure blood. The language is almost dead, as is the religion." Stephen sighed. "Intermarriage and cultural assimilation have even made them look like the Japanese now. They're still twitching, but extinction is unavoidable."

"But they're *people*!" Dan protested. "People can't go extinct . . . can they?"

Stephen gave Fitch a dark frown before he looked back at Dan. "Let's find out, shall we?" He cleared the screen a second time and began typing new instructions. "Let's redefine the guidelines to show the human race now that Sil is among us." The screen flickered and a world map came up, smaller to accommodate the expanded area, and covered with lush green. The counter reappeared at the top right, set at 1,995.00 "This program will run in increments of one month; therefore, when the counter says 1,995.06, you will be looking at June 1995." He hit the enter key and a tiny red dot appeared in Los Angeles. "Here are the new parameters: It's 1995, and the predator makes its first contact with the indigenous species and reproduces, bearing one male offspring. The offspring matures in six months—a more than generous estimate given how fast Sil matured—and successfully impregnates thirty indigenous females."

Stephen's gaze flicked to the team as he began running the program; they all watched the computer screen with growing horror. His own palms felt damp and cold. "We don't know for sure, but given that the mother is still a slower-growing species, we'll assume the gestation period is two weeks. To keep the program parameters simple enough for us to visually consider, we will also surmise that the indigenous mother will expire upon giving birth. Realistically, the predator female probably *won't* die after reproducing, and may even proceed to another breeding cycle. We don't know." He took a deep breath and ran the back of his hand across his clammy forehead before continuing. "For argument's sake, we'll speculate that the rate of offspring will be fifty-fifty—half male, half female. At the present time we must conclude that the alien species exists in this environment with no natural predators. Thus each generation will be able to proceed at this rate of procreation."

For the first time the computer gave a warning sound—*bleep!*—and the single red spot instantly appeared in places around the globe.

"What happened?" Press demanded. "I figured it would be fast, but—"

"The predator has established itself in every place an air link is available," Stephen announced. "The miracle of flying."

Suddenly the world map exploded in red splotches, like someone had stood over it and let loose with an atomizer of scarlet paint. From the centers of the established spots to the most remote areas around the globe, the red began to spread. Larger cities swelled and ebbed, swelled and ebbed, then the red swept across Africa with barely a pause.

"Oh, my God," whispered Laura. "This is *terrifying*."

The counter spun to 2,002.4—April, about seven years in the future. The red splotches were everywhere— from virtually uninhabited Antarctica to the broiling center of the Australian outback. The Pacific Islands were quickly obliterated, and the green resistance in Japan was hardly more than a pulse. As island after island yielded, the red splotches grew into a wave that spread across China and beyond.

Behind Stephen, Fitch gave a strangled cough. "This is preposterous," he choked out. "Pure speculation—"

"Shut up," Press said in a steely voice. "I don't think we want to hear you right now."

"It's like an epidemiological map of a viral infection," Laura murmured.

"A what?" Press asked.

"A foreign organism," Laura explained, "entering a system and taking it over completely."

"As in an intergalactic virus," Stephen said softly.

"More like a retrovirus." Laura's eyes were wide as

she stared at the screen. "One that changes faster than the host organism can defend against it."

Dreading the outcome, Stephen watched with the rest of the group as the red closed in on the remaining major cities. Holdouts of green disappeared, each with a nasty, metallic *bleep!* from the computer. For some unknown reason, as the remainder of the world was engulfed in red, the last of the green held tight in Finland and actually expanded a little; then it, too, was overwhelmed. With a final, stretched-out alarm noise that reminded Stephen of a flat-lining heart monitor, the global map showed only red.

Silence filled the room, then Dan pointed hesitantly at the screen. "Where are we?"

"We're the green," Laura said as gently as she could.

Dan stared at the others, his face full of terror. "There *is* no green."

Press responded, but Stephen saw that he couldn't meet the empath's eyes as he said the bleak words.

"That's the point, Dan. There is no *we*."

25

Sil was closer to Santa Monica, but the familiarity she'd expected wasn't there. Viewing the Pacific Coast Highway as a pedestrian gave her a totally different perspective, detail magnified a thousandfold. The highway was beautiful, lush and sunny, with wide, clean streets that seemed the antithesis of Sunset Boulevard in Hollywood. Traffic was abundant, but not the bumper-to-bumper mass that allowed pedestrians to amble into the street at will. People here waited on the corners for the traffic lights to change from red to green before they tried to cross, and it wasn't a fraction as crowded as Sil was used to.

About a quarter block in front of Sil, a young boy who reminded her of the kid in the train station zipped along on a skateboard. She watched him as she walked, interested in the skateboard and the way he worked at learning to control it. It was evident that he wasn't an expert—yet—but he was certainly enthusiastic in his efforts as he twirled and stopped, then did a chopping hop-jump that looked like he was leaping over something invisible before landing on the skateboard again. Coming to the corner, Sil saw him glance at the red light facing him in exasperation, then at the vehicles moving along the roadway. Too impatient to wait, the boy gave a sturdy double push with his right leg and launched himself into the street. Halfway across, the front wheel of the skateboard dropped into a rut and the skateboard flew out from under him. He pitched forward, his arms pinwheeling for balance, then gave a cry of surprise as an oncoming truck, a white Toyota 4-Runner speeding along at fifteen MPH over the posted limit, slammed on its brakes.

The driver's face went white as the brakes locked and the 4-Runner slewed sideways. Sil watched the boy trip and fall to his knees, then saw too late that the truck was swerving right for *her*. She screamed and threw her arms up instinctively as it jumped the curb and struck her, and was amazed when the ground and the trees switched places. The impact knocked her into the air and backward a good twenty paces.

The sound of shattering glass filled her ears as she landed, giving her a quick, disconnected memory of her escape from the compound. Dazed, she struggled unsuccessfully to sit upright amid a thousand sharp-edged pieces of glass, the remains of a glass-walled bus stop at the side of the road. The backs of her arms and legs stung from dozens of glass cuts and she couldn't get her mind to focus, couldn't find the right commands to bring her to her feet. Her vision was blurred and disjointed, but she recognized the kid on the skateboard as he began yelling something at the driver of the truck, who promptly leaped from the cab and took off down the street at a full run. He left the truck where it had stopped, door open with the engine stalled.

People were running toward her from every direction and Sil knew she should get up and leave before they got to her and started asking questions. But something was wrong with her shoulder, and when she looked she found a ragged gash running from the center of her collarbone straight across to her arm. Pinkish-white shards of bone glimmered deep within the wound and that side of her body was drenched with blood. Seeing the injury was a sort of nerve trigger, and Sil was unprepared and unable to block the agony that blasted through her arm and across her chest. She tried again to rise but blackness took her suddenly, sweeping her down and into painless unconsciousness.

♦

"This is an emergency," John Carey told the cellular operator as he swung his '66 Mustang to the curb. "I'm at Santa Monica and Wilshire. A woman just got hit by a truck. I think she'll need an ambulance. And you can tell the cops that the guy driving the truck ran off and left it in the street, so it's probably stolen." He hit the power button on the phone and shoved it under the driver's seat as he shut the engine off and yanked the parking brake into place. Besides the boy on the skateboard, he was the first to reach the woman's side. The way she was sprawled on the glass at the side of the road made her look like one of those crash-test dummies the car manufacturers were big on using to show the public the perils of not using seat belts. Heart pounding, he fumbled at her wrist until he found a pulse, strong and steady despite the blood that soaked her skin and nylon jacket from neck to belly. One of her shoulders looked terribly twisted beneath the fabric and she had cuts everywhere from the broken glass. He didn't know what to do next—try to stop the bleeding? Most of it seemed to have already stopped. He wasn't a paramedic, but he remembered that she shouldn't be moved, and none of the people gawking around him and the woman could offer any advice.

In the end, they simply stood by the unconscious woman and waited for the ambulance.

♦

"The patient's name?"
Standing at the admitting station of Santa Monica

Hospital and Medical Center, John Carey gave the emergency admissions nurse a blank look. He wanted to ask her if she understood English or was just plain crazy. Instead, he repeated himself—for the third time. "I have no idea. She's a hit-and-run victim. I just happened to see it."

The white-uniformed woman glanced at him sharply, as if she didn't believe him. Pinned to her top pocket was a name tag that said M. MADBAR. She was dark-skinned and exotic looking, like a Persian dancer out of *Arabian Nights*; she was also very cranky. "I can't admit her without some sort of insurance information," she snapped. "If you can't assist me in completing these forms, she'll be treated in the ER and then transported to County-USC Medical Center as an indigent."

"Oh, for God's sake," John said with an exasperated glare at the young nurse, "how many times do I have to tell you I don't know? Here—just put it on my credit card. I'll straighten it out with her when she's in shape to fill out your stupid forms herself."

"Fine." Nurse Madbar snatched John's Visa card from his fingers so sharply that she pinched him. "If you'd have given me this to begin with, we'd be finished by now."

John started to remind her that the patient was a total stranger, then gave up. Sitting there and pointedly ignoring him as she hammered at her computer keyboard, Nurse Madbar was just another robot starting up the red tape.

◆

Sil came to stretched out on a hospital gurney. The shredded nylon jacket was gone and a hospital gown, still folded in a neat rectangle, had been draped across her rib cage below her bared breasts. Most of the blood had been cleaned away and a young, dark-haired doctor with dusky skin swabbed carefully at the gaping wound on her shoulder. A harried-looking nurse set a tray with surgical tools, sutures and bandages on a cart at the doctor's right and accepted the syringe of blood he held out. "Get a lab workup and type on this right away," he ordered. "We'll need X rays, an orthopedic surgeon, operating room and anesthesiologist. I can't fix this here—the damage is too extensive. She's going to need surgery to set this shoulder properly." The triage nurse nodded, whipping the privacy curtain around the cubicle before ducking out with the blood sample.

Sil blinked and tried to push up on her elbows, groaning at the pain that shot through her. "Now, don't move," the doctor told her firmly. "You were hit by a motor vehicle, a truck, and the ambulance brought you here. I'm Dr. Shah. We've finally got all the bleeding under control and we don't want it to start again. It looks like we're going to have to send you to surgery. You'll need—hey! Wait—don't get up! *Stop it!*"

Sil ignored the white-coated doctor and sat up, swinging her legs over the side of the gurney. Her arm and shoulder throbbed terribly, so much so that it was difficult to think about anything else. There were other things going on, things she must do and others she must avoid, and her mind was too foggy to pull it all together right now. She did know, however, that she mustn't stay here, in this place of needles and medical people so much like the complex at which she was nearly killed only a few days ago. She had to leave before it was too late, before the people from the compound traced her whereabouts. To be in sharp enough shape to do that, she had to take care of the problem with her shoulder.

She turned her head until she could see the flesh of her shoulder and the sizable tear in the meat and muscle that Dr. Shah had temporarily closed with large butterfly clamps. When she moved even a fraction of an inch, Sil could feel the jagged ends of the bones grinding against each other. She focused on the skin, muscle and bone, really *concentrated*, walling out the pain, the monotonous harping of the doctor, the constantly yammering PA system and the strident noises from the rest of the emergency room, blocking them from her consciousness until she heard nothing but the essence of her own body. For a few moments her view of her surroundings faded, replaced by a more fundamental, moving panorama of blood, skin and bone rearranging itself, repairing damage that to Sil seemed only a temporary, albeit painful, inconvenience. When her vision cleared again, the butterfly clamps had popped off and all her miserable wounds were gone, her thoughts were lucid once more, and Dr. Shah's prattle had ceased. Now he was staring at her with an expression of utter disbelief.

"Y-y-your shoulder," he stuttered. "It w-w-was . . ." His eyes narrowed. "What the hell's going on here?" he demanded. "Airborne hallucinogens? Some kind of practical joke? I'll bet Cooper from ICU put you up to this." He reached for Sil's arm but she pulled out of reach. "You tell him I'll have his ass on a platter—"

"Dr. Shah!" A different triage nurse poked her head through a slit in the privacy curtain. Her gaze swept and dismissed Sil. "Are you available? We just got a child in with third-degree burns over sixty percent of her body—some kind of stove explosion. Can you—"

"Coming," Dr. Shah barked. He spun on his heel and started to stalk out, then paused halfway out of the cubicle, his olive-skinned face seething. "Be sure and tell Cooper I didn't think this was funny and I'll be in touch with the hospital administrator regarding this matter." Then, with a snap of the plasticized curtain, he was gone.

Cooper? Sil didn't know anybody by that name but she was grateful for someone else to take the heat. It only took a few seconds to shake out the hospital gown and slip it on; a hard tug all the way around and it could barely be distinguished from a cutoff T-shirt. A quick glance outside the curtain and Sil scooted out of the ER via the first door she found and kept going; if anyone noticed that the ripped hospital gown didn't exactly go with the black miniskirt, they didn't say anything.

At the end of the hallway, a handsome man saw her coming toward him and jumped to his feet, hurrying to meet her. "Are you all right?" he asked urgently. She let him enfold her hand in his larger one as he began walking with her to the exit. His eyes were a remarkable light blue and full of sincerity. Ginger-colored curls fell over his forehead. "I was sure you were badly hurt."

"I'm okay," Sil said. He started to let go of her hand, but she entwined her fingers around his and smiled shyly. "What's your name?"

"John," he answered, looking bewildered. "John Carey. I can't believe—I mean, I *saw* you, all the blood and everything. It must be a miracle or something."

Sil smiled wider. "Yes," she agreed with a nod. "A miracle. But I'm okay now. Can we go?"

"You're well enough?" he asked anxiously. "The doctor said you can leave already?"

"Oh yes," Sil answered. "He said I'm completely healed."

26

"I haven't found anything that looks relevant," Laura said. Still at the team's makeshift headquarters in Stephen Arden's room at the Biltmore Hotel, she'd been linked to the computer network of the Los Angeles Police Department for more than an hour. "Lots of murders, but none that fit what we know or anticipate about Sil's behavior."

Slumped on the chair next to the writing desk across the room, Press snorted. He ran his hands through his dark hair, then stood and walked to the window. "You're not going to, either," he said. "I've never known a cop who was current with his reports. They *hate* paperwork, and they're almost always at least two or three days behind."

"I can't believe that," Fitch commented. "That's not the way you catch a criminal or cross-reference evidence." The scientist folded his arms. "You watch too much television."

"Don't be a moron." Press didn't bother to turn around. "The only time they keep up to date is when they're tracking a serial killer who's in full swing.

There's nothing in Sil's three victims to tie them together. Yet."

Laura sat back. "I think Press is right, Dr. Fitch. The computers are a dead end."

"What do you mean, *yet?*" Dan asked.

"Reproducing problems aside, he means if we don't get her off the streets right away, sooner or later one of the police departments is going to get its reports punched in and start comparing victims," Stephen replied, joining the conversation. "Software that routinely checks the crime-scene statistics and figures is commonplace among all but the smallest venues. The commanding officer at the Central Area Station in downtown L.A. is already suspicious about the connection between the murder at the ID and the guy in Hollywood Hills. It's no secret Robbie Llewelyn was at the club before he died, and the Central Area commander is asking questions we're not prepared to answer. Seeing the army troops everywhere doesn't help matters."

The phone rang and Fitch reached for it as Press went over to stand by Laura. He peered at the computer screen. "Don't give up hope, though. We're still tracking the credit cards, plus there's an APB out based on the videotape."

Laura eyed him doubtfully. "That's not much help."

Press shrugged. "Even if the local flatfoots aren't up on their paperwork, they still have shift briefings where they get the rundown on what's on the hot sheets, et cetera."

"The murdered man's car has just been found in Santa Monica," Fitch broke in. "It ran out of gas."

"What'd I tell you?" Press asked scornfully as they all grabbed for their stuff and hurried out. "You can kill somebody in L.A. and never get caught, but everybody in the world knows when you rent a room or hoist someone's car."

◆

"What did you expect to find, Doctor?" Laura stood with Stephen, Press and Dan at the front bumper of the stolen orange Puma. "This is not a human being we're dealing with, and she won't behave like one."

Fitch peered into the car for at least the tenth time. "I don't know," he admitted. "Matches maybe. Food wrappers. *Something.*"

"I doubt she'll smoke," Laura said. "She probably won't eat much either."

"Everybody has to eat, don't they?" Dan joined Fitch at the driver's door of the car, studying the black leather interior with interest.

"Usually," Laura said. She pulled a three-by-five notebook from the back pocket of her slacks and flipped through a couple of pages. "But nothing relating to food or sustenance has been found since the sleeper compartment on the train, remember? We don't know what her life span is—long or short—but she doesn't appear to be eating right now. She may have completed that phase of her existence altogether."

"You mean she'll never eat again?" Press asked, startled. "If that's the case, she can't live very long, can she? Every living creature requires energy to keep functioning."

"True enough. She may not eat right now," Stephen noted, "but that's not to say she won't start again if she breeds. She may require extra nutrients to support the growing offspring."

"Or she may breed, then go through the whole cycle all over again," Laura added. "Eat, enter a sort of hibernation, and reproduce."

"You mean she might go into another cocoon?" Dan asked. "That's really scary, don't you think? Who knows what she'd come out looking like a second time."

Fitch's forehead creased. "I think that's unlikely—"

Robert Minjha hurried over. "We might have something," he told Fitch. "Seems a doctor at Santa Monica Med Center says he had a female patient who healed a severe shoulder wound in front of his eyes. Apparently he thought it was a practical joke by a coworker involving hallucinogens, then the blood work came back on the woman." Robert's arched eyebrow said the rest. "It's only a couple of miles away."

"Laura, you and Press go," Fitch said. "We'll wrap it up here and meet you there. Keep us posted if you go anywhere else, and for God's sake, don't confront her by yourselves!"

But they were already out of earshot.

"This area is called Pacific Palisades," John told Sil as he set a pair of tall, frost-covered glasses on the table. She watched as he filled them from a pitcher of ruby-colored liquid. "Cranberry juice," he said at her questioning look. He laughed self-consciously. "I guess I'm kind of a health-food junkie. Nothing radical, but I . . . you know. Pay attention to things, I guess." John Carey's attention to details was evident in his home and the carefully planned area in the rear of his house. Even the trees overhanging the fenced yard had hundreds of tiny white Italian lights woven into their lower branches.

Sil accepted the glass of cranberry juice and raised it to her lips for a sip, recoiling slightly at the tart flavor. John's home was spectacular, far nicer than Robbie's modern A-frame in the Hollywood Hills. This place was more of a mini–Tudor mansion set back on at least a half acre of rolling green lawn. The rear of the house, where she and John were now, was surrounded by a high chain-link security fence backed by heavily leafed trees that blocked them from anyone's view. Off to the side was a full-sized swimming pool covered by a green

canvas tarp; John had told her the pool liner had
cracked and was under repair. It didn't matter to Sil;
she'd seen swimming pools on television and thought
they were too big to encourage intimacy. She felt John's
eyes on her and picked up the glass of cranberry juice
again, rolling it back and forth between her palms to
feel the crispness of the ice coating as it melted. Her
eyes traced the area behind the house again. "John,"
she said brightly, "what's that?"

"What's what?" He followed her pointing finger.
"Oh, you mean the Jacuzzi?"

"Ah," Sil said. "The Jacuzzi." She let herself slide farther back against the warm plastic of the lounger, enjoying the heat and the feel of the sun where it striped
across her feet. Her shoes were off, tossed carelessly
under the patio table; she wished she could get rid of
the rest of her clothes and feel the sunshine and John's
hands all over her body.

John watched her for a few minutes, then reached
for a sports bag at the side of his lounger. He groped
around in it, then held up something that looked like
a black box with a glass eye on the front. A camera—
Sil remembered them from the compound, and also
from advertisements on television. "Do you mind if I
immortalize the moment?" he asked. "I'm kind of an
amateur camera buff but I try to be polite about it.
Some people don't like having their photograph taken.
Besides, I'm just starting in the hobby and I take terrible pictures." He grinned at her. "But it's fun seeing
them develop. I really love the Polaroids. What do you
say—is it okay with you?"

"Sure," Sil said. She wasn't sure what she was agree-
ing to, but her response seemed to please John and he
looked into the camera a few times, then positioned it
facing her on the arm of another lawn chair. With a
controlled move, he pressed a button on the camera
then sped back to her side and threw an arm around
her shoulders. Before she could ask what to expect, a

tiny red light began to blink on the camera and it made a whirring sound. Sudden light flashed weakly in Sil's eyes, making her blink and illuminating the dark green foliage behind them. As John went to retrieve the camera she hoped he hadn't felt her tremble when the flash had startled her. When he returned with the Polaroid, she watched as he pulled two sheets of paper apart, then carefully set the thicker one on the table and stared at it intently.

"Here it comes!" he said excitedly. "Look!"

"Wow," she breathed. Sitting next to him, Sil gaped at the developing image and started to touch her finger to it. He caught her hand.

"No, no," he warned. "Don't touch the print area while it's still developing. It'll mess it up." The photo was off center and taken from too far away, but she could still recognize both herself and John and it made her grin with delight. John beamed at her. "Do you like it? We'll take some more later, okay?"

"Yes," she agreed, and smiled up at him. "Oh, yes."

28

"We see a lot of unusual things in the emergency room," Dr. Sugata Shah told Laura and Press. "Crackheads, gunshot wounds—people do amazing things to other people, not to mention to themselves. But this girl . . ." He trailed off and his gaze wandered to the ceiling, where he seemed to lose himself in the study of the light fixture.

"Yes?" Press prompted. "What did she do?"

Dr. Shah squinted at the light, then rubbed his eyes. "My first thought was that she'd slipped me some sort of hallucinogen, perhaps in mist form. I have a . . . *colleague* in the trauma intensive-care unit with whom I have had an ongoing debate over an article published in the *New England Journal of Medicine*. I thought perhaps he had sacrificed common sense for a foolish practical joke. However, I did take the blood sample myself, I trust the nurse who delivered it to the lab . . . and I know what I saw."

"And what did you see, Dr. Shah?" Laura could barely stop herself from shaking the young doctor to get him to simply *tell* them the meat of his story. The men-

tal reminder that he had no idea of the circumstances
or the peril did nothing to heighten her patience.

"She re-formed her bone structure and healed herself
in front of my eyes," Dr. Shah said in a modulated
voice. "We didn't get X rays, but my preliminary appraisal of her injuries indicated a compound fracture of
the left clavicle plus a possible fracture of the left hu-
merus. She had extensive soft-tissue damage and a severe laceration in the injured area."

"Excuse me, Doc." Press held up a hand and
scowled. "Did I hear you say *healed herself*? Did I get
that part right?"

Dr. Shah met Press's glare without blinking. "Yes,
you did, Mr. Lennox. She *healed* herself. When she got
off the gurney, she had no broken bones or cuts, and
she was not bleeding. She walked out of here under her
own power."

"Fascinating," Laura said.

"And you let her go?" Press demanded. "Just like
that?"

Dr. Shah spread his hands. "How could I have
stopped her?" He began ticking off points on his fingers. "She was not unconscious, she was not injured,
she was not confused." He shrugged and folded his
arms. "She did something I literally can't explain, but
at the end of it all, Mr. Lennox, Dr. Baker, she was not
injured."

"But you did get a blood sample?" Laura asked.
"Which is when you realized this wasn't a joke."

"Yes."

"May I see the results?"

"Certainly." He handed Laura a folder and watched
as she quickly scanned the contents. "You don't seem
surprised," he said as she glanced at Press and nodded,
then closed the file.

"I'm not," she responded. "It's what I expected."

"It's her?" Press asked.

"Yes." Laura tucked the folder under one arm instead

of returning it and offered her hand to Dr. Shah. "Thank you for your cooperation, Doctor. We'll stop at admissions on our way out and see if we can trace the woman you started to treat. Since she was never technically a patient, I'm sure you won't be needing these test results."

Dr. Shah opened his mouth to protest, then changed his mind. His black eyes were very sharp. "I can't help wondering how my call to the Santa Monica Police Department ended up being routed to you two," he remarked. "Dr. Laura Baker ... I've heard of you and your work. You're a molecular biologist, aren't you? If my memory is serving me correctly, you're a Fellow with the National Academy of Science." He turned his gaze to Press. "And what do you do, Mr. Lennox?"

"Me?" Press gave the doctor a charming smile. "Why, I'm just here to be kind of the go-between, Dr. Shah. Just call me a ... *negotiator*."

♦

"A negotiator? That's an interesting title."

Press chuckled as he watched Laura's fingers fly over the computer keyboard at the admitting station. The outraged admissions nurse had stormed off in the direction of the employee lounge when her scathing call to the hospital administrator had resulted in a green light for Laura and Press. Laura had promised to return control of the woman's console in under five minutes; she was almost ready. A good thing, since three irritated people were already pacing the waiting room and muttering about tests and the time, and what the hell were appointments for, anyway? "It's part of my ongoing private contest to see how many words I can stretch to be a synonym for mercenary," Press finished.

"Is that what you are?" she asked without looking away from the screen. "Someone who hires out for the best price?"

On the computer monitor, screens full of data were

flashing by too fast for Press to follow and one side of his mouth turned up mockingly. "Not a chance. I prefer the smaller paychecks of Uncle Sam."

Although it didn't extend to her lips, Press saw the area around Laura's eyes crinkle with amusement. The smile lines disappeared as she leaned forward. "Here we go, no thanks to the friendly admitting staff. The guy who came in with her is John F. Carey. There's nothing else on him in the hospital's records, so he's never been a patient here himself. It says in the comments section that he's no relation, just a witness to the accident. I don't get it. Why would he offer his credit card for a total stranger?"

"Hell," Press said, leaning over her shoulder to read, "Nurse Friendly likely pried it out of his wallet. He probably figured he'd straighten it out later."

"No address or phone," Laura said as she jotted down the name and credit-card number, "but I can get that from the laptop in the car."

"I hope you realize that hospital information is confidential," a female voice said harshly from the other side of the counter. "Releasing it without authorization can result in fines and imprisonment."

Press had to bite the inside of his cheek when he saw Nurse M. Madbar standing with her hands on her hips and glowering at them both. He thought he'd make it, but the urge became too much. He made his eyes widen as far as they would go in a parody of innocence. "Of course. But we're only going to use his credit-card number to redecorate our living room."

The nurse's jaw dropped. "*Excuse* me?"

"We'll keep it all confidential, of course." Laura's voice was smooth and soothing as she stood and pressed a key that cleared Carey's information off the screen. "My associate has a zany sense of humor, that's all." She gave Press a severe look as she returned the area behind the console to Nurse Madbar's control.

"That wasn't funny." The young woman sniffed.

"Any more than when that young woman walked out on Dr. Shah." Without another word, she presented both Laura and Press with her stiffened back and began typing earnestly.

"Come on, hotshot. I can trace Carey's whereabouts in the car. Let's get out of here before you endear yourself to someone else around here."

"Hey, they love me," Press protested as he followed her back to the gray government sedan waiting in the lot. He opened the door for her and she slid in and typed her password into the computer, then did a network link to the system at Fitch's headquarters. By the time Press climbed behind the wheel, Laura already had full information on Carey displayed on the computer screen.

"Here we are," she said as he started the car. "It's an address in the Palisades on Wildomar. Phone number, too."

"We're on the way," Press said. "Try and get Carey on the phone. If he answers, tell him to get out of the house . . . and leave Sil behind. Then call Fitch and tell him where to meet us."

"How long before we get there?" Laura asked as she began dialing on the cellular phone.

"Beats the hell out of me," Press answered. "Maybe not before dark, but I live in Greenwich Village, New York, not the Palisades, remember? While you're trying to call this guy, look in the glove box for a map."

"Got it," Laura said. "Damn, the guy's got his answering machine turned on. Should I leave a message?"

"Sure," Press said dryly. "Tell him he's thinking about copulating with a monster from outer space."

"Thanks, smartass," Laura said as she disconnected the call, then dialed Fitch. "After that, I'll ask him what color he thinks we should use for the living room." Despite the light words, her eyes were wide and worried.

"I guess Carey's on his own until we get there."

◆

"How much farther?" Press demanded. The seat belts around both him and Laura locked into place as he barreled around another curve on Sunset Boulevard at full speed.

"Not too far," Laura estimated as she scrutinized the map with a magnifying glass and penlight. "We're at about 14500 now, and Wildomar's past 15700. There're at least a dozen streets in between—well, how about this!"

"What?"

"There's a street coming up that's actually. named Carey."

"Too bad the guy doesn't live there instead," Press ground out as he whipped the sedan around another curve. "He'd be a helluva lot closer to safety if he did."

◆

"What's next?" Press swung the car tightly to the left, following the yellow line so closely that a car going in the opposite direction blared its horn. "It can't be much farther."

The map jounced in Laura's hands as the sedan hit a bump. "Left at the next street—that's Wildomar. Carey's home should be the third on the right." She tossed the map over the seat back and let it fall to the floorboard, then grabbed for a handhold as the sedan fishtailed around the final turn.

"Finally!" In spite of the wild ride, Press braked quietly and made sure the car rolled to a silent stop in the driveway of John Carey's house.

29

The water in the Jacuzzi was hot, much more so than Sil had expected. It felt wonderful—silky and sensual against her skin, like the touch of a lover who knew every inch of her. She'd left her clothes in a pile on the cedar deck, not caring if they got wet or ended up smelling like the fragrant wood. In fact, she didn't care if she ever put them on again. The soft outside lights and the tiny bulbs twinkling in the tree branches ringing the patio were far enough away to let the single underwater light in the hot tub make her skin glow like soft cream.

Sil didn't know what to make of John Carey. At a deeper level, she thought that had his mind-set been more like Robbie of Hollywood Hills, they would have mated by now. At another level, she *liked* that he was shy and unsure of himself. But she was starting to get impatient. She'd been here all day—how much longer would it take?

"Come and get in with me," she purred. "The water is *very* nice." She smiled invitingly.

Standing at the edge of the tub, a plush bathing towel wrapped around his waist, John still looked unsure of himself and when the telephone rang inside the house, she thought for a moment he'd go to answer it. Instead, he reluctantly pulled his towel free and tossed it on a nearby lounger. She was dismayed to see that underneath he wore a loose pair of royal-blue swim trunks. As he stepped into the Jacuzzi and lowered himself into the steaming water, Sil moved to his side and began tugging off his swim trunks.

"Hey!" John protested. "Wait a second—what are you doing?"

"You don't need these," Sil said sweetly.

Although he seemed less than overjoyed, John finally slipped them off. After a moment's hesitation, he leaned forward and kissed her tenderly. She stayed very still for the moment, enjoying the soft feel of his lips against hers, the way his tongue just barely grazed her bottom lip. "You don't say much," he said huskily.

Sil smiled slightly and shrugged, a small motion she'd seen him make before when he didn't seem to know the answer to a question that wasn't very important. "You know I like you," she said softly.

"I know," he whispered.

His breath was warm in her ear, incredibly arousing. It was all she could do to keep from snatching him to her. "I don't think it's too soon for us to be together," she managed in a silky voice. She dipped one hand under the water and searched until she found his knee. "Do you?"

"No," he said hoarsely. "It's not t-too soon."

His fingers brushed one of her breasts once, then again. She strained toward him and kissed him harder, let her fingers find the velvety hair along his belly and travel down. His fumbling hand stopped her before she could go any farther. "Hey," he said with a nervous snicker, "that's a little *too* fast."

"I want you to be inside me," Sil said urgently. She stroked the side of his face but he didn't reciprocate.

Instead, he pulled even farther away from her in the water.

"I—I seem to have a problem." John wouldn't meet her eyes at all now.

"What do you mean?" she asked suspiciously. She tried to think of the things that could have gone wrong, but she was a novice at this. Was she not attractive enough? Perhaps he was thinking of someone else, anonymous competition like the girl at the ID that Sil had eliminated. Sil's hand went to her hair; the ends were wet and plastered against her neck. Maybe that was making her unappealing. "Don't you think I'm pretty?" she asked aloud.

"Of course I do," he said in a placating tone that she wasn't sure she liked. When she said nothing, he scooted back to her side on the bench and took her by the hand. His fingers rubbed hers, creating little waves of pleasure that expanded outward, creeping into her arms and spreading into her chest and belly. "We'll get there, baby. But there's no hurry, okay? Just relax. Take it easy and let things happen naturally."

Sil nodded, even though she had no idea what he was saying or why he would want things between them to move more slowly. She reached to kiss him again, letting her tongue probe his lips and teeth. The clean, just-brushed taste of his mouth made her want him more, but he pulled back again. "You're so passionate," he said. "I really love that."

He was saying all the right things, but his voice was too tense and his anxiety was contagious. When he drew back yet again, Sil watched him through half-closed eyelids but made no move to follow him. She wondered if he was expecting someone, maybe some other woman who shared this house with him, someone he had conveniently "forgotten" to mention. Jealousy flared, and on the heels of that, anger. He didn't find her exciting because he had given too much of himself elsewhere and he wasn't strong enough to couple with her, too. He had seemed so nice, caring and considerate, but she'd been wrong in thinking he was a suitable mate. Still, she wasn't ready to give up; after all, she needed someone to father her child, not a lifelong companion.

She tried kissing him again. He returned her kiss as if he'd enjoyed it and she could sense his ardor increasing, smell the sexy scent of passion-induced perspiration beginning to layer his skin. Finally he was getting into it, losing himself in the physical sensations she was bringing out, and when she raised herself off the underwater bench and slid her legs around his lower body, he pulled her tight against his chest and moaned against her neck.

Panting, she tried to maneuver herself over him, but felt resistance once again. Frustration abruptly welled in her; what was the matter with this man? She started to say something to him about it, demand an answer, then a faint sound eased into her ears, something apart from their heavy breathing and the sounds of desire, faint but distinctly different from the muted gurgling of the Jacuzzi. Sil scowled savagely as she gazed over John's shoulder in the direction of the house, trying to see more than the patio furniture and close-cropped hedges would allow. Unmoving against John, she tilted her head and strained to hear again. Had she really heard . . . ?

Yes. Footsteps, coming up the front pathway to the house.

30

Ringing the doorbell and banging on the front door proved futile, but Press would've bet next month's paycheck that John Carey was home. The front of the house was dark except for the soft-bulbed carriage lights flanking a double-wide oak front door with beveled-glass insets. The door turned out to be locked and moving quietly, Press motioned for Laura to follow him around the driveway running along the north side of the house. As expected, he found a row of immaculately clean trash and recycling bins next to a sliding-glass door through which they could see a darkened area with a small glass-and-chrome table and two tan leather chairs—the breakfast area. On the far side of the room, low light trickled from another doorway, probably the sink or stove light from the kitchen. When he gave a tentative push on the recessed handle in the door, the glass door moved easily aside.

"Come on," he whispered.

"I can't believe he left this door unlocked," Laura murmured crabbily. "Why not leave the front door wide open too?"

Press shrugged, his eyes checking every shadow as

they stepped cautiously over the threshold. "Guys do that all the time when they take out the garbage. It's like losing the remote control and finding it on the coffee table. He'd check it later and lock it before going to bed."

Laura shook her head but didn't comment. As a matter of principle, she flicked the latch to "lock" behind her as she slid the door closed, then followed Press into the recesses of John Carey's house.

♦

"What is it?" John asked. He watched Sil for a second, puzzled. "Do you hear someth—hey, wait. You're right; someone's at the front door." In a single smooth movement that Sil didn't see coming, he used the buoyancy of the water to lift her weight from his lap and rotate her so that she was once more sitting next to him on the underwater bench that ran around the inside of the Jacuzzi. "I'll be right back."

"Wait," Sil entreated. "Don't go, please. I—I want a baby."

John froze, his eyes nearly bulging with shock. "*Excuse* me?" This time he made no effort to disguise his retreat. "Whoa, lady. I think you've got the wrong guy here. We only met today, remember?" He raised an eyebrow and reached for the swim trunks he'd folded over the side of the hot tub, all trace of his earlier intentions evaporated. "Tell you what," he suggested in a voice that made it clear he wouldn't tolerate an argument, "I'll get the door. You get dressed, and we'll talk about this after whoever's at the front door leaves."

The sight of John turning his back on her infuriated her more than anything she'd encountered so far, even that foolish, sickly Robbie trying to force her. Cloaked as he'd been in the scents of cigarette smoke and liquor, she'd had no way of knowing about Robbie until he'd washed himself clean in the shower, but John was healthy and able-bodied, yet he was outright rejecting her offer to mate and produce offspring, *insulting* her.

"There's nothing wrong with me," Sil hissed. "*You're* the one who's flawed." She clawed at him and yanked him backward into the water before he could cry out. When he opened his mouth to yell, she shoved his head under the water to keep him quiet, holding him in place with one hand. The knocking had stopped but she thought she heard another sound, that of a door opening, but John was making too much noise, splashing furiously as he tried to come up for air. Impatient, she smacked the side of his skull against the underwater light next to her knee; the light sputtered and went out, but John continued to fight, his struggles growing more feeble by the second.

In the new darkness of the hot tub, she felt the change coming on her and surrendered to it. Along with the rest of her body, the hand restraining John slid around his neck, lengthening and bulging with muscular knobs and sharp-ended fingers that forced past his lips and teeth and filled his mouth until he could no longer close it. By the time the appendage erupted from his lower abdomen in a watered-down rush of blood and internal organs, John Carey was already dead, his lungs filled with hot, chlorinated water. When she surged out of the tub and left his corpse floating facedown, Sil was unlike anything that had ever existed on the face of the earth. A few seconds later she was over the rear fence and gone, vanished into the surrounding woods.

♦

This time Press was prepared. Following instructions, McRamsey had sent back to the complex for Press's MP5SD4, and the submachine gun felt like an old and trusted sidekick in his hands, as though he could shoot blind and the weapon would aim itself for him. Laura Baker, he had to admit, wasn't being nearly the pain in the ass he'd thought she'd be; she followed orders, stayed safely behind him, and didn't make a sound, moving with a catlike grace he found enticing and worthy of future reflection. "There," he muttered. "Out on the patio. Stay here." She nodded, then promptly followed him as he moved toward the French doors that led out to the back, blowing the hell out of his belief that she would follow his orders. Sliding the screen aside, he crept out with her at his heels. "Uh-oh," he said in a hushed voice. "Too late."

"Why?" Laura peered around him, then saw the body floating facedown in the Jacuzzi. The water was an ugly shade of diluted crimson. Her mouth turned down and her gaze flicked to the wide patio and the thin trees surrounding the house. "She can't have gone far," she said. "Look—the patio stones are still wet and she left her clothes on the lounge chair. Plus she left a trail."

"Call Fitch," Press told her. "I'm going after Sil—and this time stay *put*." When she nodded grudgingly, Press took off for the fence, following the angle of the wet footprints that led from the wide stones of the patio onto the grass. A glance over his shoulder verified that Laura hadn't come after him; standing next to the hot tub, she already had the cellular phone out of her purse and next to her ear.

A stirring on the other side of the chain-link fence made Press crouch, the 9mm sub ready. First the grass rustled, then the disturbance moved quickly into the tree branches, something swift and unseen moving just beyond the wan glow thrown by the veranda lights. To his right, unlatched and open about a foot or so, was a gate leading from the grounds and beyond; Press didn't know if the swinging motion he saw was real or his overactive imagination. He pushed through it and looked longingly back at the Carey house; it seemed safe and very far away. The low lights from the tall windows were no more than soft yellow slits way out here, and with a start, Press realized he could no longer see

Laura. She must have gone inside, he decided as his gaze searched the trees. That would certainly be preferable to standing next to the dead man while waiting for Fitch and his crew to arrive.

He took a step forward, noting that underfoot was nothing but sparse, moldering leaves—no telltale crunch or breaking branches marked his passage and it would provide the same cover for Sil—or whatever she'd become.

A noise overhead made Press tense. Leaves and branches rustled lightly overhead, indistinct from the cloudy night sky. Something was up there, but it seemed too small to be anything like Sil—

Before he could talk himself out of it, Press let the gun drop to hang by its sling at his side, grabbed a sturdy branch, and hauled himself off the ground. He swung his legs over and twisted until he was upright and balanced against the tree trunk with one hand; the other had the Heckler & Koch out, set to full auto fire and cocked without a conscious command.

Something fast scurried at him out of the blackness. Small and fleet, Press nearly shot the frightened squirrel before it veered off the branch and raced out of sight up the main trunk. His exhale of relief almost turned into a tumble when Laura's chiding, amused words came from the air below his feet.

"Very impressive. You can come down now, Tarzan. The rest of civilization has arrived."

As Press did a double swing to the ground and again let the gun drop down to his side, neither he nor Laura felt the sharp blue eyes that watched them through a knothole in a neighbor's fence twenty yards away.

◆

Dr. Fitch's face was white in the glare of the spotlights sweeping across the expansive patio and rear yard of John Carey's home. "I want six blocks cordoned off in all directions," he told the master sergeant of the Special Forces Unit. "Helicopters, searchlights, dogs—get it all out. We're not screwing around here. I want this woman found within the hour." The officer nodded stonily as Fitch marched back to join the rest of the team at the hot tub. "She can't have gotten far," he said to Press. "Carey's body is still warm and his car is still in his garage."

"No kidding?" Press's eyes were unreadable in the wildly flickering lights. "Gee, I think I heard that line in that last six movies I saw."

Fitch regarded him angrily. "This is not a joking matter, Lennox."

"Oh, I thought finding this guy with his intestines ripped out was real funny, Doc—about as funny as having to go after the thing that did it," Press shot back. "And I really like your line about how the body's still warm—considering the guy was found floating in a hot tub."

"You guys can argue about this latter," Stephen cut in. "Right now Dr. Fitch needs to get his forensic examiner to check Carey and see if there's evidence he had sex before she killed him. He—" Stephen frowned as he saw Dan off to one side, staring into the scarlet-stained water. "Dan? Are you all right?"

The black man blinked, then scrubbed at his face with his hands. When he looked at Stephen, his eyes seemed slightly out of focus, as if his thoughts were far away. "I was just realizing that the sight of blood used to scare me, but now I think I'm getting used to it," he said faintly. "Sometimes I think that's the scariest part about this."

"Guys?" Laura called from a spot near the end of the patio. She motioned for them to join her. "One of the security men found something you should see." When they got to the edge of the patio, the microbiologist led them through the fence, then off to the right. After a short distance they could see several of the MPs next to the high redwood fence that separated John

Carey's property from his neighbor's land to the north. One of the soldiers gave a final tug with a crowbar and a two-foot-wide section came free, leaving an opening to the other side. At the foot of the gap was a loose mound of dirt, and when they crowded around it, they saw a burrow curving several feet down, until it disappeared beneath the underside of the fitted boards. Another soldier, covered with earth, wriggled out of the hole on the neighbor's side of the fence.

"It goes all the way through," he told them unnecessarily.

"Christ," Press said, "no wonder we couldn't find her. What is she—some kind of giant gopher?"

"*Damn* it." Fitch shoved his hands in his pockets, then headed back toward the house. The rest of the team followed wordlessly. "She's slipped away again, hasn't she? It took us what? Ten minutes, maybe more, to find that . . . burrow, or whatever you want to call it. We still have no idea how fast she can run, if she got a ride from someone on the road, or hell—if she even looks the same as she did on the motel video. Sure, we can go house to house and ask, but we can't force people to let us actually search without getting some serious backlash from the local authorities. What a *mess*." He stopped by the driver's door to the van, waiting for the rest of the group to climb inside.

"Well," Stephen said, "we got closer this time."

"*Closer?*" Fitch's voice rose until he was almost squeaking. "What do you think this is—a kid's *game*? Is that what I'm supposed to tell the National Security Council when they ask for results? That we're *closer*?"

Stephen spread his hands helplessly. "Sorry, Doc. Just trying to think positive."

"I don't need positive thinking." Fitch was practically yelling now, punctuating his words by thrusting two stiffened fingers into the palm of one hand. "I need you people to use your expertise and *find* this woman."

"Creature," Laura said mildly. "She's not a woman."

Fitch whirled to face her. "Whatever she is, she shouldn't be running free!"

"Hey, Fitch." Press's voice was icy. "You created her, and you lost her. It's your fuckup that the rest of us are trying to fix, so before you quit screaming for the night, be sure to find a mirror and include your own reflection."

"That's very clever, Lennox," Fitch said bitterly, but he made a visible effort to calm himself before continuing. "Can anyone speculate about what her next move will be?"

"I found this on the living-room table." Dan held out a Polaroid print and everybody gathered around to study it. "Do you think it's her?"

"Maybe—I think so. But I doubt we'll get any more off this than we did the motel video. They're just too small in the print." Press shook his head.

"It's a pity Carey wasn't a better photographer," Fitch said as he took the photo from Dan. He opened the door to the van and held the picture close to his eyes under the faint glow of the vehicle's overhead light. "The way he positioned the camera must have made it take a light reading off the patio light behind Sil rather than the area beyond the fence. Everything in the front of the shot is too dark—you can barely see their faces. It's as useless as everything else we have so far." His shoulders slumped. "Climb in," he said morosely. "We're taking off."

"Where're we going?" Dan asked as he levered himself into the backseat.

"We're all beat," Fitch replied. He turned the ignition key and waited for Stephen and Dan to get settled and snap their seat belts into place. "Press, you and Laura meet us back at the Biltmore. We'll go over what we have, shower up, maybe grab a bite before sacking out. We need to clear our heads and start fresh." He gazed blankly out the windshield. "We've got to come up with something, we've *got* to. As of right now, we have no idea where she is."

"Dr. Fitch?" Robert Minjha strode to the driver's side window, disconnecting a call on a handheld telephone. "I just got the report on Carey and the water in the hot tub. There's no evidence of ejaculation."

Laura looked up in surprise. "So Sil hasn't managed to mate yet."

Dan smiled a little. "I think we interrupted her."

"Well, I guess we did!" Fitch said sarcastically. "Come *on*, for crying out loud—give me something I can *use*, will you?"

"And what flashes of intelligence have you come up with lately, *Dr*. Fitch?" Press asked testily.

Fitch ignored him. "Let's head back," he said again. "We'll get some rest and tomorrow night we'll go back and stake out the ID."

"You've got to be joking." Press's eyebrows shot up. "She's not stupid, you know. She isn't going to repeat herself."

"I agree with Press." Stephen leaned forward on the front seat of the van, his elbows resting on the dashboard. "I doubt she'll go back there—the place yielded a poor specimen. Everything we know about her says she learns exceptionally quickly. Her skills at selecting a mate will have progressed significantly by now."

Fitch looked exasperated. "Look," he explained, "she's been in Los Angeles for three days. She may not have been successful at the ID, but it is what she knows. Can any of you do better?" He waited pointedly for a few moments, but no one responded. "I didn't think so. Besides, I'd rather we try the ID again tomorrow night than spend the evening sitting around the computers at the Biltmore reminiscing about how close we were and waiting for some elusive 'break.' "

By way of good-bye, the doctor started the van's engine and put it in gear. As he pulled out of Carey's driveway Press saw Dan waving from the open rear window. He held up the Polaroid and returned the gesture. "Good detective work, kid!" he called as the vehicle made the turn out of the driveway and went out of sight on the main road. Hell, Press thought dourly, the photograph *was* the only thing left at the house that meant anything.

Of course, he wouldn't want to say that to John Carey's family tomorrow morning.

31

By the time the search helicopter passed overhead, Sil was already set for transportation.

She made her move in the parking lot of a twenty-four-hour Liquor Mart at the corner of Sunset and Fairfax, across from the Directors Guild of America Building she'd admired before. The Liquor Mart was ringed with lush vegetation and fairly crowded, a lot nicer than the ratty places by her motel in Hollywood. Sil was in a hurry but not foolish, and she waited until a woman in her late twenties who looked Sil's own size parked a car on the end and went inside. When she came out about ten minutes later with a small paper bag of groceries, Sil was ready.

No one else was around their cars when Sil sprang. The woman had the driver's door open and was leaning inside to swing the paper bag and her pocketbook over onto the passenger side, and Sil took advantage of her victim's off-balance stance to shove her bodily across the front seat. Checking the lot quickly to make sure no one had seen, Sil reached inside the car and sank the fingers of one hand into the driver's thick, shoulder-length hair. Sliding her other hand under the struggling woman's thighs, Sil lifted her clear of the driver's seat and middle console and swung her over to the passenger side of the car like a stuffed toy.

"Give me your clothes," Sil commanded without letting go of her handful of brown hair.

"Who are you?" the woman wailed. "What do you want?"

"I just told you," Sil repeated impatiently. "Your *clothes*. Hurry up—and be *quiet*."

"No!" The woman tried to pull free and when that didn't work, she took a swing at Sil and began clawing at the hand buried in her hair. Easily dodging the weak punch, Sil was acutely aware that she was stark naked, streaked with dirt and wet leaves, and sitting behind the wheel of another person's vehicle. Any moment could bring disaster, and she decided that babying the owner of this small taupe-colored Mazda 323 was a risk she could no longer afford. Instead of struggling further, Sil bounced the woman's forehead hard on the dashboard. When her prisoner went limp, Sil hurriedly pulled the woman's sweater off her and put it on, then jostled her unconscious victim onto the floorboard.

This car, Sil discovered, was different from Robbie's orange Puma. With one less pedal and a gearshift that remained stationary unless you wanted to go in the opposite direction, it was a simpler machine to learn and required little effort to drive. She preferred being naked and feeling the night air against her thighs and back, but it wasn't possible; loath to do it, she nonetheless pulled around to the back of the building and took the woman's blue jeans, socks and pair of purple-and-white Nikes that weren't quite big enough. Still senseless, the driver never felt a thing as Sil tied her hands and feet with a length of rope she found in the back, then thrust her under the overhanging shelf of the hatchback. Finally, Sil dumped the contents from the grocery bag, crushed it into a tight ball, and shoved it in the woman's mouth.

Guiding the Mazda carefully back to the front lot of the market, Sil reparked the car in a different spot facing Sunset Boulevard, angled slightly in the direction of John Carey's house. She reasoned that the people who were looking for her, including the doctor from the complex, would opt for Sunset to get to the expressway rather than the more crowded Hollywood Boulevard. Although the woman who owned the car came to after a while, her muffled thumps from the rear of the Mazda were easy for Sil to ignore as she sat, waiting, her gaze fixed solidly on the street.

While she waited Sil thought about the brown-haired man who had braved the darkness without hesitation to come after her. In her mind's eye, she remembered the way his sculpted profile had looked, silhouetted against a backdrop of leaves and night sky. Broad-shouldered, audacious and confident, fearless even though he had no idea what his opponent could or couldn't do.

A child by him would be strong and cunning, a supreme hunter. The thought of mating with him made her blood race. After all, nothing was impossible, right? What had that woman at the ID told her before Sil had eliminated her?

All's fair in love and war.

32

"Ninety-nine percent of our genes are useless now," Laura told Press as she drove. She thought it was kind of amusing that he'd taken off his shoes and stuck both stockinged feet out the window, like a carefree teenager. "They are, however, a dictionary of what's been useful on this planet throughout time."

"For everything?" Press asked curiously. "Not just for humans?"

"You got it. Genes carry instructions for all sorts of things. The gills of a fish, for instance, or the webbed feet of a frog."

"But we don't have those things," Press said, holding on as Laura took a curve to the right at a brisk pace. She was determined not to lose sight of Fitch's van on the roadway in front of them. "Christ, that man drives as erratically as he thinks."

She shrugged, never taking her eyes off the street or the van ahead. "Fitch is a dreamer, that's all. But it *is* too bad he didn't invest more time in a solid blueprint before going ahead with the physical part of his project. If he had, maybe we'd be studying his creation— working *with* it, instead of hunting it down."

"Yeah," Press said as he pulled his feet in and groped around the floorboard for his shoes, "back to the hunting down part. You were talking about gills and frog feet."

"Those instructions are still in our genes," Laura told him. "They're just turned off. Now it's junk from the past, silent and primitive history. We've seen so many things in Sil, so much *power*. Maybe the instructions from the alien part of her DNA has given her the ability to turn all those things on and off at will. If that's the case, she could access our entire genetic history."

"What are you saying?" Press asked slowly. "That we could be fighting the entire animal kingdom?"

Laura stole a glance at him. "Worse. In theory, she could have things in her bodily makeup that never developed in us, or perhaps did but are now extinct. Attributes we don't even know about." She drove in silence for a moment, then continued, her voice low. Her face was expressionless in the green backwash of the sedan's dash lights. "Here's something you can appreciate in your line of work, Press. Instead of some weird space creature, think of Sil as an object, a *tool*. She'd make an excellent biological weapon if something out there thought humankind was nothing more than a galactic weed that should be eradicated before it spreads throughout the universe."

Press stared at her, unnerved. "So what you're supposing is that she's the cure and we're the disease."

"I'm not supposing anything," Laura replied. "Only speculating."

"Jesus," Press muttered. "Human weeds. Now there's a happy thought." He rubbed the back of his neck, then focused on the car's on-line computer, still powered up and ready. "Let's tackle a cheerier subject," he suggested as he began tapping keys on the console.

"Like what?" She glanced sideways at him.

"Like . . . *you*." Not an accomplished typist, it took him three tries to get SEARCH: BAKER, LAURA [DR.]

spelled properly at the C:\ prompt. Three seconds of
PLEASE WAIT, then Press was rewarded with BAKER,
LAURA [DR.]: 17 WILDWOOD DRIVE / SIMI VALLEY. He read
the data aloud to her and smiled. "Simi Valley . . . nice
out there?"

Laura smiled in return as she pulled into the
drive-up of the Biltmore behind Fitch's van and cut the
engine. "I like it," she said. She left the keys in the ignition for the valet and climbed out without looking at
him. He barely heard her next sentence.

"You should check it out sometime."

♦

Although Dr. Fitch had already gone up to his suite,
Dan and Stephen were waiting in the lobby when
Laura and Press came in. "Anyone hungry?" Stephen
asked with a bright-eyed look at Laura.

She couldn't help but grin as from the corner of her
eye she saw Press's expression darken. "No thanks," she
said. "I'm too exhausted to do anything but sleep."

"I'll have something to eat with you," Dan offered.
"I'm starved. How about you, Press?"

"Not before bed," he answered. "It'll give me nightmares. I'll hold out for bacon and eggs in the morning."
He nodded good night to the two men and walked toward the elevators with Laura. She pressed the call button, but when the car arrived, Press changed his mind
about getting on. "You go ahead," he told her. "I'm going to pick up a paper. I'll see you in the morning."

" 'Night," Laura said with a wave.

Press gave her a return salute just before the doors
closed, then turned and made his way back through the
lobby to the newsstand near the front doors. It was
locked, but the first stacks of *Times* had already been
delivered. Press dropped a couple of quarters on the
second stack and a quick zip of his pocketknife got him
the top paper from the pile closest to him.

The elevators were slow in the early hours of the

morning, and he was already scanning page three by the time the LED floor indicator flashed back to 1 and the mirrored doors opened to admit him. Immersed in his newspaper, Press stepped into the empty car without looking up and pushed the button for his floor, not even noticing when the doors slid shut.

In the farthest corner of the Biltmore's lobby, Sil watched with hungry eyes as the LED floor indicator winked its way to 9 and stopped.

33

The man with the dark hair and eyes opened the door to the hotel room as soon as she knocked, as if he had been waiting for her, as if he had known she would come to him. He stood to the side and signaled without faltering that she should come in, although she was sure she saw recognition in the penetrating gaze that swept her up and down. She could feel her desire for him radiating from her, almost visible in the air between them like heat waves shimmering above a car engine on a bright day. When she reached for him and cupped his face in her hands, he didn't back away. He just stood there, looking at her, waiting, yet when she kissed him he seemed surprised. Suddenly afraid he would reject her like all the others, she stared at him and held out her hands pleadingly, her eyes wide and blue.

Then they were together on his bed, their naked forms already entwined in the act of love, him on the bottom, her on top and riding a crest of pleasure so powerful it shortened her breath and made her giddy. His body was hard and lean, charged with strength and maleness; she could feel him inside her, huge, stroking and filling her with heat with every sensual shift of his hips. When he closed his eyes, she thought he was going to come and she tensed with anticipation, her own blossoming orgasm making her moan. Still moving underneath her, he sat up without pulling out, wrapping his arms around her as he opened his eyes. As she stared into them, nose to nose, they were darker than she remembered, almost black. Shocked, she saw them change to a lighter color, then shift again, brown to blue to green to gray to nothing more than round, colorless orbs in his skull.

Whatever pleasure she'd felt was gone, driven away by fear. He smiled at her but the expression was . . . wrong somehow, elongated in the jaw and full of teeth that shouldn't be there. She tried to pull away but couldn't; his arms were wrapped tightly around her and they were overly extended, too, filled with far more might that she had ever known. She wanted to scream but no voice came out of her mouth when it opened. His body, still joined with hers, began to mutate in earnest, growing dozens of barbs and tentacles. Pulling out of shape, it lost its healthy flesh coloring in favor of a jellylike transparency that reminded her of the cooling grease in the pans below the hot dogs in the train station back in Utah. Vital parts throbbed within it, moving a faintly purplish fluid just below the skin surface with each pulse.

Horrified and struggling pointlessly, she could do nothing as the lover within her arms gripped her body and re-formed himself into a being much like the dark side of herself. As the spikes erupted from his chest and punctured her ribs and the softer organs beneath, even her shrieks were soundless.

♦

Sil awoke at dawn with a stifled scream, her skin running with sweat and her eyes only inches away from a photograph on the nightstand. Encircled by a fancy plaster frame with painted tulips at its upper corner, the photo showed the woman Sil had abducted last night standing on the deck of a boat with her arms around a tall, slender man of indeterminate age. There was nothing sexual about the way the two clasped each other, no tilt of the head or flirtatious curve of either's body.

The woman's name, Sil recalled, was Marlo Keegan; she'd learned that and the appropriate address by going through the purse on the front seat of the Mazda before leaving the Biltmore to come to this house. It was a small place, decorated with a lot of ruffled floral prints and pastel plaid fabric; lace curtains hung in front of bright white miniblinds and ceramic knickknacks crowded the furniture atop crocheted doilies. Very frilly and feminine, and for Sil, quite comfortable.

Rubbing the sleep from her eyes, Sil rolled on her other side. The owner of the house, Marlo, was awake and staring at her. Her prisoner was still tied securely and Sil had found silver duct tape on a shelf by the back door when she'd dragged her victim inside. She'd used the tape to reinforce the bonds, finally twining a length of tape around Marlo's ankle and her own to ensure that the woman could not free herself without waking her captor.

Sil regarded the Keegan woman impassively. "Who is the man in the photograph? Does he live here, too?"

"It's m-my brother." The answer was strained. "He lives in Dallas."

Brother? Sil didn't know what a brother was. Dallas, too, was a mystery, but not important enough to think about. She had other things on her mind. "Do you ever have nightmares?"

"Y-yes." Marlo's response was shaky. "I think I'm having one right now."

Sil cocked her head, perplexed again, but decided not to pursue it. "I have them," she said. "I think they tell me who I am."

Marlo said nothing for a moment. Then: "Why are you doing this to me?"

"To . . . save my life, I suppose." Sil sat up on the bed and ripped apart the strand of duct tape running from her ankle to Marlo's, then hugged her knees. The down comforter was soft and warm and she didn't feel like getting off the bed yet. "I don't know where I'm from, what I am, or what I'm doing here. Do you?"

"If you're asking if I know who *you* are, the answer is no," Marlo said cautiously. "And I don't *want* to know."

"Really?" Sil studied the bound woman. "Why do you think you're here?"

"I don't *know!*" Sil's prisoner began to whimper. "Please, let me go—I won't tell anyone. I won't do anything to hurt you, I promise. Please—"

"Yes, you would." Sil swung her legs off the bed and stood, jouncing the mattress. "You just don't know it yet."

Certain that Marlo wouldn't escape, Sil left her to sob into a pillow and began to explore the small house. Most of the furniture was still fresh looking though not expensive, as if the house were a recent purchase that its proud new owner had tried to fill. An interesting place, and it made her wonder what Marlo Keegan did for a living and what she was like as a person—not that Sil would bother to find out.

The yellow-and-white kitchen was small and efficient, without the clutter of the other rooms. She found what she was looking for under the kitchen sink, thrown into a disused box with a bag of potting soil so old that the plastic sack was cracked in a half-dozen places. When she walked back into the bedroom, the woman on the bed cringed at the sight of the rusted pruning shears in Sil's hand.

"What are you going to do with those?" Marlo's voice was shrill with panic.

"Be quiet," Sil said in a steady voice. "I have to think." She held up her left hand and looked at it carefully, then let it drop it to the top of the nightstand. Hanging her thumb off the front edge of the piece of furniture, Sil positioned the pruning shears precisely between the first and second knuckle—

"Oh, dear God," Marlo whispered, her eyes protruding from her face.

—and cut it off.

The Keegan woman retched and shut her eyes, tucking her chin hard against her chest. When Sil didn't cry out, she opened her eyes and watched, stupefied, as Sil held her hand up attentively between them. Arm wavering slightly, the raw wound on the end of Sil's hand did not bleed; instead, the flesh in the middle of the injury, its edges pinched together by the pruning shears like the ends of a small sausage, began to squirm and pull apart. Gagging again but unable to look away, Marlo's gaze flicked from Sil's face to her hand and back again, each new glance marking the progress of Sil's regeneration. In less than sixty seconds, Sil's hand was whole again.

Sil had brought Marlo's handbag inside last night and set it next to the alarm clock on the nightstand. Now she opened it and slipped her severed thumb inside, zipping it into the smaller lipstick pocket at the top. She gave brief consideration to taping her captive's mouth shut, but it seemed too much trouble. And what if she began to cry? With her mouth covered, the prisoner could suffocate if her nose became blocked. No, Sil decided, better just to get it over with.

Before Marlo Keegan could yell, Sil grabbed the woman's left wrist and shoved the pruning shears against her thumb; a hard *snip!* and the woman's thumb fell to the sheets with a messy splash of blood. Marlo did scream then, loud and long enough so that Sil finally slapped her to put an end to the maddening racket; the blow rocked the woman's head back and against the headboard, stunning her enough to dwindle her screeching to an incoherent babbling that Sil could at least tolerate. Marlo's pale cheeks were wet with tears of agony as she curled in a fetal position atop the comforter.

Sil dashed outside now, before the day's traffic

started building and cars began passing on the roadway. Driving back to Marlo Keegan's house last night, she had seen without really registering the trash cans dotting the roadway where driveways met the curb. Today was trash pickup day—and to make things more perfect, Marlo had set her garbage can out last night, before her fateful trip to the Liquor Mart. A quick nudge into the contents, and Marlo's thumb was destined for a permanent trip to an unknown landfill.

Back inside, Sil quickly finished the remaining tasks. She was ready to go within a half hour, and this time the only thing she had to hunt for was the five-gallon gasoline container next to the lawn mower in Marlo's storage shed.

◆

The view down Nichols Canyon from the road at noon was spectacular, ruined only by the small group of metallic rods and electrical transformers far below, at the foot of the incline. Sil had chosen this particular spot along Mulholland because of those same transformers, carefully committing the area to memory. Street names, landmarks, a handful of houses with features that set them apart from the rest—all of this coalesced into an effective mental map that would guide her back here later.

Sil had learned her lesson with Robbie's Puma, and she'd stopped at a gas station early in the morning after leaving the Keegan home. She wanted to spend the morning learning the area and working out the strategy for tonight, not skipping from vehicle to vehicle and juggling baggage in the meantime. Now she parked the taupe-colored Mazda beneath the shade of a handsome California live oak on a tiny street called Doña Nenita. The tree made her pause because it smelled strange, like nothing she'd encountered so far. She found the scent vaguely erotic and couldn't decide if it reminded her of men or chlorine bleach, or both.

Not far from the electrical substation in Nichols Canyon, Doña Nenita nonetheless offered Sil a number of retreat options, which included both Mulholland and Nichols Canyon Road, should the need arise. She didn't really want to take Marlo's cumbersome handbag with her, but it seemed that a woman was expected to have some sort of pocketbook all the time; grudgingly Sil slung the strap at an angle across her chest so it wouldn't slide off. She locked the car doors and cracked the windows an inch on either side to vent the gasoline fumes coming from the backseat.

The fresh air felt and tasted good after the warm, gas-laden air of the Mazda, and Sil took her time, enjoying the exercise and the sun. She noticed that the birdsong in the trees bordering the road ebbed and flowed according to the traffic that whizzed past. As she headed vaguely southwest it wasn't that long before she found what she sought at the corner of Laurel Canyon and Oakdell—a full-service Mobil Station. There was a telephone box not far from the open garage doors and she stepped up to it and picked up the receiver, pressing it to her ear so she wouldn't be conspicuous as she surveyed the mechanics working in the station and the cars parked outside.

It took some time, but finally she understood the process. She was ready the next time a mechanic closed the hood on a car, backed it out of the garage, and reparked it in the line of cars to the side. Waiting until the mechanic returned to the garage, Sil hung up the telephone receiver and casually walked over to the car he'd just pulled into the spot, a white-on-beige 1984 Oldsmobile Cutlass that was bigger than anything she'd driven so far. She slid inside the car, closed the door gently, and checked the ignition; as she'd anticipated, the keys were in it.

Fresh from a tune-up, the Cutlass started with a quiet purr, and no one paid any attention as she backed out of the parking spot and drove away.

34

"I still think this is a waste of time."

"Take the toothpick out, Press," Laura said. "You sound like you're talking around a branch in your mouth."

Press snatched the sliver of wood from between his teeth and stuck it in his shirt pocket. "Well, thank you, Miss Manners. Your tactfulness is certainly appreciated."

"Anytime, Mr. Lennox." She gave him a smile so absurdly vapid that he had to laugh; after a moment Laura lost it and joined in. Her laughter died away as the lights of the ID glinted through the windshield of the van. "Oh, joy. It seems we've arrived."

"What the hell," Press said as they all climbed out, "it's a free night on the town." His tone of voice, however, didn't quite match the cheerful words. He offered his arm to Laura. "Shall I escort you inside? I see Bruno over there recognizes us, so I doubt we'll have as much difficulty as the last time."

Laura playfully slapped his arm aside. "No thanks, Tarzan. I can walk upright fine on my own. Just follow me."

His eyebrows raised in mock affront. "Forgive me for dragging my knuckles, Dr. Baker. Please—lead on. I'll study your stride and learn how you balance so well."

"Just watch your step, Lennox," she retorted.

"If you two are finished clowning around," Fitch said sharply, "I'd appreciate you taking a post by the stairwell to the rest rooms and watching the crowd. Or would you prefer to stand on the sidewalk and flirt some more?"

"Duty calls," Press said with a slight salute. "You order and we obey." Without further comment, he trailed after Laura. At the front entrance she nodded politely to Bruno and showed her government ID card; as with Dan and Stephen, he waved the remainder of the group inside without bothering to look any closer at their credentials.

At least they were dressed casually enough to fit in with the crowd, although the men's blue jeans and short-sleeved shirts and Laura's jeans and snug blouse were a far cry from the provocative outfits worn by most of the patrons. In the excitement of their first visit to the ID, neither Press nor Laura had realized how much heat actually built up in the huge room after a couple of hours and a full crowd. Stationed at the head of the stairs in the back, they found the air sweltering and filled with thick layers of cigarette smoke. Vainly trying to wave the smoky air aside, Laura stood next to Press and watched as Fitch, Carey's Polaroid picture in hand, found the manager of the club and spent a good ten minutes aggravating him.

"I can't believe people still put this crap in their lungs," Laura finally complained. "Haven't they learned *anything* by now?"

"Nah," Press said. "I only quit a year ago myself." He grinned. "Don't tell me you never wondered why I just 'happened' to have a Bic in my pocket back at the research lab."

She shrugged prettily. "I didn't think twice about it. I thought it was a guy thing."

"Like toothpicks."

Laura grinned. "Exactly."

"A behavior specialist you're not." Stephen, with Dan dallying behind, joined them by the staircase.

"That's your field, not mine," she replied, her eyes scanning the throng of men and women. "Speaking of which, what the heck are we doing here?"

"Not much," Stephen admitted. He coughed delicately into his hand, then shook his head. "I need some air—there's way too much smoke in here for me. And I hate these nighttime hours—I'm usually in bed by eleven-thirty. I'm going to slip into the van and put the seat back for a while, take a short rest. We're getting nowhere here, anyway."

"I guess nature boy can't take it." Press's tone was more joking than harsh as the three of them watched Stephen retreat. "He kind of strikes me as a ladies' man, but I wonder where he goes to cruise if he can't do the clubs. This place closes at three—hell, in New York they're plenty of places with licenses until six in the morning."

"I think he knows you two like each other," Dan said innocently. Despite the uneven lights flashing across their faces, Laura's blush was still noticeable. "Besides, he told me this feels like a wild-goose chase."

"Really? And what do you feel, Dan?" Laura watched him closely.

"I'm not sure," the soft-spoken man admitted. "It's easy for me to pinpoint what someone's feeling, but usually only if I'm close to that person. This place is like a big blender, with way too much stuff going on too close together to segregate anything. Plus, I've never met Sil in person, just seen the aftermath." He scrutinized the patrons of the ID for a few moments and scratched his head absently. "I just don't know why she would want to come back here . . . unless she had a plan." His black eyes were unfathomable. "Maybe we shouldn't forget that this woman—"

"Creature," Laura reminded him.

"—is awfully smart," Dan finished. "We talked about this before. She second-guesses us because she can think like the human part of her, and outsmarts us because she can think like the . . ." He frowned. "What's the word I'm looking for?"

"Unknown," Press said.

"Well," Dan said, his expression troubled, "I thought we'd called her something else, but I guess that fits, too." He didn't say anything else for a few seconds, then he glanced longingly toward the exit. "I don't like it in here," he said gloomily. "There's too much going on in too small a space. I think I'll go out to the van and talk to Stephen."

"Okay, Dan," Press said. "You guys come back in when you're ready. Take your time—we'll be here." Dan nodded and disappeared into the swarm of dancers, oblivious to the bodies swaying around him. An attractive young woman with short, spiked blond hair sidled toward Press with an engaging smile; he purposely turned his back on her and she sulked away in the direction of the dance floor. "So," Press eventually asked, "what do you think the creature's looking for, matewise?"

Laura rubbed her arms and gazed around the club, wishing she'd worn something other than the short-sleeved satin blouse; despite the warm interior, she didn't feel comfortable in here. "Who knows? Most females choose for resources and dominance in the group."

"You mean like the dominant male in a pride of lions?"

"Something like that, although lion prides don't necessarily work that way all the time. In more sophisticated cultures and when given a chance to decide for themselves, women consider humor, ability to express intimacy, and sensitivity to their feelings."

Press's eyes narrowed as he considered this. "And our girl?"

Laura deliberated the situation honestly before answering. "She's been alive for a little under three weeks, and she's spent nearly a third of that time fighting for survival. For the most part I don't believe she understands human beings or the way we live. Children learn the most during their earliest years, and who can translate what that time period means to a life-form that develops to maturity in about fifteen days? Her existence so far will have taught her that to maintain freedom she must constantly be on the run, and to mate she may have to kill. In actuality, I think she'll look for qualities that will help her offspring survive in a hostile environment. Good reflexes, strength, daring, shrewdness."

"In other words," Press cracked his knuckles idly, "she'll choose like an animal."

"You make it sound derogatory, but yes—I suppose she will." Laura's eyes sparkled beguilingly in the fluctuating lights. "That principle is still very much in practice, Press. While human women don't generally end up with the strongest of their species—for the most part we've become far too populous for that—many are still *attracted* to the more powerful, physically appealing men, whether they admit it to others or not."

"Ah." He nodded, then gave her an impish grin. "With all that competition, no wonder guys have started bathing regularly."

◆

Dan Smithson stepped out the side door of the club, trying to guess where Fitch's aides would have parked the van. It was doubtful they'd have taken it off to the main lot and relegated it to the next available space— that was too far away. More than likely they would have slapped a government permit in the window and brought it around to the back of the building. With that in mind, he turned and headed that way.

A row of Dumpsters were pushed against the building, all overflowing, too packed to completely shut. The smell in the warm night was overpowering; he wrinkled his nose and tried to hold his breath as he passed them, then froze when something fell to the ground in the shadows between the last two.

"Dr. Arden?" He took an uncertain step forward. Colored lights washed down the passageway behind him, but not strong enough to reach all the way back here. The sound came again at ground level, louder, and his hands started to tremble. He didn't like this at all, he shouldn't be out here by himself. Something was moving toward the front of the trash bin, almost into the light, and he had no clue as to where Stephen had gone or if the professor was even all right.

Dan nearly yelled aloud when something scampered from underneath the Dumpster on his left and angled across the sidewalk, then paused to regard him inquisitively. Two white-ringed eyes stared up at his face, bright brown despite the darkness. A second later the raccoon was joined by its mate, chittering busily and rubbing at the fur of its face with tiny-fingered paws that made Dan remember what Dr. Baker had said about them being able to open things. For a moment man and animals regarded each other, then the raccoons raced one another to the cover of a line of low bushes planted at the edge of the sidewalk.

Relieved, Dan decided to go back inside. Better the noise and heavy air of the club than this nerve-racking seclusion. Turning on his heel, he glanced around the bushes by his feet to reassure himself that the raccoons were gone. He started to step forward—

—and nearly walked into the arms of the she-creature.

He couldn't begin to conceive how she'd gotten up

to him so quietly. She stood less than two feet away, close enough to touch, *too* close for Dan to let himself exhale. In human form, Sil was lovely, as beautiful as any of the supermodels whose faces and figures were plastered all over the United States and the world. Would he see her transform to her alien shape? Please God—he didn't *want* to.

"It's . . . you," he heard himself whisper. He stumbled backward and she came with him, matching him step for step. Any second she would pounce on him, and when the image of John Carey, eviscerated in his own hot tub, flashed in Dan's mind, he scrunched his eyes shut and threw up his hands in an instinctive effort to ward her off when she came toward him again.

The expected strike never came. Peering from behind his forearms, Dan saw the alien woman hesitate, as if she were appraising him. If she decided he posed a threat . . . in his head he visualized his own hand, saw himself cross his fingers for good luck. He lowered his arms slightly and his eyes locked with hers, such a clear, calculating blue, the color of an exquisite ocean with a deadly undertow. She held the gaze, fixing him in place, then abruptly dashed into the darkness.

With her retreat, Dan's paralysis broke. "She's here!" he screamed. "Dr. Arden, she's *here*!" He bolted out of the side passageway, nearly braining himself on the rear quarter panel of the van where the professor had reparked it at the front to better watch the crowd. He saw Stephen sit up from his slouched position in the driver's seat in time to glimpse Sil as she jumped into a beige-colored Cutlass illegally parked only a few car lengths away. Dan was still yelling at the top of his lungs and government agents began pouring from every doorway and corner of the old movie palace; as Sil cranked the engine of her car and jammed the transmission into reverse, Press and Laura sprinted out the doorway of the club. Panicking and unfamiliar with the vehicle, Stephen tried desperately to start the van and succeeded only in stalling the engine when he pumped the gas pedal and simultaneously turned the key in the electronically controlled ignition.

Sil's car wasn't the only one parked illegally. A glitzy, black-lacquer 1968 Impala low rider had squeezed into the space behind Sil's Oldsmobile; it was older and heavier, but no one had told her that. She floored the accelerator and rammed the Impala hard, shoving it backward and onto the sidewalk with a crunch of metal and a shower of sparks, heedless of the people shrieking and scattering in every direction. Spinning the steering wheel of the Cutlass, she shoved the gearshift to drive and mashed the accelerator again; engine howling, the newly tuned auto leaped out of the parking space and sped down Formosa toward Sunset.

Mouth open, Dan watched Sil escaping. The parking lot and entrance of the ID were total bedlam: screaming people, some Hispanic guy practically in spasms over his mangled Impala, agents running everywhere while trying to decipher rapid-fire orders spewing from the red-faced, infuriated Dr. Fitch as he rushed around on the sidewalk. Somewhere a switch was flipped and the entire scene was thrown into eye-dazzling white-on-white by emergency high-illumination lights mounted in the usually dark corners of each of the ID's second-floor windows. All those people, a dozen engines racing but hopelessly entangled in a traffic jam, doing nothing but filling the warm night air with racket and exhaust. So many soldiers to fight the war, but not a one going after Sil—

Except Press.

Dan saw him whirl in the midst of the massive confusion. Press's expression was a perfect picture of frustration when he realized there was no way he could get a vehicle out of the mess in time to give chase. With Laura hurrying after him, Press opted for dodging the chaos entirely, both of them circumventing the cars to get to the main entrance to the parking lot. As they reached it someone was turning in and gaping toward the activity at the front of the club. The guy was older and balding, and totally terrorized when Press stepped bodily in front of the moving car and aimed his submachine gun at the windshield. The driver lurched to a stop with his mouth hanging open, white-knuckled hands griping the steering wheel.

"Get out!" Press shouted. He waved his government card in the air in front of the driver. "I need your car *now!*"

The man didn't argue; in addition to the 9mm pointed at his head, there were too many blue-suited government types running toward his vehicle to bother. He clawed the door open and fell out, landing on his butt on the sidewalk and gawking at Press and Laura as they hastily climbed into the car. As the automobile roared off with Press behind the wheel, Dan saw that the guy on the sidewalk looked like he was going to cry.

Staring after the car that Press had commandeered, Dan realized it was a silver-gray 1995 Jaguar XJS.

35

Sil didn't know anything about automobiles other than the basics of operation and that they need fuel in order to run. The one she was driving had been damaged when she had forced her way out of the parking place in front of the nightclub but that was to be expected, and while the rear underside of the car was making a lot of noise, it still seemed to perform the same. She was, however, quite taken aback at the blatant difference in the power and maneuverability of the vehicle pursuing her and the one she was driving. Scowling as she whipped the car north onto Nichols Canyon Road and left Hollywood Boulevard behind, she could easily see that while she had to fight to keep the Cutlass stable around the curves of the roadway, the sleek, silvery car tracking her had no problem hugging the twisting ribbon of concrete. She swung far too wide around a curve at the intersection by Delzuro and obliterated the glass-and-metal telephone booth on the corner; the resulting damage to the left fender and the front end made her wonder anxiously if the car was too crippled to continue. The only thing that kept her pursuers from swinging around and cutting her off was the traffic on the opposite side of the roadway. But she had to hurry; soon they would barricade the entire area, close it to outside traffic, and then those small diversions would be gone.

In spite of the scenery hurtling past the car and the spiderweb of cracks that marred the windshield, Sil recognized the roadmarks. Above the squealing of the tires, the heavy sound of search-and-destroy UH-60L Blackhawk helicopters buzzed the roadway not far above. It didn't matter; she was close enough to the substation now to believe her plan was going to work. With her left hand holding the wheel and never taking her gaze off the road, Sil reached back with her right and unscrewed the filler cap on the plastic container of gasoline she'd filled up at a service station this morning. Tossing it aside, she tipped the can forward and let it wedge itself upside down in the space between the front and the backseat. Gas fumes immediately permeated the car's interior.

The Olds almost lost it on the last curve to the right before Sil's destination; the two Blackhawks that rose above the ridge on the highway ahead of her startled her enough to nearly make her turn too soon. Fighting her own reflexes, she headed straight for the lead one and was practically blinded for her effort by the high-intensity spotlight that snapped on directly into the windshield of the Cutlass.

As the helicopter pulled up, banked and headed back toward her, Sil stomped the brake and twisted the steering wheel to the right, intentionally leading the Olds into a turn that made it skid off the road and careen down the embankment, ripping its own path through the heavy brush. With the vehicle bouncing down the side of the canyon, she shoved the driver's door open, then reached over and hauled Marlo Keegan out of the cramped passenger-side floorboard. Leaving her arms and legs tightly wrapped with the heavy duct tape, Sil snatched at the square of adhesive covering the woman's mouth until it came off. Her captive immediately started screaming, but with the crunching of metal, the grazing of the heavy branches along the sides of the car, and the hammering of the helicopter blades, her long shriek was just one more little noise amid the pandemonium of the chase.

◆

"We're about a mile up Nichols Canyon Road," Laura hollered into the microphone of her small radio. "She just took out the telephone booth at Delzuro. You've got to try to cut her off on Mulholland. Don't let her get to a more crowded street!"

"Jesus!" Press swerved to avoid the shards of glass and twisted metal spraying the roadway, the remains of the telephone booth. Aptly named, the twelve-cylinder Jaguar clung to the road like it was digging claws into the street surface. "I don't know how many times I could've gotten around her and forced her to the side if it wasn't for oncoming traffic."

"Don't give up," Laura said stonily. "We'll get her."

Press's short laugh startled her as the XJS swung right, then left again. "Give *up*? I'm sorry—I don't think I know what that means!"

They shot around another curve and Laura pointed. "Look out—she's losing it!"

The car in front of them had been a cream-puff early-model Olds before Sil had slammed it into the Impala in back of her at the ID; now it was beat to hell, its trunk permanently smashed closed above a back bumper Press was sure would let go at any second. They couldn't see the front where it had smacked into the telephone booth at Delzuro, but he was sure she'd hit it hard enough to cave in the right front fender and probably loosen that bumper, too. It was amazing that all four tires were still intact, but now she seemed to have lost the remains of whatever driving skills she had acquired during her short period of freedom. For no apparent reason, the brake lights flashed and the Cutlass went into a skid that sent its front end plunging at full speed through the heavy foliage on the right side of the road. Sliding, the car plummeted down the incline.

"What the hell!" Press hit the brakes and downshifted to first, leaving a trail of rubber behind the car as it screeched to a stop a couple of yards beyond the hole in the underbrush. Yanking his seat belt free, he leaped from the car and ran to the edge of the street, then almost lost his balance on the edge of the sharp drop-off. He backed up a few steps and squinted down the slope; he could hear the metal grinding and trees breaking, but seeing anything was impossible.

"Should we follow her?" A half-dozen other vehicles skidded to a halt around the Jaguar, and Laura had to shout to be heard over the noise of racing engines and the helicopters diving at the tops of the trees below. Press opened his mouth to reply, but before he could get the words out, they heard a crash and saw blue-white sparks erupt somewhere in the black tangle beneath them. There was a series of harsh sizzles and the sudden, acrid smell of burning transformer oil swirled up, followed immediately by the deafening sound of the car as it exploded. Every streetlight in sight went dark.

"Shit," Press said crudely. He craned his neck forward, trying to see something beyond the dancing orange-and-red shadows. "I think she plowed into an electrical substation. This makes absolutely no sense— she didn't stand a chance this way. Why would she run off the road?"

Laura peered down the path the Olds had battered through the foliage. "Maybe she wasn't as smart as we thought."

The words didn't fit the look of doubt on Laura's features, and Press snorted as he wiped his forehead with the back of his hand. "Right. She's been ahead of us every step of the way so far, so now she's going to run her car into a bunch of electrical poles so it'll blow up.

Sorry, I didn't know she had a death wish. I thought the point of the game was that she was trying to live."

As Laura started to reply one of the helicopters swooped out of the air like a huge black bird; there was a whistling noise and a moment later something heavy and loud rocked the side of the hill five hundred feet below. Press and Laura stumbled and grabbed for the surrounding shrubbery. By the time they found their footing, a fireball mushroomed from the valley floor, dousing the area with red-and-orange light. A second helicopter followed and fired another incendiary rocket, the backwash from its rotor creating churning circles of burning brush just visible down the track left by the Cutlass.

"Oh, good Christ," Laura said in disgust as she and Press struggled to their feet. "Not only have they ensured we won't find any remains, they'll probably burn up Nichols Canyon while they're at it."

"I guess Fitch was listening when I bitched him out about the idea of taking her alive," Press shouted. As if to punctuate their words, one of the Blackhawks circled over Mulholland and returned, firing a third incendiary rocket. This one overshot, and they glimpsed a line of fire ripping through the undergrowth, then speeding into a small backyard; a second later the fireball rammed into something solid. With a roar, someone's home went up in flames. "What did I tell you?" Laura said bitterly. "How'd you like to come home from work and find that? Assuming, of course, you weren't already there and *in* it."

Press straightened up and rubbed his face with his hands. The fire sent a warm orange glow all the way up to the road, but the light didn't reach his eyes, which were still dark and troubled. "I don't know," he said gravely. "It'd be hard, but . . . knowing what we do—or maybe what we *don't*—isn't it better this way than to have any part of her survive?"

♦

Forty-five minutes later the entire team was assembled above the crash site. The streetlights were still out but Fitch's assistants had several generators feeding oversized spotlights, and a multitude of headlights and high-powered flashlights finished illuminating the area. Press couldn't decide if the situation reminded him more of a beehive or a black comedy.

"All right," Phil McRamsey told Dr. Fitch, "we've blocked the road in a big loop, including Woodrow Wilson and Laurel Canyon. The news crews are going completely ape-shit. We're going to have to feed them something."

"I don't care what you tell them," Fitch said. "Just don't tell them the truth. Handle it."

"Am I the only person here who thinks it's awfully convenient that Sil turned up at the club like that and just by coincidence Dan saw her out by the Dumpsters?" Press looked at the rest of the group skeptically. "Or—imagine that!—an electrical substation just *happens* to be at the bottom of the hill that her car skids down? No one else has *any* doubts?"

"What's to doubt?" Fitch retorted. "Trust your eyes— she was at the ID, and the car she was in was incinerated. Seeing is believing, and every one of us got an eyeful."

"Excuse me, Dr. Fitch?" Fitch's other aide, Robert, held up a sealed plastic bag. "We found what looks like a severed thumb."

"How the hell did you manage that?" Press demanded. "There's nothing left of the interior of that car except ashes and smoke!"

"It was jammed in the fireproofing of the driver's door," Robert said. "The door broke off during the crash."

Press's eyes narrowed. "So the car door was open *be-*

fore it hit the substation." He looked hard at Dr. Fitch. "She may not have even *been* in that car, Doc."

"We've already verified the presence of a body." Minjha said. "And you saw her driving the car."

"Let me see the thumb." Laura held out her hand and Minjha dropped the bag onto it, then offered her a penlight from his coat pocket. "That's strange," she murmured. "It looks . . . *pinched* off rather than torn. No ragged edges."

"If you saw the wreckage of the car down there, you'd understand how easily that could have happened," Minjha said. "The miracle is that the thumb didn't burn up with the rest of the body, not that it's a clean cut. Maybe her hand got in the way when the door was torn off."

"Perhaps," Laura said, but she looked troubled as she snapped off the light and handed it and the bag back to Robert. "Have it checked against the computer records to make sure. If it's Sil's thumb, we'll be able to prove it by genetic identification. And be sure to call my room at the hotel tonight to confirm the match," she reminded him sternly. "If I don't hear from you, I'm going to assume the worst." The aide nodded and tucked the plastic pouch into his side pocket.

"Great." Xavier Fitch rubbed his hands together briskly and glanced quickly at each of them. His gaze stopped on Press, then he dug in his pockets for the keys to the van. "Then that'll be it. This job's done, Lennox. Tomorrow you can all go back to your careers and normal lives. Congratulations on a job well done." He turned his back and walked away without another word.

They stood for a few moments without speaking, then Stephen cleared his throat and addressed Laura and Press. "That was a damned harrowing car chase. Are you two all right?"

"Sure," Laura said. "Besides, what could have happened? Jaguar or not, Press and I never came within ten feet of the creature."

Press grinned. "That pretty much sums it up, I think. A hard chase and a few bumps—hell, nothing a good meal and a drink or two won't cure."

"Now there's an idea," Stephen agreed. "We could meet back at the Biltmore, whoop it up a final time." He looked over at Dan. "What do you say, Dan?"

"Me?" Dan had crossed his arms and was still staring oddly after Dr. Fitch. "I'm pretty sure Dr. Fitch thinks we're all assholes and is glad to be rid of us."

While Stephen and Laura gaped at Dan, all Press did was burst into laughter.

36

Returning to Marlo Keegan's house had been much easier than Sil envisioned. The people who hunted her had dropped two firebombs on the stolen Cutlass after it plowed into the substation and exploded, then carelessly destroyed another house with a third one. Between their arrogance at assuming she was still in the car and the resulting chaos from the burning home, Sil had slipped through the surrounding yards and woven her way down the neighboring streets until she was back on Doña Nenita. The Mazda was parked where she'd left it and had cleared of the gasoline fumes since she'd transferred the gas can to the Olds. The drive back to Marlo's home was uneventful.

Remembering one of the commercials she'd seen on television, Sil stopped only once, at a large-chain drugstore. She was in and out of the store in less than ten minutes, resisting the urge to dally in the aisles and examine the strange and colorful merchandise. She paid for her single item with cash from Marlo's wallet.

Now Sil stood naked in front of the bathroom mirror and stared at her reflection. She hadn't been very skilled with the scissors but she had used the photo-

215

graph on the box as a guideline and was nevertheless mildly pleased with the outcome. The shoulder-length blond locks were no more, and the woman in the mirror sported a short, shaggy-ended head of black hair. Tilting her face from side to side, Sil decided she liked it. The image was totally different and worked surprisingly well; the inky color made her skin look shockingly pale and her blue eyes seem overly large and luminescent, like some kind of moon child forever secreted from the sun.

She picked up a comb from the vanity and pulled it through the new, shorter style, then almost dropped it when something in the other room started ringing. Pulse pounding, Sil hurried out of the bathroom and searched until she found the source of the racket, feeling foolish to discover it was only a telephone. She started to return to the bathroom, then stopped when the ringing cut off in midnote and a recording of the dead woman's voice came out of the Phone-Mate, a cream-colored box hooked to the telephone by a couple of wires.

"Hi, this is Marlo. I can't come to the phone right now, but if you'll leave a message, I'll get back to you just as soon as I can. Thanks for calling."

A second later a man's voice floated out of the speaker.

"Hey, sis, how you doing? I'm back in town and thought I'd catch you at home, but I guess I'm too early. Don't forget, we're supposed to go to Century City tomorrow to look for an anniversary present for Mom and Dad. Call me when you get in and let me know what time is good for you, okay? I'll pick you up. Talk to you later."

The last word was followed by a click, then the machine on the dresser made an internal metallic sound and cut off. Silence once again filled Marlo's small bedroom. Who was this person who expected the dead Marlo Keegan to return his call? The voice had said the two had made plans for tomorrow—when Marlo didn't call, would he come here looking for her?

Sil went to the closet and began rummaging through the clothes. No matter; within an hour she'd be gone from this house forever.

♦

The entertainment in the back corner of the Biltmore's Grand Avenue Bar consisted of a three-member band, all very talented and in their early forties. One man played the piano, another had a double-cutaway Gibson ES-335 guitar, and the third member—a middle-aged woman who looked as if she took better care of herself than most females half her age—had a strong, lovely voice that reminded Press vaguely of Barbra Streisand. A nice overall effect, he thought somewhat testily, if you were into soft jazz and hadn't grown up in the 1960s with an ear for good old rock and roll. These days his tastes tended toward the alternative bands with a hard, fast beat. Whatever Press's personal preference, the couples gliding across the parquet dance floor seemed to find the excellently rendered tunes soothing, if not exciting. From the corner of his eye, Press saw Xavier Fitch come into the bar; the doctor noticed the group and hesitated, then chose an empty table on the other side of the room.

"Well," Dan said cheerfully, "I guess we won." He sounded proud, as if they had all orchestrated and seen to flawless completion some massive and complicated military maneuver.

Stephen gave the younger man a tolerant smile and glanced at Laura. She looked very winsome in a snug black dress with a sloping, lace-trimmed neckline. "We won. Science lost." She gave a small, one-shouldered shrug that made her seem more feminine than her answer.

"I didn't think we'd get her this way. Not this easily," Press said. He looked dashing but vaguely stiff in tailored black slacks and a gray suede jacket. Even to his own ears, his voice sounded curt.

Stephen deliberated a moment before responding. "What gives, Press? You sound like you're going to miss her."

Press started to reach in the pocket of his shirt for a toothpick, then remembered what Laura had said earlier about sounding like he had a branch in his mouth. He picked at his fingernails instead. "I . . . had respect for her, that's all. I might not know how she really felt, but I could appreciate the hell of being thrown into a situation you didn't ask for and having to deal with it. I suppose that's why I still don't understand the outcome."

Stephen gave him a comradely clap on the shoulder. "Look," he said as he leaned forward, "this may have been a miserable job, but I still enjoyed working with all of you. We had a great dinner and Uncle Sam's paying for the drinks. Let's oblige that fine old man and start putting this behind us." He raised a hand in the direction of the bar. "Waiter, when you have a chance, we need assistance," he called merrily. "A round of nerve medicine for the table, please!"

"A glass of water will be fine. Or maybe an iced tea," Dan said as the waiter came over to take their order. "I don't drink."

Stephen waved aside Dan's objection. "Don't worry, Dan. Tonight you will. And you've just told me exactly what to order for you." He sent a fetching smile in Laura's direction. "How about for you, Dr. Baker?"

Laura's fingernails tapped thoughtfully against the tabletop, then stopped. "No, thanks," she said finally. She turned her face toward Press. "Would you like to dance?"

Press blinked. "Me?"

"No, silly," Laura teased. "I'm asking your guardian angel." She gave him a comical roll of her eyes.

Press looked flustered for a second, then uncrossed

his feet and stood. "Sure," he said. "Why not?" He offered Laura his arm and glanced apologetically at Stephen, who gave him a sheepish grin and sat back in defeat. On the way to the dance floor, Press and Laura nodded at Dr. Fitch as they passed his table. Concentrating on his drink, the other man saw them but didn't acknowledge the greeting.

Laura stopped on the dance floor, turned, and stepped easily into Press's arms. The number from the band was slow and easy, another soft piece of music that fit perfectly with the extravagant, richly paneled bar, abundant fresh flowers and low lighting. He might not care for the music style, but Press grudgingly admitted to himself that the band knew their market.

"So," Laura said after a while, "do you have family back in the Big Apple?"

Press thought she felt good in his embrace, warm and soft. Holding Laura this close had triggered thoughts of lots of things, none of which had anything to do with family or New York. It took a conscious effort to focus his thoughts and answer her. "Family? Not much. An older sister, that's all. She doesn't live in New York though, and my mom and dad are gone."

"I'm sorry." Laura tilted her head back to look at him. He'd never seen her eyes this close and found them flecked with bits of green. Even her hair was a surprise; the gentle candlelight lamps around the bar revealed strands of strawberry blond among the soft, shining red. "How about a girlfriend?"

There was nothing joking in Press's answer. "They don't hang around very long," he said. "I've got too many secrets."

"Tell me one." When he didn't answer, she gave his hand a gentle squeeze. "I know what you are, Press. And what you do. It doesn't scare me."

He rubbed her thumb with his own, enjoying the tingles of attraction the touch was causing. "You're no ordinary woman."

Laura chuckled and he felt her breath against his jaw; warm and sweet, it smelled like the butter mints in the crystal bowl back at the table. "How did you get into finding people? Were you a police officer?"

For an instant the room shifted out of focus, then Press pushed away the old memories. "No, I was never a cop. My father taught me," he said at last.

"He hunted people down, too? Like you?"

Press shook his head. "No. He *needed* hunting down. My sister used to send me out to find him before my mother did. It saved everybody a lot of grief."

"Where was he all the time that you had to go after him?"

Press gave a careless jerk of his head that didn't fool Laura at all. "Various girlfriends," he answered. "He was a very traditional guy."

"Ah. So you went from there to joining the army," she said, deciding to steer the subject away from family and his less-than-happy recollections.

"It was something to do. I got into finding AWOLs before they got too deep into trouble to get out without ending up in the slammer. People—normal ones, anyway—nearly always follow a pattern. For instance, if they go bowling every Thursday night, they could be halfway around the world, but come Thursday night—"

"They go bowling," Laura finished for him. Her eyes were veiled in the more dimly lit area of the dance floor. "So for all your ability to find people, you haven't done very well for yourself."

He hesitated before answering. "No . . . I guess not."

Laura's face tilted toward his, her lips close and warm and sweet. "I wouldn't want to never see you again, Press."

Laura's voice was softer than he'd ever heard it and she moved more snugly into his embrace. She felt so nice, like she belonged there, and Press was opening his mouth to tell her so when something else caught his attention—a woman he hadn't noticed before, sitting at the bar with her back to the dance floor while she talked animatedly with the young, good-looking bartender. Long and lean, platinum-blond hair spilled down the center of the woman's back and the loose silk top she wore over skintight black leggings did everything to tease the imagination. He'd seen that hair before ... he'd seen that *attitude* before.

Press let go of Laura's shoulder and backstepped, his hand diving into the holster under his jacket to retrieve the SIG-Sauer he preferred to carry in normal circumstances. Laura gawked, then followed as he elbowed his way roughly through the other five or six couples moving slowly across the parquet flooring. With their complaining still burning in his ears, Press grabbed the shoulder of the woman on the barstool and spun her to face him.

"*Freeze!*" he ordered, shoving the barrel of the pistol under her chin.

The woman paralyzed in his grip stared at him with wide, brown eyes the color of chocolate. Her face was round and pixielike, her eyelashes and arched eyebrows several shades darker than her obviously bleached hair. Below an upturned button nose, lips the color of overripe strawberries had formed a circle that silently said *I'm-going-to-scream-any-minute!* Reflex kicked in and the semiauto was holstered and out of sight before she could inhale enough to start. "Hey, now!" Press said as loudly as he could manage. "My mistake! No harm done, just a case of mistaken identity, that's all. Sorry—I apologize."

The couples on the dance floor had stopped in midstep and the bartender's face was scarlet with fury; he looked ready to leap over the counter and pummel Press. Before he could, Press swung an arm around the shaking woman and turned her stool back toward the scrupulously polished bar. "Bartender, the lady's drinks are on me tonight." He flipped out his wallet, pulled out a hundred-dollar bill and tossed it atop the bar.

"Whatever she wants, and buy yourself a couple rounds besides. Keep the change."

"Just a minute, pal," the bartender said hotly. He was leaning on clenched fists. "Your money's big, but that doesn't change the fact that you just pulled a piece on one of my customers. I'm calling the cops."

"It's all right, sir." Before the bartender could reach for his cordless telephone, Laura cut in front of Press and came up with the government identification card that Fitch had given her at the start of the project. "I'm Dr. Laura Baker. This was just an accident, that's all, the result of too much pressure. The young lady does bear a strong resemblance to someone we were hun—ah, looking for."

The blond woman was holding tightly to the rail that ran down the edge of the bar, but starting to recover enough to look angry. "Well, for God's sake," she said shrilly at Press, "next time, whyn't you look first, you freakin' maniac!" She tossed her head defiantly, but there was a glassy, scared look to her eyes that might have been tears. "I need something to calm my nerves. Guy's ruined my whole evening."

"Come on, Press. Let's go." Laura turned him toward the doorway out of the bar and gave him a little push.

"Sorry," he offered again over his shoulder as he led the way. Wincing, he saw that the woman at the bar had turned whiny and now seemed bent on detaining Laura long enough to chew her out for Press's indiscretion.

"My blood pressure's sky-high," she complained as she thrust her hand forward. "Feel my wrist—I bet my pulse is two hundred. I don't feel so good."

Laura obligingly settled her fingers across the woman's wrist and checked the second hand on her wristwatch for a count of six. "Nope," she told the anxious woman, "steady at about ninety-eight. That's pretty good, considering you're consuming alcohol." She touched a finger to her forehead in a parting gesture.

"Thanks for your understanding. Enjoy the free drinks." She tried to scoot away, but Press's mistaken target was still bellyaching.

"But he scared me so *bad*. He could have shot me!" The blonde tossed her hair again. "He's crazy, that's what he is. I could have had a coronary."

Laura shrugged and turned away. "Look at it this way," she said without looking back. She was grinning at Press but she was also a marvelous actress; her voice was unaccountably icy as she walked away. "At least he didn't squeeze the trigger. You *could* be dead." She left the woman with her mouth hanging open.

Unfortunately, Press discovered in the hotel lobby that the grin Laura had sent his way wasn't sincere, either. "What the hell were you doing in there, Press?" she demanded. "You came very close to killing an uninvolved civilian. Is this the kind of top-notch work you do?"

Press was seldom at a loss for words, but she had him on this one. "I—I thought it was Sil. I saw the blond hair, and the way she moved . . . I thought it was her."

"She's *dead*, Press. Remember? We found the severed thumb and the aide left me a message saying it matched genetically. The tests we did proved it was her."

The coldness was back in Laura's voice and it hurt to have it directed at him. And she was making perfect sense, of course . . . except everything in his gut was screaming *No way, it's just too fucking easy.* "You've got your tests," Press said aloud, "and I've got my instinct. Don't you see how the whole thing is so convenient, Laura? This is not a stupid creature. Sil came to the ID because she *wanted* us to chase her, and I think she made it look like she died in that car because she knew that's the only way we'd stop looking for her."

"Fine," Laura snapped. "Now let me tell you what *I* think. *I* think that as long as you believe she's still out there, you've still got your mission. You don't want this job to be over, do you? You want to keep going with it!"

"Maybe you're right," he admitted. Why, he wondered, in a world where people could cross a full day's time zone and talk to each other from different sides of the globe, did getting something across to the person standing right in front of you have to be so damned difficult? "But maybe it's—"

"I have to go to the ladies' room," Laura said abruptly. She whirled and stalked away.

"—not for the reason you think," Press finished lamely.

But he was speaking to empty air.

At first Sil didn't understand what happened to make the dark-haired man pull a weapon on the blond woman at the bar, but it wasn't hard to figure out as she watched his red-haired companion defuse the situation and send him out to the lobby. The blonde who'd been threatened was still griping about it to the bartender when Sil rose and walked casually to the exit. The dye in her hair and the darkness of the hotel lounge had apparently rendered her all but invisible—even to the esteemed Dr. Fitch from the compound. Sil found it absurdly funny that he'd sat not two tables away from her for the past half hour, nursing a drink and catching everyone in the room—including Sil—in his sharp, hawklike gaze at least twice. This was the man whose biochemical makeup had helped make the blueprint for her own, her *father*—she had finally learned the right word—in a roundabout way, yet he never sensed she was fewer than fifteen feet away. So close, and the only emotion Sil saw was when the scene at the bar had brought a sneer to his lips that he'd hid badly behind his glass of Crown Royal.

Sil got to the door of the lobby in time to see the

redheaded woman stride away without listening to the remainder of what the dark-haired man was saying. After a few seconds he started back for the lounge and Sil did a half turn that put her face in the shadows as he passed. She didn't want to approach him for the first time in the bar with the rest of his group—the same people who had joined with him in the effort to destroy her. Alone, he probably wouldn't recognize her, but to face all five of them at once was sheer stupidity. That dark-skinned one, especially; there was something ... *peculiar* about him that no matter how she tried, Sil couldn't identify. A foolish decision unavoidably made without enough forethought: she should have killed him in back of the ID when she'd had the chance.

Slipping back into the lobby, Sil left the dark-haired man and his two male companions behind with the solitary Dr. Fitch. The redhead had gone into the ladies' room across the lobby and Sil headed that way, smiling to herself at the ridiculous thought that entered her head.

Of all places, it seemed she was destined to always take care of the competition in the washroom.

◆

"Hi, guys," Press said. Between the fuckup at the bar and Laura storming off, he felt like an ass all the way around. "Mind if I join you?"

"That's a dumb question and you know it." Stephen waved at one of the empty chairs. "Don't sit on anyone's lap while you're at it—although that *does* sound like more fun." He grinned at his own humor.

Without warning, Dan reached over and patted Press's hand, as if he were comforting a young boy. "Don't worry, Press. She still likes you, I'm sure. I wish somebody would like me *half* that much. That would really be something." Press felt his face redden and was saved by the arrival of the waiter with drinks for

Stephen and Dan. "What do you call this?" Dan asked, dubiously eyeing the extra-tall glass in front of him.

Stephen beamed at him. "You wanted iced tea, I ordered you the next better thing. Try it—it's a Long Island Iced Tea."

"Has it got any tea in it?" Dan held up the frosted glass and shook it, as if he could see the liquid through the glazed exterior. "I was going to ask for decaffeinated so I wouldn't have trouble sleeping."

Press and Stephen both chuckled. "Trust me," Stephen assured Dan, "you won't be worrying about sleep after one of those."

Dan shot him a final look over the rim of the glass and took a long sip through the double straw, then another. "Hey!" he said in surprise. "This tastes *great!*"

Press started to question the wisdom of drinking it too fast, then realized he was too late; the whole blasted glass was already empty.

♦

This rest room was bigger and cleaner, a lot fancier than the one back at the nightclub. Pastel floral wallpaper covered the bottom half of the outer sitting-room area, stopping at a white-painted Victorian chair rail that ran along three of the four walls. A settee and several chairs were scattered around the small room, while above the chair rail was a narrow ledge built to hold purses, toiletries and ashtrays. The fourth wall was covered in bamboo-textured paper and divided by the two doors, one leading into the sitting room from the lobby and the other leading into the toilet area from the sitting room. The three walls above the ledge were solid mirrors, and it was at the middle one of these that the redhead stood. Unnoticed in the doorway, Sil watched as the woman—her rival—sprayed herself lightly from a small bottle of cologne, then plucked a tissue from a nearby box and blotted carefully at the corners of her eyes.

Stepping nonchalantly next to the woman, Sil inhaled. The perfume the redhead had sprayed on herself was unnaturally sweet, but light and inoffensive. It masked the clean, more natural scent of her body and Sil wondered suddenly if spraying yourself with something like this made you seem more attractive to a potential mate.

"I—may I help you?"

She was standing too close to the redhead and had inadvertently made her uncomfortable. Sil took a step back. "Your fragrance," she said, thinking quickly, "it smells so lovely. May I try some?"

"Sure." The woman bent her head and dug into her pocketbook. "Just a sec, I just dropped it in—here you go." She held out the tiny bottle and Sil took it from her palm. "It's Shalimar. Cologne, not perfume, so it won't be too strong. You can be generous."

Sil had no idea what all that meant but she aimed the nozzle at her neck as she had seen the redhead do and gave it two short pushes. Sweet scent swirled around her, settling on her skin and clothes, coating the insides of her nostrils. Sil handed the bottle back to the woman and watched as she dropped it into her purse. "Does it work?" Sil asked. "On your boyfriend?"

The redheaded woman's eyes slid away from Sil's face and found her own reflection. Staring at herself, the woman's gaze seemed suddenly remote, and when she spoke, her voice was clipped. "I don't have a boyfriend."

Sil didn't believe her and didn't bother answering. Instead, she closed the distance between her and the redhead. Lips pulling back, she reached for her adversary, feeling the ends of her fingers start to contort—

Behind her, the door to the rest room flew open hard enough to bang against the wall behind it. Sil made a garbled sound into her hands that she hoped resembled a cough and twisted past the redhead as the woman picked up her handbag and moved away from the mir-

ror. Sil remembered seeing the three women who entered the rest room at a table near the dance floor
earlier in the Grand Avenue Bar. Laughing, two of
them flopped onto chairs in the sitting area while the
third one ducked into a stall in the other room. Grit-
ting her teeth, Sil saw her chance to eliminate the redhead slip away . . . for now.

♦

Leaving Press to sit at the table with a morose look on
his face, Stephen wound his way through the light
crowd and went to the bar for a couple more drinks for
him and Dan. When Stephen had left the table, Press's
Grolsch still sat untouched, condensation dribbling
down its side. Glancing back to see Press staring at—
through—his beer bottle, he decided Press was taking
the whole thing with Laura way too seriously. Granted,
the woman was lovely and intelligent . . . brave and
composed, too, considering some of the things they'd
seen over the last few days. But in a couple of hours she
would head back to her home in the Simi Valley and
Press would be flying back to the East Coast. What had
Press hoped for, anyway? Stephen had been involved in
a number of long-distance romances in his college days,
none of which had worked out and several of which
had turned out to be a royal pain in the ass. With the
width of a country to separate them, the enchantment
was doomed to dwindle rapidly.

Stephen paid the bartender, picked up another two
Long Island Iced Teas, and started back to where Dan
was watching him from the table. Skirting the edge of
the dance floor, he saw the prettiest woman besides
Laura he'd seen all evening. Tall, with shapely legs
showing beneath a floral, earth-toned blouse and miniskirt, she had short black hair and crystalline blue eyes
that met his gaze without flinching and didn't look
away. Aggressive women did not intimidate him—in
fact, he preferred a lady friend to be confident and

more than a little assertive ... especially in certain areas. Brashly he held up the frosted Long Island Iced Tea in a gesture of invitation. When her eye contact broke and she disappeared into the crowd, he dismissed it with a muttered, "Oh well, her loss."

At the table, Press had finally started working on his beer and Dan reached eagerly for the glass Stephen offered. "Yum," he said as he sucked a generous amount through the straw. "I like these!"

"Better be careful how fast you drink 'em," Press warned. "They can go to your head pretty quick."

"Like Laura?" Stephen quipped. "Hey—there she is. Maybe you can talk her into rejoining us."

Press followed the nod of Stephen's head to where Laura was standing uncertainly in the doorway. With a contrite expression, he signaled her, trying to get her to join them. She looked undecided, then she shook her head and made a motion with her hand that told them she was going to bed. With a final wave of her fingers, she headed out of the bar.

Stephen watched as Press's mouth went into an "I screwed up" downward twist and the other man picked up his beer bottle and drained it. "What was all that commotion at the bar?" he asked after Press was finished swallowing.

Press picked the bottle up again and turned it thoughtfully, then began to pick at the label. "A ... mistake," he eventually answered. "I thought the woman was Sil."

"Sil?" Stephen looked surprised. "I thought we were past that business. I mean, the creature's dead and we're all heading home tomorrow morning, right?"

"Sure," Press said agreeably. "The lady just looked so much like her from the back that I freaked a little, that's all. Everybody makes mistakes."

Stephen started to say something about how that could be dangerous in Press's line of work, then decided that would be pretty tactless. "And Laura got upset?" he asked instead.

Pressed nodded. "I guess I freaked her out, too." He looked around for the waiter. "Maybe I'll get another Grolsch."

"Are you going to take it with you?" Dan asked, startling both Stephen and Press. The empath had thankfully stopped guzzling his drink at about the midpoint of the glass.

Press glanced quizzically at Stephen and the professor shrugged. "Beats me."

"Am I . . . going somewhere?" Press squinted at Dan, but he looked steadily back, unruffled.

"Laura's room, of course."

"Of course," Press repeated.

"Well," Dan said, "she might be off to bed, but she still wants to see you."

Press deliberated over this for a moment, then pushed the empty bottle aside with finality and stood. He gave his jacket a quick check to make sure he looked presentable. "Hell's bells," he said with a small smile. "Why didn't I think of that?"

♦

Sil waited until the door to the elevator was halfway closed, then waved her hand through the opening, trying to trigger the laser switch that would reopen it. The dark-haired man was inside and she got a glimpse of him pressing the door open button while she stepped in. "Thanks," she said.

He nodded, then tapped 9. "What floor?"

She hesitated, then went for a higher number. "Ten, please." He didn't say anything else as the floors began to click past and she could feel the desperation building inside her. What now? This was the mate she'd sought so desperately, but he would also kill her if he knew who she was. Emotions warred inside her—desire, anxiety, and most of all, fear. The man standing only three

feet away had all the qualities she wanted for her offspring, but he was as unreachable as if he were on the
other side of the world.

Something—a rough spot on the oiled cable,
perhaps—made the elevator vibrate slightly, sparking
an idea in her mind for conversation. "I'd hate to be in
one of these things during an earthquake, wouldn't
you?"

He nodded again, more solemnly. "Boy, that's a fact."
Watching him discreetly, she saw his nostrils flare as he
inhaled, saw vague recognition flash across his features.
"Nice perfume," he said. "I like it."

"You do?" Ah, she thought, a chink in the wall. At
last. She gave him her brightest smile. "My name's
Nicole."

"Press Lennox." His gaze slipped back to the floor indicator.

"Are you new in town?" Sil asked quickly. "I haven't
been here very long."

He chuckled. "I'm so new, it's not even my town. As
a matter of fact, I'm headed back to New York tomorrow." Sil started to say something more but the elevator
stopped with a small bounce and the doors slid silently
open. "Excuse me," he said, stepping around her. "This
is my floor. Enjoy your stay."

Disappointed and unable to think of anything else to
say, Sil nodded and watched him go. At the last instant, her finger found the door open button and
pushed it firmly.

◆

What am I doing here? Press wondered. Despite Dan's
recommendation, he could think of no good reason
why Laura would want to see him, and a dozen why she
wouldn't. Better judgment be damned, he knocked on
her door anyway, half expecting her to ignore the
sound. She could be sleeping, she could be in the
shower—

"Who is it?"

"It's . . . me," he said in a low voice. "Press."

"I know who *me* is," she said wryly as she opened the door and waved him inside.

Press stepped through the doorway into a room pretty much like his own but a little more floral, as if someone at the registration desk had taken the time to realize that this should be a room for a woman. The lighting was softer and vaguely romantic. Laura crossed her arms and stared at him, waiting.

"What is it, Press?" she finally asked.

He opened his mouth and shut it again. "I'm . . . sorry," he said at last. "I didn't mean to act like an ass in the bar. Sometimes I get so wrapped up in things, I can't let go."

She uncrossed her arms and held out her hands, palms up. "Some things are good to let go, you know?"

Press wasn't about to pass up the opportunity to take her by the hands, then step closer. She smelled so good, like the woman on the elevator. Correction: this was how Laura *always* smelled—that was what that dark-headed woman had reminded him of. He was close enough to pull Laura's arms up so that they clasped him around the neck, and she didn't pull away when his arms slid to either side of her small waist.

"But some things shouldn't be let go of right away," she said softly.

Laura's face was tilted up to his. Her eyes were big and an incredible midnight blue above coral-brushed lips that looked soft and inviting. Before he could have second thoughts, he dipped his head forward and covered her mouth with his.

She responded without hesitating and a jolt of electricity shot through him. For a second Press felt like all the air had been sucked out of him, then it all came back in a rush as Laura's tongue explored his mouth. She pulled back, then nuzzled at his neck. "Mating is dangerous," she murmured with her lips pressed against his skin. He was holding her very tightly now, feeling her hands run over the muscles of his back and leave lingering washes of heat as they passed, like a hot tide of oil. "A kiss is assurance that neither party will bite."

She nipped at his neck again and he sunk his fingers into that gorgeous head of red hair; it felt like strands of silk. "What's wrong with biting?" he asked hoarsely. He tried to kiss her again but she licked at his lips and ducked her head, rubbing her cheek against his. The movement of her softer skin against the tiny stubble on his face made a quiet rasping sound that was oddly erotic.

"Nothing at all," she answered, "as long as the teeth and mouth are used in a nonaggressive way." Chest to chest, he was still gripping her waist and now she slid her hands over his and pulled them free, then brought them around and between them. She gave each palm a light kiss, then deliberately settled them on her breasts. His gasp of surprise was simultaneous with her sigh of pleasure. "Most men try to skip this," she told him breathlessly. "They don't know it, but seduction is their greatest weapon."

"Weapon for what?" Press asked. He felt her start to move forward and went with her, loath to lose the feel of her body against his. Something collided with the back of his calves—the side of the bed—and he bent his knees and sat. Laura followed his downward motion and kept going, pushing until he was on his back and gazing up at her.

"To conquer," she answered. He lifted himself obligingly as she tugged his jacket off. Press thought for a second that the side-holstered SIG-Sauer might spoil the mood, but she only waited patiently as he slipped it off and lowered it to the floor. Then her fine hands were stroking his chest and arms again, slipping inside the fabric of his shirt to feather warmth across his chest. His hands reached to hold her and discovered a zipper running down the back of the enticing black dress. He fought the urge to pull it all the way down as she stretched out next to him, then snuggled closer. Instead, he inched it open, enjoying his own anticipation as much as hers.

"I always thought the woman conquered the man," Press said in a husky voice. "Now you're saying that men conquer women?"

"Both." Her fingernails dragged lightly down his side, then glided along the line of his belt, just far enough inside it to be alluring. She followed the belt around to the front button of his slacks, paused for a heart-stopping second, then moved on. "To conquer," she continued, "the female willingly surrenders. A woman tests and selects, then tries to convince a potential mate to make a commitment. A man, on the other hand, must seduce."

Their mouths met for a deep, fiery kiss as the zipper yielded enough for Press to slip the dress down around Laura's shoulders. The skin along her collarbones was creamy pink and lovely, sprinkled with a thousand pale freckles. He wanted to touch every one of them with his tongue. "Did I pass the test?" he managed.

As the dark fabric fell away completely, Laura's ocean-blue eyes sparkled at him above her smile.

"Ask me again in an hour."

38

Stephen tapped Dan on the arm. "How about those two over there?" He pointed to a couple of women a few tables over. Nicely dressed in tailored business suits, they each had a drink in front of them and were deeply engaged in conversation. "I bet they'll like unusual guys like us. Let's go talk to them."

Dan shook his head and looked at Stephen as if he'd grown an extra nose all of a sudden. "Forget it," he said. "Women *always* think I'm weird, and I *always* know it."

"Nonsense," Stephen said briskly. "Come on—let's go have a chat. They look far too intelligent to be that shallow." He got up but Dan stubbornly stayed where he was; after a second Stephen shrugged and walked over to the other table by himself. "Good evening, ladies. My friend over there—" He started to point back at the table, then realized Dan *had* gotten up and followed him. "Uh, right *here*—wants to know what two, interesting, glamorous-looking women like you are doing without a chaperone?"

"Excuse me," Dan said, "but I don't think—"

"My friend Dan Smithson," Stephen said with a flourish. "And I'm Stephen Arden. We—"

"I don't feel right in here, Stephen," Dan interrupted. His gaze started flicking erratically around the room. "Something's wrong."

Stephen didn't know whether to be impatient with Dan or just flustered. "Come on, Dan. Don't be afraid—we're doing just fine here. These women are very nice. One of them even said she was attracted to you." The two businesswomen shot each other an amused glance, but said nothing.

"Somehow I doubt that," Dan said firmly, "but good try, Dr. Arden. I have to go, and I wish you'd come with me."

"No thanks. I'm going to stay around the bar for a while." Stephen smiled engagingly down at the women.

"Okay." Dan turned away. "See you tomorrow."

"Good night, Dan. Sleep well." As Dan walked away Stephen turned his full attention on the women. "So," he said, "I teach at Harvard University. Comparative anthropology." If anything would get him an invitation to join them, the college-professor thing was it—it always worked. Both women were brunettes, with only a year or two difference in their ages. It would be a hard choice, but life was full of choices, wasn't it?

"I lived in Boston once," the prettier of the two said. "For a year. Froze my butt off, too." She scooted her chair to the side and Stephen smiled to himself. All he needed was another chair—

"Here's another screwdriver, sweetheart," said a male voice from behind him.

Stephen's stomach gave a hard flop, but he was proud of himself for the smooth and expressionless way he made it look like he was leaving anyway when their boyfriends came back with a fresh round of drinks.

◆

Sil had seen which door the dark-haired man entered, but the sound of the elevator opening had frightened her enough to make her duck into the vending-machine service room. A good thing, too; as she stooped in front of the ice machine, the dark-skinned man she'd confronted behind the ID passed in the hallway. Would he have recognized her? She wasn't sure, but instinct told her not to take the chance; something wasn't right about him and how he related to her. Deciding it was best to avoid him, Sil stayed put until she heard a door open and shut.

Finally the hallway returned to silence and she stepped out of the service area. Glancing cautiously around, she walked quickly to the fourth door on the left, the one she'd seen her quarry enter. But when she put her hand on the doorknob and started to turn it, Sil froze. Sounds drifted through the varnished wood, breathy and barely distinguishable. The sounds of—

With a black scowl on her face, Sil moved to the next door over and put her ear to the wood. Nothing moved inside, but when she tried the knob on this one, it was also locked. Wrapping her fingers around the brass knob, she tugged it experimentally, gauging its resistance. She could easily break it—

"Did you lose your card key, ma'am?"

"What!" Sil's head whipped around. One of the ninth floor's housekeepers stood not three feet away, watching her curiously. "Oh—yes, I did." Card key? There was a little box above the doorknob with a slot across it and red-and-green lights below it—that must be what the woman was talking about. Sil still had the Keegan woman's pocketbook and now she pretended to dig through it. "It's so *little*." She tried to sound exasperated.

"Here," the woman responded in a conciliatory voice, "I'll let you in. You could spend all night trying to find it. Be sure to call the front desk right away and tell them you need a replacement."

"Thank you," Sil said, relieved.

The housekeeper stepped forward and used a master key from a ring in her pocket to open the door, then waved her in. The housekeeper stopped the door before it could fully shut behind Sil. "Just one thing," she said.

Sil's eyes narrowed dangerously. "What's that?"

"When you fill out your comment card—you know, the one in your guest packet? You might mention that Lee Anna helped you out. You know, in response to question number eight."

"Lee Anna," Sil repeated. "Of course. I sure will." She had no idea what the housekeeper was talking about, but the woman nodded her appreciation and pulled the door closed. As Sil glanced around, her teeth ground together in frustration when she saw that there was no adjoining door to the room the dark-haired man had entered. Separated by a wall, she could sense his presence when she pressed against it, almost *smell* his male scent through the wallboard and paper. There was something else, too, the sounds that had nearly made her break through the door in the hallway.

The sounds of mating.

Sighs, whispers, the sweetness of flesh against flesh. Sil could recognize the dark-headed man's voice as he murmured, knew the tone of the redhead's as she replied. The *redhead*—she should have killed her in the ladies' room when she'd had the chance. Now she had stolen Sil's mate and Sil might never get him back.

The sounds of pleasure from the other side of the wall increased and Sil felt heat and desire flush her own body in unintentional response. Pressing herself against the wall, she could imagine what his hands on her would feel like, what it would be like to touch him, stroke his skin, *have* him. She *needed* that man, more than the woman in there, more than anyone else. Jealousy ran through her in physically painful streaks and her hands ran down the satiny wallpaper, unconsciously forming claws. She would go in there, she thought wildly, and kill the woman and claim the man who should have been *her* partner. He would see her strength and appreciate her desire, he would—

Something *clacked*! behind her—the door lock—and she whirled, her breath coming in short gasps. Her gaze tripped hastily around the room, but there was no other way out. Trapped, she waited anxiously as the door opened and closed and she found herself facing a different man from Dr. Fitch's group, the one who had offered her a drink in the bar downstairs and whom she had rejected.

"Hey," he said with a frown, "how'd you get in here?"

"The maid," Sil said. The story formed in her mind so quickly she didn't even pause. "She was in here checking your room, so I acted like it was my own and walked in." He stared at her and she knew he was debating whether or not to believe her lie. He was, she saw, a handsome man, too. Not as resourceful or bold as the other, he was here and available and would nevertheless make a suitable substitute.

"I remember you from the bar," he said doubtfully. "It's damned strange to have you blow me off there, then show up in my room."

"I'm sorry I didn't take you up on the drink downstairs," she continued quickly. She let her eyes drop demurely for a moment, then met his gaze again. "You were with all your friends, and I don't . . . do well around a lot of people." Sil gave him a lazy, sexy smile. "But I do much better one-on-one. My name's Nicole. What's yours?"

He seemed to relax a little, dropping his card key on the dresser and coming closer. "Stephen, Stephen Arden. So"—he tilted his head quizzically—"Nicole—what can I do for you?"

"Actually, I . . ." Sil glanced around again to assure herself that everything was okay, then stepped as close to Stephen as she could without physically touching him. "I'd really like to . . . you know. Get to know you better." She reached out a finger and played with the tip of his shirt collar, but held herself back from anything more.

"Really? Me?" Stephen's cheeks went red and he looked incredulous, but his responsive smile was beaming. "Well, hey—that's great! How about a couple of drinks? Or maybe you're hungry—I could get room service—"

"No, no," she cut him off. "When I said I wanted to get to know you better, I meant now." She slid her hands down her chest, over her breasts, then up and under her blouse, slowly pulling it over her head. "I want you," she whispered unexpectedly. "All of you. Right *now*."

Stephen's mouth dropped open, then his hands began groping for the buttons on his shirt. "Jesus," he said in awe. "This kind of stuff *never* happens to me!"

Sil tugged at her skirt until it slid over her thighs and dropped around her ankles. She stepped out of it and kicked it away, standing before him in nothing but lace-and-silk panties and black patent-leather high heels. "I want you *now*," she purred.

She opened her arms and he didn't need another invitation. He was all over her, hands everywhere on her bare skin. She arched to meet him, finding the buttons on his shirt where he was too slow and ripping them open to feel his warm skin against hers. They bumped lightly against the dresser, then the wall, finally found the bed and tumbled onto it. She didn't need foreplay or the flowers and wine and diamonds she'd seen on the television and in the magazines; she was ready *now* and by all appearances, so was Stephen. His shoes and socks were gone by the time they got to the king-size bed, and he couldn't wait to get his slacks off, moaning when she tugged his briefs past his hips and fondled him. His skin was smooth and covered in fine black hair that felt soft and sensual against her skin. His mouth and lips were everywhere, until she couldn't take it any longer and straddled him on top of the deep green bedspread. A quick yank and the black bikini she wore went sailing onto the floor, revealing a patch of body hair more than a few shades lighter than the black-dyed hair of her head. Stephen never noticed.

"Wait!" he gasped as she started to lower herself onto him. His hands gripped her upper arms. "What about protection?"

Protection? From what? Sil ignored his question and shrugged free of his hold, then dipped forward to kiss him. Her breasts brushed the muscles of his chest as she drew her nails deliciously up his thighs, feeling the coarser growth of leg hair scrape along the pads of her fingers.

"Nicole, we shou—*oh, Jesus!*"

She slid onto his body anyway, and the two of them cried out in unison as they began to move against each other.

♦

Dan's mind wasn't really focused on the television until he saw a reed-thin model with platinum hair who looked like Twiggy in an obscure sort of way do a computer-aided swirl and come around to face the camera with black hair instead of blond. Geez, he thought as the television shots flashed by and the commercial's music blasted through the inadequate speaker in the television, now she looks like Liza Minelli.

He'd tossed the remote at the foot of the bed and now he searched for it and hit the mute button, wanting silence but unable to bear nothing at all. He pulled himself upright and swung his legs over the side of the bed. It was a damned nice room, a lot better than anything he'd ever stayed in, and in a way it was too bad the job was over and they were all going home tomorrow. He liked his teammates, Laura, Stephen, especially Press. Dr. Fitch . . . well, Dan felt terrible for him. The man had let himself become so involved with his work that he'd lost touch with the rest of the world and could no longer make or keep friends. There were things Dr. Fitch wanted that he would never get—a wife and family, love and companionship—all because of his single-minded devotion to science. Dan could feel need radiating from the man every time he was close to him, but there was nothing to be done about it. Sil, made with Fitch's chromosomes, had been the daughter he'd never fathered and never would. She had filled that need for a short—*very* short—time, and now that she was dead, Dr. Fitch's hopes and dreams had shattered and his heart had become an empty black hole into which Dan dared not sink too far.

Stephen Arden was another matter. Successful and good-looking on the surface, the ladies loved him most of the time. But they never *stayed*, and that's what he needed most in his life, even if he didn't—or wouldn't—realize it. Stability, someone on whom he could depend beyond a single night of ecstasy . . . he unknowingly drove away his more suitable female colleagues by fawning attention on the front-row airheads who giggled over him during his lectures. No wonder he had been so bewitched by Dr. Baker.

The most well-rounded of them all, she was a saner, younger version of Dr. Fitch. She didn't know it, but if she wasn't careful, she could end up just like the doctor.

And Press—

Press could change things for both Dr. Baker and himself, if he'd only try. Another solitary man filled with bleakness, and pain, too, from emotional wounds so far back in his childhood that they were only shadows of misery now.

For some reason, the emotions tonight were too much for Dan and he stood on wobbly legs and went into the bathroom. He felt surrounded by loneliness, nearly suffocated. And something else was nagging at him, like a word on the tip of his tongue that drove him crazy as he struggled to remember. He tried but couldn't find it, not yet.

At the sink he adjusted the flow from the faucet to lukewarm, then lowered his head and splashed his face. Cold water was too much of a shock and Dan never used it—wouldn't even drink it, much less put his hands under it. As he raised his face to the mirror, the sheen of water on his skin under the fluorescent fixture made his dark skin look eerily light, almost Caucasian, but when he grabbed a hand towel and rubbed his roughening cheeks, the illusion disappeared. He grinned at his reflection, his teeth white and strong below tired, bloodshot eyes. Can't hold that trick for long, he thought. Even if I dyed my hair like on that commercial, it wouldn't work for very—

Dan's mouth dropped open.

Blond hair, black hair.

A flash memory of a tall, exquisite woman with platinum hair in the back passageway of the ID, her eyes the color of tropical water in the sunlight.

Another memory, a glimpse across the bar as Professor Arden offered a Long Island Iced Tea to a woman with a dark, shaggy haircut that reminded him, outlandishly, of the woman in that commercial.

Blond hair. . .

Black.

Sil!

39

Someone was in the room with Professor Arden.

With a sinking feeling in his gut, Dan stood outside the door. Nobody inside was trying to be discreet, and the sounds finding their way through the barrier were explicit enough for Dan to know that if he knocked, he'd probably be ignored. If Press was in his room, he wasn't answering either. That left Dr. Baker or Dr. Fitch; Dr. Fitch had a private suite on another floor and Dan didn't think he wanted to face the scientist with what he was thinking. His mind made up, Dan strolled one door over and knocked on the door to Dr. Baker's room.

"Dr. Baker—Laura? It's Dan." He knocked again. "Please open the door." He heard movement, finally, and gave it a few seconds before rapping on the wood again. "Laura, please—it's urgent! I really need to talk to you." His knuckles were starting to feel bruised.

Laura's voice came through the door. "Hang on a minute, Dan."

Relieved, Dan waited. About thirty seconds later the door was jerked inward and he stared straight into Press's face. Trying not to look annoyed, Press was struggling to pull on his shirt while behind him stood Laura, fastening the tie belt on one of the Biltmore's plush terry-cloth bathrobes.

"Press—I–I'm sorry!" Dan exclaimed. "I went to your room, but you weren't there." Dan shuffled his feet, feeling like an idiot. Under ordinary circumstances he wouldn't have been surprised—hadn't he told Press that Laura was waiting for him? But tonight his mind was all mucked up with theories about Sil and an overload of strong emotions from the rest of his team. No wonder it had taken so long for him to slip what he had seen in the lounge into place.

"Well, I wasn't there," Press said dryly. "What's the problem?"

Dan opened and closed his mouth several times before he figured out how to start. "I've just had this terrible *feeling*, all evening—"

"The whole time?" Laura asked over Press's shoulder. Her face was flushed but her eyes were keen. "Even in the bar?"

"Later," Dan admitted. Standing in the hallway gave him the inexplicable sensation of vulnerability, but he was too embarrassed to step through the door into Laura's room. "I was in my room, lying down with the television turned on. Channel surfing, that's all. Then I saw this commercial, combined with how I'd started feeling downstairs, and I realized that nothing is . . . damn it! I don't know how to explain it. Nothing is *right*." He looked at them both, his eyes wide. "I think—I think Sil is alive. I think she's *here*."

"A commercial made you think this?" Press looked nonplussed.

"It was something about hair dye. You know the hype—blond today, brunette tomorrow, that stuff. The thing is, I thought I saw a woman in the bar who looked familiar, and I remember seeing Dr. Arden offer her a drink."

"Did she take it?" Laura demanded. She looked completely alert now, already moving to find her regular clothes. "Did she talk to him?"

Dan shook his head, then had to step partway into the room to be heard because both Laura and Press were going for their things. While Press shoved his feet into his shoes, Laura scooped a pair of jeans and a white shirt from an upholstered chair and hurried to the bathroom. "No, not then. She ignored him. But that was a while ago, and the commercial got me so upset that I went to Dr. Arden's room. There was somebody in there with him."

Press looked up sharply from the task of lacing a black-and-army-green pair of running shoes. "Did you knock?"

"No." Dan twisted his fingers together nervously. "I was too scared. There was a lot of noise—you could hear it, hear *them*, doing . . . you know." He looked terrified. "I'm telling you, Press. I think he's with Sil and he just doesn't know it."

Laura came out of the bathroom, a pair of Nikes in her hand. "Did they sound like they were having sex?" Her face was white.

Dan nodded and Press snatched up the telephone. "Give me Xavier Fitch's room," he barked into the receiver while yanking the SIG-Sauer's holster over his arm. "And keep it ringing until he picks it up!" He glanced at Laura.

"I'm ready," she said simply.

He started to say something to her and Dan, then turned his attention to the phone instead. "Fitch," he snapped, "Sil is alive. Get down to Arden's room on the ninth floor, *now*."

He didn't bother to say good-bye.

◆

"That was fabulous, Nicole," Stephen whispered in her ear. "I enjoyed it immensely. How about you?"

Sil was on her side, her mate's hard body curled behind hers spoon fashion. One of his arms supported his dark head on a pillow and the other had slipped around her waist to hug her to him. "Mmm," was all she needed as a response, and she could tell by the way he hugged her that he understood. She'd thought it was incredible—the mating, the desire, the orgasm, *Stephen*. Everything she'd dreamed of and beyond—so far, the pinnacle of her short life.

Sil slipped out of his grasp and rolled over. She had so much to tell him that she didn't know where to start. Stephen smiled when she faced him, his eyes so dark and sultry and mirroring all the wonderful emotions raging inside her. How to start?

With something truly magnificent, of course.

♦

"What the hell is this all about, Lennox?" Dr. Fitch growled. "Your overworked imagination again?" Fitch's close-cropped hair was mashed flat on one side, evidence that he'd already been in bed. He was awake enough but he'd never looked as disheveled as he did now.

"It me, Dr. Fitch," Dan offered. "I'm the one who got everybody together."

Fitch looked around. "Where's Arden? Inside?"

"Yeah." Press's mouth was a grim slash. "And Dan seems to think he's got your little creature in there with him but doesn't know it."

"*What!*"

"I think she dyed her hair, Dr. Fitch." Dan's voice was urgent. "Plus, I'm sure Stephen was trying to talk to her in the bar when he didn't realize who it was—"

"And now he won't answer," Laura finished for him.

"Break the damned thing down," Fitch ordered. "If that doesn't work, then shoot the lock. Just get it open."

"Christ," Press said. Inspecting the door, he backed

up as far as he could, until he bumped into the wall behind him. "Dan, I hope to hell you haven't got this wrong."

◆

"Don't answer it," Sil murmured. "I have something wonderful to tell you." The hammering on the door came again, and this time she thought she heard Press's voice calling out.

"I really should answer him," Stephen said. "It could be important."

"I felt it, you know." She looked at him with wide-eyed marvel.

"Felt what?"

Sil looked away, feeling dreamy and drowsy, like she could sleep for a week if she could just find a safe place to do it. "It's started."

"What's started?" Baffled by her words, Stephen had temporarily forgotten about the knocking at the door.

The corners of her mouth turned up in a small, sweet smile. "Life," she whispered, and pointed to the sleek, fair skin of her belly. "In here."

Stephen gave her an affectionate glance and reached to caress her face, his gentle hands running down her jawline to her neck, and beyond. "Darling," he said indulgently, "there are many cultures in which the women claim they know the exact moment of conception, but it's basically only superstition. The likelihood of this happening the first time we met and made love . . . well, it's—"

"You don't believe me," Sil said indignantly. He opened his mouth to reply but she touched a finger to his lips to stop him. "Then feel for yourself." She took his hand and pressed it flat against her abdomen.

His hand looked large and rough across the concave span of her stomach, but his tolerant expression disappeared when something pulsed beneath his fingers. A second later the movement came again, and this time the surface of the skin visibly rippled as the life growing within her began to swell enough to expand the walls of her abdomen. Stephen yanked his hand away and his throat worked as he tried to speak. The best he could choke out was "Holy *shit!*" as he scrambled off the bed and as far away from her as he could get. "What *are* you—oh no, oh my *God!*" Standing at the side of the bed, he took a couple of jerky steps backward as he stared at her with eyes bulging with recognition.

Something crashed into the hallway door, startling them both. Sil was off the bed in an instant, her lips pulling back over her teeth in fear. Lennox was trying to kick in the door; so far it held, but it wouldn't the next time. Disappointed by Stephen's reaction and rejection, trapped in this room with no avenue of escape, she felt her human countenance slip away and dissipate entirely. The feeling was almost like falling and she went with it, relishing the split second of free-fall as her flesh and bone structure instantaneously re-formed, the surge of raw power that felt much more natural than the previous fragile camouflage of humanity. Stephen began to scream and Sil swung to face him, irritated at the harsh, repetitive noise; it only took a flick of her long, beautiful tentacles to end it for eternity.

The door to Stephen's room gave way as it was struck again, and Press Lennox and his comrades spilled through. Press led the way, fighting to regain his balance after the assault on the door, the rest tumbling over each other at his back. Before they could compose themselves, Sil drew herself up to her full height and shrieked at them, her voice loud and high enough to make their hands automatically slap over their ears and make their eyes water. She would not endanger her unborn offspring by plowing through them physically— there was too much danger that one of their weapons might accidentally find its mark. She chose the closet instead, not caring that the entire group saw her dive into the small, dark space.

And, laughing in her piercing, alien voice, she burst through its far wall into the outside hallway and fled . . .

To freedom.

40

"Don't bother checking," Laura said. Her mouth twisted. "He's dead." Fitch turned away with a sick sound and left Dan, standing there with his hands over his mouth.

"Come on, Laura. We've got to stop that thing." Press grabbed her by the arm and pulled her away from the twisted, bloody thing that had been Stephen Arden only a minute before. As they raced down the hallway they saw Sil far ahead, her oversized body skidding on the loose carpet runner as she turned into the fire stairwell. "We're heading to the basement," he yelled over his shoulder to Fitch and Dan. "You guys get in the stairwell and drive her all the way down. The fire door should trap her at the bottom—just be careful!" The elevator doors opened and they leaped through; Press was punching the close door and Parking 1 buttons before the doors had completed their cycle. They saw Fitch and Dan sprint past on their way to the stairwell; Fitch's pistol was out, but Press had to wonder if he'd have the gall to actually use the weapon. "Come on, come on!" Press slapped at the Parking 1 button again, and finally the car began to move.

Press's face was furious. His gaze was glued to the floor indicator as the elevator descended. "What are the chances she got pregnant, anyway?" he said, half thinking aloud. The small elevator magnified his voice, making it sound more frantic than it already was. "But in case she is, we've *got* to get to her before she gives birth. I mean, we can't have two of those things running around out there, right?"

Laura laughed a little hysterically. "Two? Are you kidding, Press? Who *knows* what kind of a reproductive system she has. She could have a dozen children . . . or lay a *thousand* eggs!"

"Then we'll find every one of them and fry them," Press said rigidly. He started to say something more but the elevator bounced lightly and the doors slid open to reveal a concrete underground parking lot. Fluorescent lights buzzed overhead, throwing lighting that was more than adequate in normal circumstances but not nearly enough to make him feel comfortable right now. As they sprang out of the elevator every noise made a double or triple echo, and oddly, they could hear footsteps in the stairwell—Fitch and Dan, pounding toward them from nine floors up. Swinging to face the fire door, Press and Laura were met with the gray, tangled edges of a hunk of misshapen metal.

"Shit!" Press said in disbelief. "I don't believe it— she went right through a steel door!"

Laura wrenched her head to the left, then the right, fear making her envision movement in every shadow between the cars. "Damn it, *damn* it!" Her voice had risen to a shout. "What is it going to take to *stop* her?"

"The weapons we need are in the van," Press said. His eyes glittered like blue ice. "I'm sure we'll find something."

"Jesus!" Fitch exclaimed as he and Dan burst through the remains of the fire door. "I was positive you were right about the fire door, but it doesn't look like it so much as slowed her down!"

"Let's go!" Fitch's van was parked at the end of the row and Press ran to it and pulled on the handle of the driver's door. Locked, of course. He spun and drew his elbow up—

"Keys!" Fitch yelled. He threw something and Press's arm stopped its reverse motion and darted up instead, snatching the small ring of keys before they could sail over the roof of the vehicle. "Otherwise the alarms'll go crazy."

"Gotcha." Twos steps to the right and he jammed the key into the lock and twisted it; the side door slid over and he was inside and pawing through Fitch's portable defense arsenal. "Grab some flashlights," he told Laura when she climbed in beside him. "Where the fu—found 'em!" His mouth stretched in a tight, dark grin and he held up a couple of flamethrowers with backstraps. He heaved one next to Laura and slung the other on his back, then reached for a Mossberg Model 590 Special Purpose shotgun with a speed-feed stock. A titanium-coated Specwar knife snapped to his belt completed the ensemble, and he and Laura clambered out of the van.

"Did you see her?" Fitch demanded as he leaned inside and seized a flamethrower for himself.

"No, she was out of the stairwell before we got down." Laura wrestled her own flamethrower onto her back. "God, how much does this thing weigh?"

"Fifty pounds, give or take ten." Press reached over and yanked it the rest of the way in place. "You know how to operate it? Short bursts, not long ones. The fuel doesn't go far."

"Just give me something to point at," she retorted. "I'll figure it out."

"I think your 'something' came through that door," Dan said worriedly.

"Which way did she go?" Fitch scanned the parking garage. "Any idea?"

"Not a clue," Laura said. "Has everybody got a

weapon of some kind? Hey—where'd Press go? Jesus, I've never known anyone who could sneak around like that guy!"

The three team members whirled as a man's scream suddenly cut through the air. Four rows of cars away, a metal door marked BOILER ROOM banged open and smacked the wall behind it with a nerve-shattering *clang*!

"*Press!*" Laura's face went white and she bolted for the open door, the others at her heels. Reeling through the opening, she staggered down a flight of creaking iron stairs and spun around the first landing, nearly ramming into the barrel of Press's shotgun.

"Jesus, Laura—be careful!" Press swung the gun back, pointing it down the dimly lit landing.

"What was that scream?" Fitch hissed from behind Laura. "Was that her?"

"I don't know," Press said. "Let's go, and for God's sake," he threw a reproachful look over his shoulder at Laura, "watch where you're going *before* you get there!"

With Press in the lead, the group inched down the last of the stairs, then darted around a corner. Press stopped them with a chopping motion of one hand. At his feet was the disfigured body of a hotel maintenance worker. "Well," he said in a low voice, "I guess she's around here somewhere. One way or the other, we're going to find her."

"If she's down here," Laura words were a pseudo-whisper that could just be heard above the thunderous noise of the boiler in the middle of the room, "we've got her trapped. There's no way for her to get out without going past us."

"Look over there." Press used the Mossberg to point at a smaller door marked ELECTRICAL at the far end of the dim room. The door was ajar and in the murky light trickling into it from the boiler room, they could barely see circuit breakers lining the wall beyond the entrance. No other light shone from its interior. Press's eyes skimmed the boiler room one last time. "There's no place else she could have gone," he said. "Come on."

The electrical room turned out to be hardly more than a large walk-in closet. The light switch was on the inside right wall but Press skipped it, unwilling to fully illuminate their own position when they didn't know Sil's. Besides, the beams of their lights, Afterburner Ballistics, were as good as directed cones of daylight in the small space and more than enough to show the farthest corner, where a jagged crater three feet in diameter had been dug into the concrete floor. "Damn it," Press said, lowering the shotgun. "She's dug her way out—again."

Fitch peered over Press's shoulder, trying to see. "But this is concrete!"

"Apparently that didn't matter to your little creation any more than the steel door did in the garage." Press and the others sidled up to the hole as he aimed his light into it; below them, a smooth-sided tunnel dropped a couple of feet, then curved away into darkness.

When she spoke, Laura's voice sounded like a tightly wound spring. "Oh, God, Press. Does this mean . . . ?"

"Yeah, it does." He swung the Mossberg's strap over his shoulder, his eyes squinting in the beams of the Afterburners. "We're going to follow. It's time to go to the *real* party." Without saying anything else, Press dove headfirst into the burrow.

"Oh, I really *hate* this," Dan said unhappily as he and the others scooted in after Press. Weaponless and bringing up the rear, he found himself wishing he'd at least picked up a pistol or a knife from Fitch's van. "Where do you think this goes, Press?"

After a moment of silence, Press answered from his position farther ahead. "Right here, guys." He waited, sharp eyes following the sweep of his light, as the others crawled out of the tunnel and found their footing.

"Where's here?" Fitch asked breathlessly. "What *is* this place?"

Press dragged the beam's light across the pipes lining the ceiling that curved high above them. "Welcome to the Los Angeles sewer system," he said in a hushed voice.

Speechless, the team gazed around. Their Afterburners did a great job of illuminating a room-sized portion of the huge pipe in which they stood, but an elbow turn in both directions sent the sewer back into blackness. As their voices faded away, other sounds moved in to fill the space: water dripping, an occasional small splash, the faint, scurrying echoes of rats moving along the catwalks on either side. A wide, sluggish river of cold, vile-colored water flowed at their feet, separating them from the walkway on the far side of the pipe. While the smell was none too pleasant, it still wasn't as overpowering as the stench from the empty cocoon Sil had left on the train.

Press turned his beam in both directions, uncertain. Nothing either way moved or made a sound that was outside of what they would have expected. "Which way do you think she went, Dan?"

Covered in dirt from the burrow, Dan's face looked sweaty and vulnerable in the harsh, compact circles of light. He stared one way, then the other; ultimately, he could only spread his hands. "I'm not sure. I just can't be certain."

Fitch grabbed the shoulder of Dan's shirt and gave it a hard yank. "Well, think about it, will you? For Christ's sake, Smithson, I thought you had some kind of extrasensory powers that would tell us this sort of thing!"

"I'm an empath, not a psychic," Dan cried defensively. "It's different!"

"Never mind," Laura cut in. "We'll find her—"

"That way," Dan said. His glance to the south end of the tunnel was tense. "Let's try that way."

"It's as good a bet as any." With one hand on the Mossberg, Press moved off in the direction Dan had indicated. Laura followed, her gaze skipping quickly around the walls and the walkway, the rancid water at their feet.

"We'll go the other way," Fitch said firmly. "That way we'll have both ends covered."

Dan couldn't move. "I—I'm not so sure we should do that, Dr. Fitch."

"Get your ass over here, Smithson." In the backwash from his Afterburner, two scarlet spots of anger dotted Fitch's white face. "I'm not going alone and you're the only one left. Come *on!*" He stalked down the catwalk a couple of yards, the nozzle of his flamethrower clenched in one hand. Above the trickling sounds of the water, the slow buzz of the double pilot light was less than comforting.

"Please, Dr. Fitch—wait!" Dan could see Fitch's back, but the older man refused to slow his gait. "I—I may have gotten it wrong. I think we should go back and get help. Dr. Fitch, wait! Don't go—" His voice choked off as a line of bubbles broke the surface of the water directly below his position on the catwalk. "I think there's something down here!" he cried.

From the corner of his eye, Dan saw Fitch, flamethrower ready, spin and start back. "Stay put!" the doctor called. "I'll be right there." Moving as fast as he dared on the slick, narrow walkway, Fitch hurried toward him.

The bubbles at Dan's feet multiplied, then abruptly disappeared. Terrified, Dan flattened himself as much as he could against the moist, curving wall behind him. His sight fastened on the water and he saw something pale and shiny—a spike?—break the surface halfway between him and Dr. Fitch for an instant. Then it disappeared below the brownish liquid.

Fitch saw it, too. With his finger on the trigger of the flamethrower, he halted at the spot and peered over

the edge of the catwalk, trying to see. Another round of
bubbles floated to the top of the slimy water and
broke—*bloop! bloop!*—but nothing else followed. Was it
Sil, or just a swimming rat?

"Dr. Fitch," Dan pleaded as the other man leaned
farther out over the water. "Come back, okay? This is
very *bad*—"

Fitch never had a chance to do it himself, but Dan
screamed for him as something huge burst upward from
the sewer water and clamped itself around the doctor's
face. Transparent tentacles flailed madly in the air below a sharklike mouth with multiple rows of teeth that
ground through flesh and bone, sending a spray of crimson blood across the moldy wall in back of Fitch's vibrating body. Still screaming, Dan glimpsed a huge,
diaphanous torso below an oversized, elongated head
topped with coils of metallic-looking hair; something
large and darker than the rest of the life-form pulsed
within its abdomen below the purplish-red tinge of vital organs. As Fitch's body toppled into the fetid liquid,
the scientist's flamethrower slipped off his back and fell
to the walkway floor, useless.

With a frenzied rush of icy water and spikes, the
creature dove back under the surface and vanished as
Press and Laura pounded down the catwalk toward
Dan's position, then slewed to a halt.

"Aw, shit!" Press swore. He reached out, trying to
snare Fitch's coat, but it was too late; bobbing leisurely,
the man's corpse drifted toward the opposite wall. Dismayed, they watched as a current took the body and
made it do an obscene swirl before it floated quickly
out of sight. "Shit," Press repeated.

Dan was dripping and shivering from the cold water
and his eyes were wide with remorse and terror when
his gaze slid to Fitch's surplus flamethrower. He picked
it up with a grunt and struggled into it. "I never
thought I could feel like I wanted to kill something,"
he said despondently. Under the false sheen of the wa-

ter, his skin had a ghastly gray overtone to it. "But now—"

"No," Press interrupted. "Don't think like that—it's not healthy. I should know." Dan didn't answer and Press scrutinized the darkened areas of the pipe. He turned to look at Laura and Dan. "We have to go after it," he said softly. "If we don't risk it, there won't be a world left for us to live in."

"Okay," Laura said. Her voice was shaking but the hands griping the stock of her flamethrower were steady. "I'm ready." She glanced at Dan and he nodded. "*We're* ready," she amended. "Let's do it."

The catwalk again, leading them farther into the sewer and away from the Biltmore Hotel somewhere above. For some reason it was inexplicably darker the deeper they went, until their Afterburners seemed like pitiful candles in the blackness. Beneath their feet the walkway turned and they followed the pipe to the right, the only sounds accompanying their ragged breathing the faint dribbling of running water and the tiny, far-away splashings of unseen creatures. Around the turn and twenty feet, thirty, then forty—

"Stop!" Dan said urgently. "She's so close. I can feel her . . . *arrogance.*"

"Arrogance?" Laura asked, bewildered.

The glare of the Afterburner in his hands made Dan nothing but a disembodied voice behind her, a ghostly phantom. "Yeah. She's . . . watching us, I think. Laughing because she sees us but we can't find her." He sounded petrified. "Viewing us as such easy *prey.*"

Press ran the light's beam rapidly along the walls in front and in back of the group, the catwalk, the water. Nothing. Finally, he tried the ceiling of the main shaft, glimpsing only glistening pipes running off into the flat blackness. He swung the beam down and over the water's surface again; they were lucky they weren't being dripped on by the moisture above them—

With a yell of recognition, he brought the After-

burner back up, aiming it at the shining area on the
ceiling. Shouting in surprise, Laura and Dan backped-
aled as the light flashed across Sil's eyes. They glittered
redly for a half second, then she released the piping and
sprang over their heads. Press let go with a blast from
the flamethrower, but she was already gone. With a
geyserlike spray, the sewer water enveloped her.

"My God," Dan gasped. "She's so *fast!*"

"And bigger," Press said flatly. "A *lot* bigger." He shot
a glance at Laura and she nodded.

"Oh yeah," Laura said, her expression stiff, "she's definitely pregnant."

"What's that noise?" Dan asked suddenly. "Hear it?"

Not too far down the sewer pipe, hissing and scrap-
ing sounds rose above the constant gush of running water. The three remaining team members rushed toward
the commotion, balancing precariously along the slip-
pery, moss-covered catwalk. A few more feet and the
Afterburners' glow reached far enough for them to see
a new opening in the concrete wall of the main pipe on
their side, this one slightly smaller than the one in the
electrical closet in the Biltmore's boiler room. Soil and
rocks were still being pumped from the opening as Sil
clawed her way into the earth. It took only a few more
seconds for Press to dash to the gap, thrust the nozzle
of the flamethrower inside, and squeeze the trigger. A
wall of flame engulfed the shaft and Press yanked the
flamethrower out of the crevice and threw himself to
the side to avoid the backwash. Then—

Silence.

Finally, Dan spoke. "I think you got her, Press."

Press peered into the hole, trying to wave aside the
stink of the burning napalm. "We've got to make sure."

"You mean we've got to go *in* there?" Laura looked
doubtfully at the burrow, bright patches of its sides still
blazing.

"Most of it'll burn out in another thirty seconds,"
Press said. He began digging at the loose dirt on the up-

per sides of the depression, shoving handfuls of it down the sides in an effort to smother the rest of the flames. He threw Laura and Dan a glance over his shoulder. "Just try not to get any on your hands, because it clings. Laura, you watch your hair."

When he decided it was safe enough, Press went in face-first, the Afterburner light leading the way. The other two followed, lights bobbing and fingers searching for purchase in the rubble. "God," Laura muttered, more to herself than the others. "Isn't this ever going to be *over?*"

"Almost," Press called back, making her jerk. "We—aw, damn it."

"What's the matter?" Dan asked from a few feet behind Laura's shoes. "Are you okay? Press?"

"There's a definite draft flowing through here." His voice was filled with frustration. "I think we're out of luck again—she's escaped."

"Where does it go?" She was trapped between Dan and Press and all Laura's light would let her see in the inky tunnel was Press's rear end and the wet bottoms of his shoes.

"I'm not sur—oh, *man.*" His voice faded for a moment, then came back. "Wait'll you see *this.*"

As they fought their way free of Sil's latest passageway, the surface on which Laura and Dan crawled unexpectedly ended. They tumbled forward, then slid about a yard before coming to a sprawling stop. "Where are we?" Laura demanded. She found her balance and stood, then her jaw dropped. "Jesus Christ! Where did *this* come from?"

The three of them were standing in a huge, subterranean cavern.

41

The small rocky outcrop on the far side of the cave was a good place to birth her offspring. She knew the group still hunted her and Sil felt lucky to have found the hidden spot so quickly; her child would draw its first breath and be on its feet long before their puny efforts let them make the first guess at her whereabouts. The stalactites and stalagmites everywhere in the cavern did a fabulous job of distorting and magnifying sound, making their clumsy movements around the rocks and strange pools of oily tar dotting the ground indistinguishable from her own. Her ledge was high up the wall nearest their left, almost completely in the shadows and invisible from the ground. While she *had* put a little distance between herself and the burrow entrance, the fools chasing her would think she had fled across the span of the cave to its farthest depths and wouldn't bother to look so close to the tunnel she had made. Adding to the airy noises filling the enormous space were the rats and the blind albino lizards scuttling among the boulders.

Her face twisted in agony and her breathing doubled, then tripled as the child within her swelled in size. Arching backward until she was bent almost in two, her mouth opened in a voiceless wail as the skin between her breasts lightened and stretched as far as it could, then split. The bones of her rib cage gleamed and then her sternum shifted, the bone matter melting to form interlocking pieces that began to push apart, one by one, to expose the pulsing birth canal beneath.

With a low, tortured grunt, the muscles of the birth channel contracted, then expelled the boychild from her body with a rush of translucent pink fluid. Chest heaving, she felt the infant roll down the side of her body and pull itself away from her. Her lightless surroundings did nothing to hinder her, and she could see him clearly—covered with birthing blood and fluid, he was perfectly formed, an exquisite example of a human child but possessed with her superior abilities at concealment and survival. Right now he would be afraid of her and want to hide, and that was good; he would also be a hungry, instinctive killer and dangerous to her in her weakened state. He was a born predator and Sil knew she could leave the boy without worry, knowing he could fend for himself while she healed in safety for a short while.

Without looking back, Sil scurried off into the darkness.

◆

"Incredible," Laura breathed. "I never thought I'd see someplace like this in person. Look over there." She pointed at the closest of half a dozen inky ponds across the rock-strewn ground stretching before them. "It could be oil, or it could tar—like the La Brea Tar Pits. Who knows what's in these pools."

"Then we'd better be careful not to get stuck in them," Dan said with unaccustomed cynicism. He looked anything but happy to be in the midst of the immense cave. "Or we'll end up like those saber-toothed tiger fossils you see in the museums."

"What was that?" Press brought his flashlight beam around and aimed it toward a noise somewhere to his right. The light caught a flash of eyes reflecting in its glare; a rat chittered angrily and ran behind a huge stalagmite banded in multicolored red and cream.

"Just a rat," Laura said. "I wish we could count on that being all that's down here." She aimed her Afterburner into the distance and watched its strong beam dissipate into nothing. Nevertheless, when Press moved off to start searching, she and Dan followed.

"This is a lost cause," Press said with a scowl after only a few minutes. They had made a vaguely elliptical search, stopping at its three-quarter mark. "This place goes on forever—probably under the whole fucking city."

Dan timidly shone his light behind a particularly large boulder, revealing nothing but more rubble and a few fleeing lizards. "She could be anywhere in here," he agreed. "Or nowhere. Maybe there's a way to the surface that we haven't found."

"You two stay here," Press said. "I'm going to go back and check the burrow opening to make sure she didn't return to the sewer behind our backs."

"How would you know if she did?" Laura asked incredulously.

"By the soil pattern," he explained. "Her body will leave tracks in the dirt just like a tire. I'll be back in two minutes. Stay *put*, you understand? I don't want anybody getting lost in here, and as long as your lights are together, they'll be strong enough so that I'll be able to find my way back to you." Light bobbing, Press strode off in the direction from which they'd come; it seemed only seconds before his footfalls faded to faint whispers.

"Great," Laura said. "Our hero makes tracks for the horizon and leaves his two sidekicks to wait it out." She bounced the base of her Afterburner nervously against her thigh.

Dan's gaze skittered along the darkness outside their small circle of light, then stopped. He could sense the feelings of something out there, up the sliding wall of soil to his left. Whatever it was, it definitely *wasn't* Sil. Instead, Dan caught flashes of softness, unfocused intelligence, hunger . . . and fear of the unknown. After a moment's hesitation he began to scale the loosely packed slope.

"Dan, what are you doing?" Laura's voice rose a notch; he caught a spark of fear in the rising volume. "Come back here!"

"It's okay," he called back. "I'm not scared—just wait there. I'll be right back."

"Yea, well," he heard her mutter, "I think that's what Press said, too. Jesus, I can't believe you guys are leaving me standing here by myself. What a *crock*."

"I'll be right back," Dan repeated. Almost to the top, he hesitated when he heard something squeal, followed by a nearly inaudible crunching sound. When nothing else happened, he grasped the jutting outcrop of a stone ledge and pulled himself upright. He could see Laura's light swinging back and forth far below, like a nightlight in an abyss. Balancing carefully on his toes, Dan could just see over another ledge, this one barely at eye level. This was where the feelings were coming from, deep and forceful in his head and heart, impossible to ignore. When he stretched to his full height and peered over, he let out a cry.

Naked and cringing, a little boy—a *baby*—crawled backward on the ledge and stared at him in terror.

"Don't be afraid," Dan said soothingly. "I won't hurt you." He wanted to pull himself up, but there was no way—nothing within reach offered a place for him to put his feet or hands.

"Dan?" Laura called. She sounded very far away. "Dan, what are you doing? Where are you?"

From farther in the distance, Press's worried, echoing voice joined hers. "Laura, are you guys okay?"

"Laura, I'm fine," Dan yelled down. "There's a baby boy up here!" He turned his face back toward the trembling child. The infant watched him with wide, frightened eyes, the skin of his face and body mottled with pinkish stains that looked like diluted rust. "I'll be right back," he said calmly to the child. "Don't go anywhere, and we'll get you out of here." Leaving his flamethrower on the ledge on which he was standing so he could have both hands free, Dan began to move cautiously to the side, searching for another way up the rest of the incline.

"There's a *what?*" Something in Laura's voice had changed, but Dan couldn't think about that right now; he had to concentrate on finding a way to get to the boy. "I'm going to climb up a different way," he shouted. "I can't get to him from here!"

"Dan, don't do *anything!*" The light far down the slope flickered and went out, then Dan heard a slapping sound. "You don't know what—damn it all to *hell!* My light's dead!"

"Just stay there, Laura. I'll be back for you in a minute, I promise." Crawling carefully along the incline, Dan finally found a set of indentations in the rocky dirt, deep enough to use as a sort of staircase. Pulling himself onto the higher ledge, he crawled back toward the baby, letting his Afterburner's beam cut a swathe of light along the ground in front of him. He could still feel the child, the emotions of hunger stronger now, and tempered by intense curiosity. Whose child was this, and how had he come to be in this godforsaken underground cave?

Almost there. He could hear the baby cooing at something, then he caught another of those odd, crunching sounds. When he found the final handhold and levered himself over, the child was bent over something, its back to him. The air in this place was cool and damp, much too extreme for an infant, and Dan pulled off his jacket. He would wrap it around the baby

so it could build up some warmth, then figure out a way
to get it dow—

The boy turned and Dan froze. A few minutes ago
he had barely been older than a newborn, hardly able
to crawl, but the child who swiveled to face him now
stood upright with no trouble. He cocked his head quizzically in Dan's direction, as if trying to make the connection that Dan and the man who had appeared on
the other side of the ledge were one and the same. Paralyzed in the act of offering his jacket, Dan saw everything that the strain of peeking over the ledge before
hadn't allowed: the reddish color streaking the boy's
skin wasn't rust but washes of blood—birthing blood—
and the heavier scarlet stain around his mouth had
come from the headless rat still clutched in his tiny fingers.

"N-nice little b-boy," Dan said shakily as the child
dropped the rat and began to toddle toward him.
"N-no—you s-stay there, n-now, okay?" Dan backed up
as far as he could and felt the edge of the rock outcropping at his heels, the cooler wash of the updraft from
the cavern floor many yards below. He dropped to his
knees, never taking his eyes from the boy's, and felt
desperately for a handhold among the rubble so he
could lower himself. His light swayed wildly across the
narrow span of the ledge, flicking over the toddler's
face and making the chubby-cheeked face pull into a
strange and unexplainable shape. Just a few more feet—

The child was still more than two feet away when it
lunged.

Dan cried out as a horribly barbed tongue the color
of dirty amber shot out of the boy's mouth and swiped
at him. He felt the fabric of his shirt tear at shoulder
level and a hot spot of pain spread across his arm and
neck, making him lose whatever precarious grip he'd
maintained on the rocks. He had one breathless moment of weightlessness, then he hit the slope headfirst,
hard enough to make him see a flash of bright white

that he thought for a millisecond was just his flashlight. Then he heard pebbles rolling somewhere else in the darkness and realized he'd lost the Afterburner in the fall, disjointedly remembered reading somewhere that the light you saw in a bad fall was your brain slamming against the inside of your skull.

The boy ... Dan could hear him coming down the slope with a surefootedness that belonged more to a mountain goat than a toddler ... toddler? The heavy noises coming from the blackness above him indicated more a boy of seven or eight, or—what did Dan know of children and their ages?—maybe eleven or twelve. He blinked and tried to clear his head, then began to move slowly along the incline, searching for his light. As the last of the sparkles cleared from his vision, he caught a faint glow a few feet farther down—the Afterburner, lodged in a crevice on the rocky bank.

The sounds above began to get louder as the child neared its prey. Fighting for balance, Dan clawed a path sideways toward the light. If he could get to it before the creature got to him, he might—*might*—be able to find the flamethrower. He'd set it at the edge of a spot on the upper edge; he should be able to stand and feel his way along the rock until he got to it. If he couldn't find it ... well, he wouldn't think about that.

Far below, he realized that Laura was screaming for Press.

◆

"What's wrong?" Press yelled. He was running in a darkness broken only by the glow of his light, a dangerous thing to do. As if to prove it, he tripped on something—a large rock—and fell, felt his left hand shoot forward to leave a good chunk of skin along the gritty floor of the cavern so that his right could juggle the light. He was back on his feet and sprinting for Laura and Dan without feeling the pain. "Laura?" he yelled. "Damn it, *answer* me! Where are you—where's your light?"

Her voice floated back to him, echoing and directionless. "Press, something's happened to Dan up on the slope. I'm going up."

"*No*! Stay where you are—where the hell is your *light*?" Moisture gleamed blackly in the beam of his Afterburner as he swept the ground with it—one of the tar pools. Press skirted its edge, forced to go slower by the treacherous furrows hidden in the sliding soil.

"He needs *help*, Press! I can't just stand here an—"

Laura's words ended in a squawk and a muckysounding splash, then she started cussing. Farther above, he could hear Dan scrambling frantically along the rocks. "Oh God, Press—I'm stuck in one of these damned tar pools! Jesus, what *is* this stuff?"

"I'm okay!" Dan called hastily. "I found my light— *sweet Jesus*!"

"What's the matter?" Press and Laura shouted nearly in unison. Press's gaze searched the upper regions of the cavern, finally pinpointed the other man's whereabouts by the glow of the faraway flashlight beam.

"It's another one," Dan cried. "A new one—her baby!" Then his voice rose in pitch. "Hey, no—stay back! Oh God, *where is that flamethrower*?"

Off to his right, Press finally spotted Laura mired a few feet inside the edge of the largest tar pit. He started in her direction but she waved him anxiously away, the nozzle of her flamethrower perilously close to the flammable pond. "Never mind me, Press—I'm not going anywhere. Get up there and help Dan."

Press didn't need to be told twice. He whirled and headed up the mound of earth toward his friend. A useless effort, though—without taking the time to search for careful footing, he lost two steps for every three he tried to take. Balling his fists in frustration, he kept at it, each unseen scrabbling making him think Dan was dying or already dead. But midway up, he heard Dan's triumphant howl.

"I *found* it!"

A jet of flame filled the air above Press, rolling from the nozzle of Dan's flamethrower like a sideways mushroom cloud thrown by an explosion. The startling red-and-orange eruption blinded Press momentarily, but not before he saw Dan's target. Already nearly as tall as a teenager, it could have been the Sil creature herself except for its smaller size. Poised to attack with ropy coils of hair spread in a Medusa-like fan above a head that might have come from a mutated praying mantis, the blast of napalm caught it full in the face and knocked it off its feet. It staggered back and fell, and Press tracked its frenzied path downhill by the rolling ball of light. A high, head-throbbing shrieking filled the air as Press let himself slide back to level terrain and saw Dan chase the life-form at an angle across the hilly area, the creature batting crazily at the burning blotches on its head with long, yellowish tentacles the entire time.

Enraged, Sil's blazing offspring spun to face its attacker. It lunged, huge mouth snapping open to expose triple rings of teeth the pale color of new ivory. Legs firmly planted, Dan two-fisted the handgrip and nozzle of the flamethrower and coated the creature with a full, two-second spray of pure heat.

Yowling in agony and engulfed in flames, it went sprawling. It got up and Dan grimaced and aimed the flamethrower again, but the life-form whirled and tried to run across the oily surface of the tar pit, succeeding only in trapping itself in the gooey black pool. Looking on, Dan lowered the nozzle of the flamethrower as the liquid floating on the surface of the pool ignited and began to burn around the creature. Catching a natural path as Sil's only child gave a final death screech, the flames hungrily enveloped it—

—then began to fan across the pool toward Laura, still fighting to free herself from the tar's sticky hold.

The interior of the subterranean cavern was suddenly filled with the red-and-blue glow of the fire. It looked like lighter fluid ignited on the surface of water, floating and licking at its own boundaries in an effort to speed itself farther along.

"Press!" Dan shouted. "The fire's headed for Laura!"

But Press was already there, feet precariously close to the edge of the tar pool as he stretched himself over the beckoning liquid. The only thing that kept him from falling face-first into the filth was the woven strap of the Mossberg hooked around one of the hundreds of stalagmites jutting from the ground. "Come on, Laura," he urged as he reached out, "grab my hand. You can do it—stretch."

"I—I—got it!" With a jubilant cry, Laura's hand slid up his wrist and locked. Grunting with exertion, Press hauled her out, feeling like he was pulling some precious treasure from an aeons-old burial place. He swung her around to dry land and she collapsed, trying to rub the black mess from her skin with one hand while still grasping the pistol grip of the flamethrower with the other.

Press let go of the shotgun and bent over her. "Are you all right?" he demanded.

"God," Laura sputtered in reply, "now I know what a fly feels like on flypaper. That was awful."

"Well, it's over now—"

"Press, look out!"

Sil! Press twisted around, then jerked his body down in reflexive response to Laura's shriek, but he wasn't fast enough. Two soiled-looking tentacles shot forward and twined about him, dragging him away. He heard Laura yelling—"Get out of the way, get out of the way!"—in the background, vaguely registered her shrill instructions to get away from Sil so she could blast the creature with her flamethrower. A great idea if it weren't for the sinewy limbs wrapped so viciously around him—and he didn't have his own flamethrower as an option. He'd left *that* next to the stalagmite off of which his Mossberg 590 was still hanging. Great preparation . . . to *die*.

Fighting for his life in a macabre dance up the side of the cavern, he felt something bang against the side of his elbow as he shoved an arm between himself and the life-form—his Specwar knife. Spikes were thrusting their way from Sil's rib cage, and Press was trying mightily to keep some distance between his chest and the creature's torso to avoid being impaled. As he dodged the teeth snapping at his face, the fingers of Press's right hand found the knife and pulled it free of the belt loop. When one of the two tentacles whipping around him came close enough, one good swipe of the high-tech military knife severed the appendage cleanly and caused enough pain to gain his release, giving him the chance to retreat farther up a wall of rock ledges to his left.

Sil roared in agony and floundered backward, the stump end of the tentacle spurting a nasty, gelatinous glop that was yellowish tinged with glistening clear streaks. Twisting, the creature nearly lost its balance, then charged at Press again, its movements filled with strength and much more agility across the outcroppings than Press's. He slashed at the air in front of it, ducking away from the dozens of daggerlike protrusions that erupted from its body. If it got hold of him with its remaining tentacle and pulled him to it, he was dead; the sharp spikes of before were nothing compared with those jutting from its skin now, and Press had the flash impression that it had only been playing with him then, like a cat toys with a mouse it doesn't consider threatening. The amputation of her limb had changed all that; she wasn't playing games anymore.

Sil slapped at him again, the backward motion of her tentacle leaving her upper torso wide-open. Press saw his opportunity and went for it, darting forward to bury the Specwar knife deep in the center of her chest before momentum brought her limb back. Was her heart there? Did she even *have* one? He didn't know the answer to either question, but he'd done *something* right, because the resulting scream from the life-form was like no sound he'd heard it make before. Long, incredibly loud, it was enough to disorient him for a second . . . enough time for Sil to launch herself and knock Press off his feet.

The battle had carried them farther up than Press realized, and the glow from the burning pool below was a madly swinging kaleidoscope of orange, yellow and red, splitting the blackness like a child's flashlight covered with Halloween paper. Pinned beneath Sil's weight, Press had just enough room to bring his leg up and under his own body in an instinctive maneuver to avoid her killing spikes; a tricky shift of balance, a bit of opportune leverage and the hardest push he could muster—

—and Sil went sailing into the empty space past the rock ledge and toward the pool of flaming sludge below.

But not before wrapping her remaining tentacle tightly around Press's ankle.

The alien's weight dragged him forward and Press clawed at the ground, frantically searching for a hold on the loose, pebble-strewn earth. His fingers dug deep grooves into the ground until the right hand scraped across a rock poking out of the soil. Press clung to it while one foot shook in midair and the other leg was pulled straight by the mass of the creature hanging on to it. He tried to kick at Sil with his free leg, but every jouncing movement made his hold loosen a little more. His endurance was running out, and to his horror Press saw that the tip of flesh beating the air where he'd hacked off the life-form's tentacle was elongating, beginning a slow, spontaneous regeneration. Soon she would have full use of her limbs again, and then what the hell would he do?

Unanticipated warmth wrapped itself around Press's

wrists below his grip on the jutting boulder. His fingers spasmed and slipped beyond the point of no return, but when he opened his mouth to cry out, Dan and Laura were there, hands locked around his as they towed him back over the edge of the brink.

"*No!*" Press gasped. "You'll pull it up, too!"

Dan's face twisted with dread but he didn't stop pulling on Press's arm. With Laura dragging on the other one and Sil hanging from one leg, Press was starting to feel like a victim of the rack—or at least a little like a human rubber band. Everything hurt and he couldn't stop the groan that escaped his lips as his thighs scraped the jagged lip of the ledge; suddenly he was over and pushing with his free leg, battering at Sil with his foot, but to no avail.

Amid the frenzy, Press caught the glimmer of something metallic shining on the ground—*his combat knife.* He reached for it but was too far away; still, Dan understood Press's intent and leaned sideways without letting go of his friend, snaring the dropped weapon. Without being told, he scooted to the edge of the precipice and began to stab at the tentacle encircling Press's ankle, oblivious to the yellow-gold fluid spurting from the wounds he was inflicting.

"Put some elbow in it!" Press screamed as the monstrosity hanging from his foot simultaneously scrabbled for purchase against the side of the rocks and tried to tug Press's body sideways to avoid the bite of the blade. "Pull it *across*—it'll cut!"

Dan abandoned his puncturing motion. With a single, swift slash he severed the alien's remaining tentacle. Fluid geysered from the open wound, coating all three of them as the thing went into free fall, its tentacle slipping away from Press's ankle like an untied piece of nylon rope.

As the Sil-creature, flailing uncontrollably, roared its final defiance and tore at the rocks on its fall toward the pool of tar below, Press righted himself and reached for the flamethrower on Laura's back. She turned her body and twisted free of the straps as Press seized it and hurled it over the side of the ledge. It struck the alien and followed it down. Before they could look over, they heard a double splash, then—

KABLOOM!

The explosion rocked the subterranean cavern and sent pebbles and fist-sized boulders pelting the entire length of the cave's drafty interior. Flaming jellied napalm and unidentifiable saffron-colored pieces of the creature splattered in every direction, and Dan yelped when a chunk of squishy yellow flesh nearly took his eye out and left a deep purple bruise in its wake.

And, finally, it was over.

Nothing moved within the cavern but the flames dying out across the bubbling pool . . . and a rat, scuttling into a dark crevice with a bit of severed tentacle.

Press drew a deep, relieved breath as he stared at the tar pit. "I could have been down there with her." He glanced at Dan, gratitude etched in the dusty lines of his face. "Thanks, Dan. *Again.*"

Dan grinned at his two teammates, not even feeling the angry bruise below his eye anymore. "I think I like my new job," he said proudly.

"It's got lot of variety!"

42

"So, tell me," Laura said. "How did you arrange this? Not many people can reserve a quarter-mile of ocean-front for an afternoon."

She and Press were sitting on a stretch of incredibly clean beach. In front of them was the ocean, wide and sparkling like an endless bowl of diamonds below the Pacific sunset. While it was a public region of Las Tunas State Beach in Malibu, the area was strangely trash-free and empty—no cars, no littler, no vaca-tioning couples with children fighting it out over whose turn it was to use the beach raft. Laura thought she'd never seen anything so beautiful.

Press lifted his face, enjoying the faint sting of the sand carried on the breeze. "You know me. I've got con-nections."

"Uh-uh. Speaking of connections, any with Dan?"

Press's lips turned up in a small grin. "We keep in touch. Seems he was only tooting his horn when he made that crack about this being his new job, though."

"Oh?"

Press leaned farther back on the beach chair and stretched lazily. "Yeah. He's out of the special-project stuff entirely. Decided he could put those empath feelings to better use with abused children."

Laura's eyebrows shot up. "Really? And they let him go, just like that? That's wonderful!"

Press shrugged. "What can they do? *Make* him feel something for them? I don't think so. Besides, I don't think he knows anything classified beyond this project anyway."

Laura looked doubtful. "That seems awful easy."

This time Press laughed. "Easy, nothing. You'd better believe they'll watch that fellow for the rest of his life. He knows it, but it doesn't bother him. Part of the reason he made a successful 'change' was that he went with the Department of Health and Human Services. Things would have been more . . . *difficult* had he tried to switch to a private employer."

"So he still works for Uncle Sam," Laura said wryly.

"Exactly."

They drifted into silence for a while, then Press leaned forward and clasped his hands. "I guess I'm still wondering *why*," he said. "They sent us what we needed to know to . . . I don't know. *Grow them,* if that's what you want to call it. Why would they go through all that trouble simply to destroy us?"

Laura gazed out over the water. "It boiled down to a fight over the most important thing in the world, Press."

"What's that?"

"Babies."

Press looked at her oddly. "Babies? What do you mean?"

"Babies—*whose* babies, more specifically. Whether the next generation was going to be hers, or ours."

Press looked at her thoughtfully, then pulled something from his pocket. When he held it up, Laura realized in amazement that it was the Polaroid shot taken of Sil and John Carey. "Hey," she said, "how'd you get your hands on that?"

"I told you," he said as he stared at it. "I've got connections." He studied the photograph for a few moments. "Look at her," he said quietly. "She was half us, half something else, a predator from so far away it was impossible to make a physical journey through space. You once suggested that we were weeds in the galaxy and she was the weed killer. I had automatically assumed it was to conquer us, take our planet or something like they do in the old science-fiction movies—but that doesn't wash because of the travel distance involved in space. So maybe you weren't that far off. Maybe we *should* be stopped before we spread."

"Now there's a cheerful thought for a lovely late afternoon at the beach," Laura commented. When he didn't say anything, she turned her face back to the ocean. "Which do you think was the predatory half?" she asked softly. "Her half, or ours?"

Laura almost didn't hear his answer. "I don't know."

He looked up at her finally and she gave him a warm smile; after a second he couldn't help but smile back. She wore a lacy camisole that made the skin of her face and arms appear smooth and peach-colored in the fading sunlight; he could smell tropical-flavored lip gloss that made her mouth exquisitely inviting. Her clear gaze was like a glittering mirror of the ocean. "What beautiful eyes you have," he said, leaning toward her.

Still smiling, Laura's lips brushed his, then moved closer for a full kiss. He barely understood the words she murmured against his mouth.

"And in front . . ."

ABOUT THE AUTHOR

YVONNE NAVARRO is a dark fantasy writer and illustrator who lives in a western suburb of Chicago. Her first short story appeared in *The Horror Show* in 1984, and since then her short fiction and illustrations have appeared in over forty professional anthologies and small press magazines. She has also authored a reference book called *The First Name Reverse Dictionary* for writers and parents-to-be. She has written one previous novel, *AfterAge*, for Bantam, and her next novel, *deadrush*, will be coming out in October of 1995.

ABOUT THE SCREENWRITER

DENNIS FELDMAN is a photographer and screenwriter. He is the author of "The Golden Child" and "Real Men," which he also directed. He lives in Los Angeles.